LaTonya Trilogy Relaunch 2019
McDaniel Publishing House (SL McDaniel)
Cover Art: Drop Dead Designs

*The word **Girlishcious®** used in this trilogy and, as spelled, is a registered trademark and brand symbol for the Latonya Trilogy series and associated products. It is also an official definition in the online Urban Dictionary.*

Dedication

I dedicate this series to my sister Brenda, brother Anthony and daughter Miss T (TiAnna) and my grandkids Dontae and AJ for inspiration and vision for writing this long overdue story. To Miss T Hair Designs and nephew Anuff, hip hop artist and producer, for lending me their names as characters in this book. Many thanks to all the focus group reviewers, including Veronica. Thanks to Zaida Zuniga for helping with my Spanish. And always and forever, my late parents Janice Rosetta McDaniel and Captain John McDaniel Jr.

Dear Readers:

I am proud to introduce LaTonya "Tippy" Ellis, a 16-year-old growing up rich with middle-class values touched by real life experiences wealth can't save her from.

Right before her senior year in Stone Mountain High, her father moves her from predominately black Atlanta, Georgia – where she was born and raised – to majority white Portland, Oregon where African Americans are less than 2 percent of the population.

The LaTonya Trilogy is a work of fiction inspired by real life events as seen through the eyes of a protagonist who finds her reality to be dangerous and often cruel.

Given the nickname Tippy at age 4, this spunky teen can be standing right behind you without you knowing – her daddy can attest. The very daddy who insists she grow up well-grounded rather than "uppity" like her mama's folk. Although her relationship with him is often painful, it is because of him she experiences multiple black experiences moving beyond boundaries, limitations and rules.

LaTonya's journey is one of joy and humor complicated by violence and abuse. This may be hard to stomach for some readers but naivety doesn't describe today's young adults – awful shit does happen!

So, get ready for drama, suspense and romance in the LaTonya Trilogy. Once you begin, there's no turning back.

Yours in truth,
Amanishakhete

1

Ain't Hell For
Bad People?

June 8, 2012
7:30 a.m. Atlanta, GA

Friday morning at the breakfast table, daddy feeds me his daily dose of bullshit! Rather than keep quiet, he makes a crazy ass announcement catching me off guard. Why does he have to be so mean? And he's damn ungrateful – him and his new family, a wifey and two twin brats. They all should feel honored to have me sitting here with their tacky asses around this white picnic table and side benches. Except for daddy who has a chair for his stocky ass.

"I ain't sitting on no damn bench inside my house," he says. "This ain't no park."

Regardless, daddy puts up with shit from his tall, boney, half his age, biracial wifey Luanne. Her tired-ass blonde naturally-curly hair droops right below her sharp cheekbones.

The two brats Jayden and Brittany are 8 years old. Both have stocky bodies like daddy except for their faces. They can't escape the Doberman features like they mama have. Ugh. I don't like them and they don't like me. They are damn spoiled. Always get what they want and can do no wrong in the eyes of daddy and his wifey.

As for me, I swear daddy hates me as much as he hated my mama.

"What I say is final!" daddy shouts.

The words "go to hell" rise to the tip of my tongue. Ready to lasso the sound of his voice punching through my forehead exploding into a throb, throb, throb. Falling echoes land on my lower intestine. Nausea. Rumble. Acid spurts upward. Detours left to right, settles underneath my armpits. Sweat dribble, dribbles breaking through melting my expensive deodorant. Boom, boom, boom pulsating blood vessels sync up with my throbbing insides. Minus the green body hue, I think this is how the Hulk feels right before he kicks ass!

I jump up from the table, pick up my plate of uneaten bacon, eggs and soggy hashbrowns throw it, plate an' all,

"Woohoo!"

The crashing sound of broken glass hits the rust painted walls right behind daddy's head. He ducks. I grin. Sticking bits of food juices slide down the wall. Makes me feel good and strong. Standing my ground, I look at daddy dead in his eyes. If he hits me, he's going down. I may end up in prison for murder at 16.

Okay, I could be another statistic. Black, an African American, a person-of-color. Regardless of how you paint me, one thing that separates me from the stereotypes is my family is wealthy. This makes me a very rich "girlishcious" teenager.

I'm LaTonya Loretta Ellis. Most everyone calls me Tippy a nickname my parents gave me when I was 4. I would walk up on them and their guests without them knowing during the most inopportune times. I'd hear juicy stuff kids at that age shouldn't. As an only child, this often was my source of entertainment, and in some cases, the basis for my unhappiness.

Lots of kids blame their parents. I'm no different even though you may think my life is a little easier because I'm rich – I mean really rich

— and you probably think I'm spoiled. Not! I have problems like any average teenage girl. In fact, I bet my cross is heavier.

Early on, I was fortunate to have 2 parents who married for love, so I thought. Now daddy has a new wifey, not my real mama nor step-mama. I don't claim the lying, cheating, backstabbing skank whose shit stinks worse than anyone, I've smelled! Pretty bad huh?

My birth parents are Robert T. Ellis and Loretta Oliver-Ellis, well-educated and socially astute. They both come from politically-charged backgrounds. Daddy gained his views over time whereas mama's were handed down through generations.

Mama's family is staunch Republican the ultra-conservative kind. They support every Republican candidate despite their ideology. They may be black, but they think they're above the average black person. The ones who are poor and middle-class. Granddaddy and gramma Oliver campaign for Mitt Romney and Paul Ryan during this year's 2012 presidential election. They believe Romney and Ryan are the answer to black folk's problems.

I live with daddy, so I learn my ideals from him. He makes sure his family understands what side of the track to stand on. Daddy talks about politics often and we support President Barack Obama. You probably guessed Daddy is a diehard Democrat. He hates Republicans especially the black ones. He thinks they're all traitors except for General Collin Powell.

"Yeah he's a good man," daddy says. "Even told his boss W to go to hell. That takes courage."

Mama was born with a silver spoon. Comes from a long-line of Oliver's — steel and land moguls dating back to the 1700s.

Daddy's a self-made multimillionaire thanks to mama. She helped him start RJ Builders and Design fast becoming a billion-dollar company, so I hear. Wealth is why wifey married him.

One of my pleasures in life is to "tippy" up on daddy. Sometimes I just stand quietly without saying anything to see how long it takes him to notice. It annoys him when he finally realizes. Probably 'cause

I'm prone to losing my cool, if the situation tempts me. This keeps Daddy wondering what I'm thinking. Like today. Am I like those kids you see on the news? The ones who snap and kill their parents – slice 'em up and leave 'em for dead.

Am I wacked? I don't know. My anger has gotten worse since mama left and I miss her badly. As for daddy, he doesn't care anymore about mama who wasn't gone a hot minute before he married Luanne who's much younger than he is. We're talking about a skank who use to be my live-in nanny!

"Stay out of this Luanne! This is between me and my daughter!"

"You damn right Daddy. Today is mama's anniversary and you don't give a shit about my feelings!"

I hate to cry, but I'm mad as hell. Crying don't stop me from defending myself though.

"You never talk about mama anymore! You want me gone too?"

Look at daddy. Paleeze. He's pointing his finger at me like he'd do mama, tryin' to scare me. "You're grounded!" he says.

"It don't matter 'cause I'm getting emancipated!" I say.

Today I decided not to go to school. Since I was 7 years old, I celebrate June 8 as Mother's Day, honoring the life of my mama who's no longer with me. At least daddy could be more compassionate. He was married to the woman for 7 years.

When daddy and me start arguing, the twins jump up, sprint over to the kitchen entrance and stand in the hall. Staring at me, eyes bugged-out. Never know, I may go off on them too.

Wifey doesn't move. Snarls at me like she always does.

I frown with my whole face daring Luanne to say something. Any excuse to kick her ass!

Luanne is no-good like my mama and gramma claimed. Probably because her daddy's a pimp and her mama was his whore. Don Juan is what they call her daddy in the streets of Atlanta. His real name is Donald Sutherland and he's black and fuggly, nothing cute about him! Mm, mm, mm. I can't fathom why any woman would want to be with him let alone be his whore. If looks could kill, you'd be dead.

My BFF TiAnna Johnson and me spotted Don Juan one day while we were on a black college tour. We were visiting a university in east Atlanta. He drove by right when we got off the tour bus. Our girlfriend Tommy Crumbs was with us. He told us he heard Don Juan stalks college campuses, hoping to pull a few girls.

"Paleeze. They're smarter than that," I say to Tommy.

"No shit Sherlock," says TiAnna.

Don Juan was in a white Cadillac Convertible, skin black as night, grinning wide showing his 2-gold upper front teeth.

TiAnna said, "He gotta have a gold penis, the Negro is ruint!"

Wifey Luanne has a hold on daddy. He rarely spends time with me anymore. Practically ignoring me unless he's yelling at me or grounding me for no reason. Luanne is up to something all right, but I'm not going to let her win.

2

A Skank Is Born

Druid Hills

In Atlanta, we lived in a beige stucco 2-story mansion gifted to mama and daddy as a wedding present from mama's parents. My formative years where I formed many happy memories until she moved in.

Our home stretched along a sprawling estate uphill from a peekaboo view of a private creek beyond the backyard pool, basketball and tennis court and my covered playground with a carousel daddy installed for my 1st birthday. We could walk there along the asphalt pathway set to the left between the pool and courts pushing through the rows of old growth maple trees guarding the mansion borders.

7 of the 24 rooms were bedrooms with private bath; a den, gym and cigar room for daddy; a game-room with movie screen, surround sound music and stocked bar for grownups only; a fuchsia-colored themed playroom with my own child-appropriate games. My special room was a hit among my select group of friends. It was themed like a miniature candy-land of non-edibles with edible ones secured inside gumball machines, behind the ice cream bar and candy counter only touched on special occasions like playdates.

We had a formal living room staged with Victorian style furniture, African and European art kin to our African and French heritage; a sitting room hidden on the other side of 2 French-Doors for intimate conversations. This room has a back entry leading into a 10-seat formal dining adjacent to the large baker's kitchen used by our cook.

My favorite room was mama's skylit meditation room for meditative prayer and yoga. Walls adorned in soft golden materials, white thick-carpeted floors with futons and large pillows, this room welcomed only natural light. Mama and me spent many quiet times watching the sunset slowly reveal the moon and stars when the night was clear. It was in here I felt the most peace as did mama. Where we built our inner-strength to face the darkness waiting to arise.

Like when I was 6, Mama hired Luanne as my live-in Nanny. Not long after, crazy stuff started happening. Luanne drove a wedge between mama and daddy causing them to fuss and fight constantly.

Sept. 15, 2000
5:30 p.m.

I'm standing next to mama in our newly remodeled kitchen. Right in front of the long taupe and coca brown granite counter, set underneath the just as long spice rack. A same-colored backsplash behind the rack, runs with the counter along the wall, stops at the stainless-steel fridge. On the other side of the fridge is the baker's oven. 3 skips behind us, the grill top island lays beneath a rack of hanging sharp knives. Pots high enough to keep me out of reach. Around us backed against the walls, wooden cabinets refinished in taupe stain coordinate with the backsplash.

Today we get the kitchen to ourselves. Mama gave our cook Miss Eloise and her husband Chester, our driver, the day off. The kitchen feels big making our laughs echo off the forest green walls.

While I'm waiting for mama to scoop me up some of our favorite ice cream, vanilla with yummy chocolate covered almonds, outta nowhere daddy busts into our space interrupting our party for 2. He's acting nutty – no pun intended. He's right up on mama standing close makes me claustrophobic. Dang. Doesn't he see me? I guess not. The devil's got a hold of him again. I look up and see right inside his nostrils. I'm glad he doesn't have boogers. When he gets mad, his nose gets wider and his lips tighten. His lips barely move making him talk funny like "ju dank I'm craaza," while pointing his pudgy forefinger in mama's face. Right between her eyes.

Daddy reaches over me with his big hands and grabs mama's arms. My turn to duck. I'm getting out the way. The fight begins: Loretta Ali verses Robert Frasier. I know all about Ali and Fraser. I saw the Ali movie with mama. You know the one with Wil Smith playing Ali. I'm betting on mama.

Daddy starts the round by shaking mama making her body look like she's having convulsions.

"Come on mama! Break loose!"

I'm jumping up and down cheering mama on while I'm standing over by the kitchen entrance near the front door. This is the best spot in case I have to run and take cover. Like inside the big coat closet not too far from me. I bet I can get there faster than daddy can. If that happens, I'm locking the door so he can't get in. I want him to get his well-deserved beat down.

Mama recovers, breaks loose from daddy's grip and runs over to the stove. She reaches for the once hot teapot and throws it at him. He ducks trying to save his ass after mama rope-a-doped him. Mama then runs to the center of the kitchen – to the island, pulls a big knife from the holder! Daddy runs to the back entrance, leading to the back hallway, down to the family room and to the back of our estate. He makes it through the door with mama right on his ass!

"Ooo, I gotta see this!" I say out loud.

I start to go after 'em but someone grabs the back of my pretty fuchsia blouse. Frowning hard, I quickly turn around force releasing the hand that grabbed me. My clothes mean a lot to me and they're not cheap. Mama buys me the best.

Hm. Wouldn't you know. It's Luanne stanky slanky. Her breath stinks all the time and she's tall and boney. She snatches me by the arm and pulls me up the stairs. I thought I liked Luanne. She once acted like a big sister not a babysitter. When we get to my room, she reminds me of how much I can't stand her stanky self. She slams my door. Huh! She got her nerve. I'm the only one allowed to slam my door. Then she yells at me, accusing me of being nosey.

"No, I wasn't," I say. "I was in the kitchen with mama when daddy bust…"

Stanky interrupts me without letting me finish my defense. Instead she says, "Stay away from dem when dey fight. Yo mama can be dangerous!"

"Ooo," I say.

This is when my dislike for Luanne takes root. She continues to say nasty things about mama pissing me off. So I mouth-off to her every chance I get defending my mama's honor. I do it despite daddy's mama – gramma Ellis – warning me to watch my mouth.

"Yo mouth gone get you in trouble wit' yo daddy," gramma Ellis would say.

I didn't care about what gramma said. I told Luanne, "I'm tellin' mama so you can get fired!"

Well she never says anything else. At least not, while mama's around. She did tell daddy though and you know what he did? He threatened me. Said he'll ground me if I ever speak disrespectfully to Luanne again. This was the beginning of me losing my edge with daddy as his little girl. All because of Luanne!

Gramma Oliver was right. She warned mama before she hired her. Mama didn't listen. She's gotta heart and wanted to help Luanne who she thought was in danger. What a joke. Luanne turned out to be the dangerous one.

After Luanne's Plan A takes shape, she launches Plan B and goes after daddy. Mama says no 16-year-old girl should act the way she acts towards a grown man. She's flirtatious. Always touching on daddy and giving him long hugs.

"It's not proper," mama would say. "You wouldn't know she was once sexually assaulted."

Several times I catch Luanne flirting with daddy and he plays it off by saying her actions are innocent. Hm. Even I know better. But daddy has grown weak when it comes to her. She manipulates him into taking her side against mama and me.

Gramma Ellis is like daddy. Easily manipulated. She thinks Luanne is "such a nice girl." That's what she said to mama, and me when we visited her in the hospital. Gramma had pneumonia. Gramma Ellis said daddy told her about mama's concerns, but she believes mama is imagining things. Then she started talking about me. Said mama should stop spoiling me. Let daddy discipline me like he should've been doing long ago.

"It won't hurt to tap her little behind every now and den," She told mama who doesn't believe in spankings.

Even if daddy wanted to, he'd better not "Unless he's ready to die," mama says.

Shoot. Like I'm a bad kid. I don't do nothing but play with my dolls most times.

Mama rarely takes me to visit gramma Ellis. She thinks she's too old-fashion and a walk-behind your man kind of woman. I heard mama tell gramma Oliver, gramma Ellis walked so far behind her man she lost sight of him. He ran off with another woman and she's still walking trying to catch up.

Gramma Oliver says, "She's way too country. She needs to learn proper English. Do not allow my granddaughter to mimic that woman's grammatical inaccuracies."

Got to admit gramma Ellis isn't cultured and beautiful like gramma Oliver. They're both around 50, but gramma Ellis's face looks wrinkled and worn. Bags underneath her always bloodshot eyes, drooped-jaws, mouth turns downward at the corners like a sad clown.

She no longer has to work. Daddy takes care of her, but she still complains about being tired. From what I know, she sits around the house all day, eating and gaining weight. She's diabetic so her doctor puts her on a diet she never keeps. Gramma doesn't do her hair either.

What little she has she keeps in small braids covered up with an old black wig when she leaves the house.

Gramma also wears below the knee box like dresses – in white, black, red and brown – with flowers or polka dots. Beige nylons come up to her knees, feet shoved in thick-wedged closed-toe shoes. Gramma Ellis could use help understanding the difference between tacky and swanky.

Jan. 5, 2001
Early Evening

Mama and daddy are gone longer than expected. So is Luanne. She leaves me home alone while she runs to the corner store – so she says. She's out for what seems like hours. When she comes back, she gets right into my face and warns me not to tell. Ooo, I wish she'd move. She smells and her breath stinks.

Later I find out her smelling funny might've been weed. I guess it also made her hair messy and clothes look like she put 'em on in a hurry. I remember her eyes being red too. Shoot. I thought she'd been crying. Almost made me say sorry for calling her a pea head.

"Could you move pea head please?" I said.

She growls at me crunching the tip of her long thin Doberman dog nose, I heard gramma Oliver call it.

"Dang! I did say please," I say to her.

Mama yelled at her once about her red eyes and funny smell, "Don't be smoking those damn drugs in my house!"

Daddy came to her rescue. Again. "Chill Loretta. At least it's not cocaine or heroin."

Hypocrite should be daddy's middle name. He talks bad about his baby brother, Unc Rae-Rae, for the same thing.

"No good pothead," I hear daddy say to mama one time when they were arguing about my uncle. Funny. They argue about Luanne and my uncle. What's up with that?

March, 9, 2001
Daddy comes home from work

And says, "How's daddy's precious darling?"

"Hi daddy," I say and give him a big hug. "Are you coming to my recital? I'm the lead ballerina because I dance better than the other girls my age."

"Of course, you're the best. I wouldn't miss seeing it."

I remember being happy. As an only child, mama and daddy spoiled me rotten. Mama put me in every "girly" activity from beauty pageants to ballot and dance classes. Pageants daddy hated. Didn't like me being all made up. He said he didn't want his little girl looking like a grown woman. Mama stopped telling daddy when we'd go and asked Unc Rae-Rae to escort us – our little secret.

My daddy also hated when mama enrolled me in The Malcolm and Denorsha Young Finishing School for children of wealthy black Republicans. Malcolm and Denorsha served as co-head masters since establishing the school in 1950, up until Mr. Malcolm's death in 1997 on the day Princess Diana died. He fell asleep one night and never woke up. Ms. Denorsha's 3 children – Alice, Teresa and Malcolm Jr. – now help her run the business.

Ms. Denorsha is 75 going strong, keeping herself busy with tons of activities. She's well-respected and belongs to groups like Omega Theta Si sorority, Jack and Jill and the Links. Ms. Denorsha is something when it comes to politics. Proud to say her family's Republican. Ms. Denorsha succeeds at turning young black girls into Prima Donnas. We earn our places among the high society of snobs.

Mama was different. She loved people and tried to instill those values in me. With my growing anger towards daddy and a deep hatred for Luanne, I'm almost ashamed to say, it's gonna take a while for me to do right by her memory.

3

Ooo
I'm Telling

Feb. 5, 2002
Around lunch time

I learn something no little kid should. But then again, my home life is colorful.

Mama's gone shopping without me. Dang. She should've woken me. Instead, she leaves me a note: *Gone shopping be home soon, Love mama.*

I'm much better after having the flu for the past several days. I'm hungry for real food, not mama's homemade chicken soup. It's good, but I'm over it.

I get out of bed, put my feet in my fuchsia slippers, pull on my matching robe, go find daddy. I think he's in his office downstairs where he usually is even on weekends. Don't know where Luanne is.

Daddy's den door is cracked. It's quiet in there until I hear a giggle like Luanne's. I peek through the crack. Daddy is sitting in a leather brown chair near his desk. His head laid back, moaning. Kneeling in front of him is Luanne, her head bobbing up and down above his lap.

What's she doing between my daddy's legs? Is he moaning 'cause she's hurting him? Maybe daddy's zipper got stuck and she's trying to fix it. Like this one time, I walked in on him and mama. Mama was fixing his zipper. I still got a scolding for not knocking.

Here I go again entering without knocking. Oh well.

"Daddy!"

His head pops up, eyes widen, mouth drops. Luanne doesn't move from her kneeling position. She just keeps bobbing her head up and down. Daddy jumps up knocking Luanne to the floor. His pants fall down around his ankles leaving him standing with no underwear. Ooo. What's that dangling way down below daddy's stomach?

"Tippy get your ass outta here!"

Luanne's head pops up. She looks at me laughing like what daddy said was funny. I'm not laughing and I don't like daddy right now. I run out of the den and out the front door – something my parents forbid me to do when I'm by myself – but I go down the stairs and out the gate. Left I go, run, run, run without looking back.

2 hours later

The police find me and bring me home to my frightened mama who grabs and hugs me tight. She called 9-1-1 after they searched the neighborhood, spoke to neighbors. Daddy and Luanne didn't notice I was gone until mama came home. Don't know how I ended up at a construction site a couple of miles away. A worker spotted me playing around a manhole and called the police.

Mama's crying but she's still mad, mad, mad. She says I could've been killed or kidnapped, sold into the sex trade. Mama always worries. She watches bad news on TV. I don't know about you, but I'm OK with mama being overly protective.

Mama takes me upstairs, leaving daddy to finish with the police. She gives me a bath and puts me back in bed. My nose is stuffy again and I'm nauseous. I had run out in with only robe on and slippers.

"Pudding you are my pride and joy," mama says. "If anything happens to you, I couldn't live with myself. Please help me keep you safe my little Tippy."

Mama places her right hand over her heart and taps twice. I do the same. This is me and mama's way of saying, I love you.

"Why did you run off," says mama.

I tell her, "Daddy yelled at me for interrupting Luanne fixing his zipper."

Mama stiffens, crunches her forehead.

I keep talking, "Remember mama when I walked in on you fixing daddy's zipper?"

Mama's face turns red, quickly changes her expression, smiles and says, "You can tell me anything even if your daddy tells you not too."

Like earlier. After the police brought me home, daddy asked me not to tell mama about his broken zipper. Right after my moment with mama, daddy picks me up, knowing I'm no baby. I enjoy the moment with my arms around his neck and my legs around his waist. He squeezes me tight, whispers in my ear, "I'm sorry baby girl but don't tell mama. It would be your fault if she sends me away."

Shoot. Made me feel smaller than I am. I go from daddy's precious darling to his attempted cover up. So yep. I started something. I told. What I did only added fuel to an already rip-roaring fire.

June 9, 2003
Special note to mama

Dear Mama,

Today I'm 8 and I'm sad you won't be here to make my day special like you always do. Daddy took me out for burgers, ice cream and cake at my favorite restaurant. His new wifey Luanne and their twin brats Brittany and Jayden came even though I didn't want them to. Unc Rae-Rae was there, which made me happy. I love my Unc Rae-Rae. He treats me better than daddy does.

When we got home, Unc Rae-Rae came in and walked with me out to our backyard. He had a special gift for me. A beautiful diary I'm writing in right now. He told me anytime I miss you, think about you or wish I could tell you my secrets, to write to you in my diary. Unc Rae-Rae says you will hear me because you are watching over me. My diary has fuchsia flowers on the front cover.

It wasn't your fault you left me, but I'm still mad. I miss you and daddy doesn't seem to care anymore. Unc Rae-Rae does. He says I remind him of you. Remember how Unc Rae-Rae would make daddy mad when he'd say to you "girl you look good as a plate of collard greens on a Sunday." I'm laughing now because he says it so funny and with a big, big smile. Unc Rae-Rae loved you mama and me too.

Mama, I hope you are happy. I will never forget you.

Love forever and ever,
Tippy

4

Daddy's Home

May 27, 2012
Right before midnight

Someone or something is shaking me out of my sleep.

"Tippy! Come on girl wake up!"

"Oooohhhkayyyy. I'm awake!" Daddy loosens his grip of my arms. He's sitting on the edge of my bed.

"Did I upset you again daddy? Sorry." Poor daddy. He looks like I feel tired, helpless.

"I'm sorry too baby girl. This has been going on too long."

"Yeah daddy I know. Makes my head hurt."

Daddy usually sits with me after my rough nights. This is when I have his undivided attention.

Lucky for me, he came home early from his Friday night poker game. He's been smoking cigars, I smell it on his clothes. Daddy likes cigars but doesn't smoke in the house. His wifey doesn't like it.

"I'll call Dr. Anderson."

"No daddy. I'm okay, really."

"Look at you shaking. Not good." Daddy grabs an extra blanket and wraps it around me.

"Your doctor is lucky I haven't fired her."

"I'm dealing much better daddy. Don't worry."

For daddy's sake, I keep the specifics of my nightmares to myself. When he asks, I tell him I can't remember. He doesn't believe me but doesn't push. It's bad enough I have to relive the horrible images. No need for him too.

The worst are the physical symptoms like the brain zapping. Brief pulsating shock waves. Dr. Anderson gives me prescription pills. They calm me down by shutting my mind down, so I can sleep. The pills have side effects, making me drowsy the next day. I can only take 'em sometimes like on weekends.

Daddy gently squeezes my hands and says, "I'll sit with you until you get back to sleep."

I may be 16, but I miss being daddy's little girl. Often, I pretend my nightmares affect me way more than they do. Then I can be his little girl again.

May 28, 2012
Late morning

Thank you, Big G. Today is Memorial Day and no school. I plan to stay home all day eat, sleep and watch movies. No Jeremy either. My boo is out of town visiting Miami University, 1 of the schools trying to recruit him. Jeremy is 1 of the most sought-after football quarter backs in the country. He's a senior at Stone Mountain High. Scouts started courting him in junior year.

Oh, damn! The phone's ringing. It's my BFF.

"Hey Tip! Get your ass up!" TiAnna is loud, making me hold the phone away from my ear.

"What!" I shout back.

"We're going to the mall so get ready," she says.

TiAnna can be demanding sometimes. Hm. Like I'm gonna jump right up. Not today.

"I ain't feeling it T. I've been up most of the night."

"Uh-oh. Another nightmare girl?"

"Uh-huh. Daddy sat with me."

"Aw ain't he sweet. How's he acting anyway?"

"Hm. Gotta have a nightmare before he acts right."

"All the reason you need to get up Tip. It'll do you good to break out of Guantanamo for a while."

"Naw T. I just wanna chill."

"Now look Tip. You being all depressed ain't good."

"Who says I'm depressed? I'm just tired."

"Girl paleeze. I can hear it in your voice. I know you."

Damn. I love my BFF and would do anything for her. But today ain't the day. Why does she keep buggin'?

"LaTonya Ellis," she says, trying to sound like daddy. "Be at the mall by 2:00. I'm buying you your birthday outfit."

"My birthday's not until next month. What's the rush?"

"I'll be broke by tomorrow that's why."

Funny. TiAnna almost never spends money on anyone but herself. But she's a good friend and knows all about my problems.

TiAnna and me met in grade school. We've gone through a lot together. Our families moved to Stone Mountain around the same time. TiAnna comes from a middleclass family – the Johnsons – and her parents work for the post office. Her mama Lydia is her daddy's wife # 2. She once dated my Unc Rae-Rae for a hot minute and before me and TiAnna were born. I asked Unc Rae-Rae about it and he shrugged his shoulders.

TiAnna's daddy Randall is daddy's height. He has short, curly, salt-and-pepper hair and is a big guy, stout with a pot belly. He's always sitting in front of the TV – when he's not working or bowling – watching sports and old school shows like Bill Cosby. His thick droopy eyelids make him look like he's sleeping when he's not. TiAnna says he's been sleeping in the TV room a lot lately. She heard him say to her mama "I get better sex with TV. It cooperates and makes noise."

19

My BFF is the Johnson's only daughter and the same age as me. Her half-brother is James Robert – we call him J.R. – is 20 years old and fine. He recently started sporting his long-groomed sideburns, close shaven beard and keeps his hair twisted. Looking at his height 6'11, he should be playing pro basketball, but he wants to be a dentist. Before Jeremy I tried to get wit' him, but he treats me like a kid sister. TiAnna's baby brother Randall Jr. is a year younger than she is. He's a cutie and knows it. Got the girls sniffin' up behind him. Just mannish.

TiAnna is having a tough time with her mama, who runs things, including Mr. Johnson. TiAnna's been complaining about her a lot. Says she's in good company since her daddy complains too. I listen but remind her I don't have a mama anymore, so she should be grateful. She could be gone before you know it.

1:30 p.m.
Going to the mall

Yeah, we have a chauffeur. Chester Young's been with us since daddy and mama were together. He's 65 and thinking about retiring.

You might think I'm pretty cool for having my own chauffeur. Then again, you could be hatin'. The truth is when mama was around, she never drove. She had her reasons.

This 1 Sunday mama and me, got into an accident on the way to visit gramma Oliver. Some drunk rear-ends us while stopped at a traffic light. I was 5 then, strapped into a car seat in the back. We were lucky mama was driving an SUV and that drunk wasn't driving at top speed. I could've been seriously hurt. From then on mama refused to drive. The same thing may have happened with Chester driving, but mama felt much safer. She'd sit in back with me, thinking she could shield me from anything bad happening.

Lazy-ass Luanne doesn't drive even though she can. She'd rather flaunt daddy's wealth, which he hates. Daddy is okay with having nice things but doesn't think we should deliberately throw it in people's faces. Like rappers. He can't stand 'em. He says touting bling, bling,

bling, fancy cribs and cars is unnecessary. This is why there are so many poor black kids going down the wrong path to get what they have.

Chester doesn't drive us around in a limo like you may think. He drives one of several family cars. We own a 6-seater olive-green Nissan van, a mauve colored Lexus, a canary yellow Chrysler 300 and a turquoise BMW convertible with a dark blue vinyl top. The convertible BMW is daddy's baby, so he doesn't allow us to drive it.

Personally, I don't like the family transportation choices, but daddy won't buy me my own car. I'd prefer a sporty convertible or smaller SUV. Daddy says my behavior ain't up to snuff even though I try to be civil. He and his family treat me like shit anyway.

Chester comes in handy when I don't wanna drive. If kids at school ask, I introduce him as my granddaddy. Only my BFF, Jeremy and Tommy know the truth.

The upside to riding with Chester is I'm free to talk about Daddy and Luanne. I tell him I believe daddy hates me like Luanne does, but I don't know why. He listens and doesn't judge.

Then he says, "Member y'all be 18 one day. Den y'all can hold' yo own and tell dat winch Luanne ta go da hell!"

Then he'll say, "I hope you and your daddy can make peace even though he's made mistakes. I know yo daddy loves you."

Chester is loyal to mama's memory and despises Luanne. He hates what she did to mama and she's downright mean to him and Eloise.

"I'da quit long time ago," Chester says. "I stay 'cause yo mama would want me to watch over you."

Chester is tall, lanky and walks with a limp. He was born with a short-left leg. His hair is fully white with matching brows, making him look older than he is. When he says hello, he nods and says, "How do."

Eloise is our housekeeper and cook, good-natured like Chester. Chester is a man of few words but short little Eloise loves to talk once you get her going. She always has a big smile on her face while talking about anything from what happened at church on Sunday, her grandkids, to some nut she ran into at the grocery store. Daddy loves

Eloise's cooking. She's true to her southern roots but makes food with healthy ingredients and saves the fatty stuff for holidays.

As a pre-retirement gift daddy bought them a house not too far from us, near where TiAnna lives. The place is big enough for their kids and families to visit. The Young's come from Alabama originally – Tuskegee and Auburn.

Chester and Eloise have 7 grown children – 5 girls and boys – Deborah, Edna, Olivette, Julia, Mollett, Chester Jr. and Johnny. They would've had 8, another girl, but she died during childbirth. Between the 7 of 'em, Chester and Eloise have 16 grandkids.

I arrive on time

And push through the crowd of people to get to the food court where I'm meeting TiAnna. I see kids I know from my school, but when they spot me, I nod or wave and keep walking.

TiAnna's standing next to Starbucks looking girlishcious as usual. She's wearing her new blue skinny jeans she bought last week from Bling West, 1 of our favorite stores here. I call her Miss Skinny Mini. She's toned and petite like her mama. They go to the gym together and do Yoga and Pilates. I go with them sometimes. The gym is where TiAnna and her mama seem to get along.

People say we look alike – same facial features – except she's shorter than I am. She's 5'5 and weighs 110 pounds. She wears a light brown and blonde mixed colored weave, cut slightly above her ears, faded on both sides and down the back with long bangs swooped across her right eye. I know that's the thing, but how can she see? I tried the swooped style once. Drove me crazy.

My BFF's dream is to open a chain of beauty supply houses. TiAnna says she hates that black women spend millions of dollars on hair products but Asians make all the money. They own 99 percent of the beauty supply houses in the U.S., targeting black women and corner the market.

What they do is manufacture the products and sell back to their own supply chains. Asians owning the manufacturing, make it difficult for blacks to get in. They won't sell to us unless it's at a premium, making black-owned stores less competitive.

TiAnna and me hate when we go into a supply house and the Asians help us even though they know nothing about us. They don't even speak. If they do, they don't smile.

"Damn! Can I get a thank you?" TiAnna says to an Asian girl at the supply house in downtown Stone Mountain.

Between the 2 of us, we spent a couple a hundred dollars. TiAnna was so mad she cussed the girl out. We stopped shopping there and started going to the 1 across town. Funny. The same girl works there and still doesn't speak. You would've thought she learned her lesson.

"Hm," TiAnna says when she sees her. "I'mo save my energy to start my own business and put y'all out of business." Then she looks at me. "I already have an investor."

TiAnna likes to volunteer my money. Money I can't physically access until I'm 18. The real big bucks. Mama left me a trust fund and daddy's the guardian; he refuses to tell me how much. Says no need to worry about it until the time comes. Huh. Can't wait. I wonder how much I have. A million? 2 million?

I'm glad TiAnna's thinking about doing something constructive rather than complain. Daddy says competition is healthy. If you don't like something, find a way to compete rather than blame. So, I'd help her out. It would be a good investment. She's my BFF.

5

Going Once

Not late but

"Hey girrrl you look cute. Better than I feel," I say to TiAnna, giving her a hug.

"Hm I see," she says, leaning back, looks me up and down. "And you late."

"What T? You don't like my sweats? They're clean," I say ignoring her comment.

Besides, my BFF is the one who's usually late. She must be feeling her cheerios or her mama must've driven her out the house. I don't plan to mention on her issues with her mama unless she invites me to.

"Dang Tip. You could've put some lip-gloss on. We gotta maintain our girlishcious image."

"Naw T. Not today."

A couple of years ago, TiAnna and me came up with the word Girlishcious. We wanted to be different from the sexually active girls. We also know we're all that, so girlishcious only applies to the two of us: We are young girls who are damn fine. We have sophistication, class and style. We act with innocent sex appeal. We must be ladies at all times – not whores.

TiAnna and me don't mind being virgins for now. We don't broadcast and careful not to put ourselves in situations we'll regret.

Unc Rae-Rae warned me to protect my cherry. He says young boys get way too hot and can't control their penises. "Don't make 'em hot if you don't plan to go all the way," says Unc Rae-Rae.

Jeremy is an exception I wanna say to my uncle. Jeremy can control his until the time is right. Buttera, I keep this to myself.

TiAnna and me know girls who've been date raped, talked into doing-the-do, or who cried rape in the middle of doing-the-do. Then they say "no means no." This girl Genevieve told us that's what she did. My BFF told her off big time. Says girls like her make it hard for real rape victims.

"Girl you need a drink," says TiAnna, grabbing my elbow. "Come on. Let me buy you 1."

We both get 1 of our favorite drinks, a strawberry smoothie from Starbucks – we love strawberries – take the last empty table.

"So, spill Tip."

"Same dream. Brutal" I say.

"Hm. Any clues?"

"Naw. I think I'm getting close though."

"I'm scared for you Tip."

"Daddy says not to worry."

"Good thing y'all got it like that. Daddeo can keep you safe."

"Um yeah. I guess."

"How's Jeremy?"

TiAnna's changing the subject. What's going on with me really bothers her, but she's been sweet about it.

"Jeremy's visiting Miami U."

"Yeah? What if he decides to go?"

"Me and Jeremy talk about it all the time. I can go to school where he goes; we'd live together."

"Hm. You ready for dat?"

"Yeah. I love Jeremy, but I plan to follow my dream too."

"Mr. Jeremy cool wit' dat?"

"Mm hm. I can be his arm-candy and follow my dream too."

"Ha! I still can't believe you want to be an Architectural Engineer. You don't seem the type Tip."

"Type or not, I'm intrigued by what daddy does."

"True dat. You an engineer, me a Princess. Ha!"

You know y'all since Disney created the movie Princess and the Frog with a black princess named TiAnna, you can't tell my BFF nothing. She takes the character to heart.

This one time, I happened to be at her house when a friend of her mama's, stopped by to visit. She had her 8-year-old daughter with her who got excited when she heard TiAnna's name.

"Are you the princess?" she says to T.

"Yes I am," TiAnna says with a straight face.

Lydia turned-up her lips and rolled her eyes. The little girl's mother laughed. I don't know if she ever told her the truth.

Late afternoon still at the mall

Bling West is crowded like always. I purposely look at expensive stuff, making TiAnna nervous. She keeps making comments like, "I hope what you looking at is gold. Hm. I ain't tryin' to spend my whole allowance. You still my girl. Don't get mad if I ask to borrow some money next week. You the one with' all the cash." I finally find something reasonably priced – a black jean skirt and a fuchsia lace top – and this makes TiAnna happy.

We leave Bling West and run into a familiar face. TiAnna's on-again off-again boo Virgil. He's Latino and Black, fine and got swag like the singer Miguel. I ain't saying they all look alike, but they could be cousins.

LaTonya

TiAnna stops about a foot in front of him — posing — her arms crossed, leaning on her right hip with her left foot extended. She pooches her lips out, looking him up and down.

"Bebé caliente," he says, holding his arms out inviting a hug.

TiAnna's angry with him so ignores the gesture. Last week she found out, he's dealing and he said he wasn't. TiAnna giving Virgil an attitude doesn't stop him from grabbing the sides of her cheeks. He leans into her slapping his lips on top of hers. From here I can see him stick is big-ass tongue into her mouth for some quick-tongue action. Then he slides his tongue across the tip of her nose.

"Stop!" says TiAnna while playfully pushing him away. Virgil falls backward laughing.

"Whassup Tippy?" he says, grinning, looking over at me.

"Hey," I say, shrugging my shoulders.

Then he turns his attention back to T. "Bebe, let me holla at you for a minute."

"Why?" she says.

"Come on bebe, don't be like dat."

TiAnna glances over at me. I shrug and say, "Y'all can drop me off." Frankly, I'm glad for an excuse to go home. My head's starting to hurt again.

TiAnna leaves her car parked at the mall and they run me home in Virgil's Cadillac SUV, the 2013 edition. I'm riding in the back seat while their upfront arguing. They both have 3 words they love.

Virgil says, "Come on bebe`."

My BFF says, "That ain't cool."

Miss Tommy told TiAnna long ago Virgil's a drug dealer. He's driven a new Cadillac since we've known him, wondering how he could afford it. TiAnna told us he worked for his daddy at some repair shop even though she's never been there. I believe TiAnna knows about Virgil but pretends she doesn't. She likes him a lot and told me she was considering doing-the-do with him until he made her mad.

4:00p.m. Roadrunner

Virgil has a knack for getting through traffic faster than anyone I know. I breathe easier when we make it to my house. Virgil stops in the middle of the street rather than pull to the side. And he's in such a hurry I can barely get out the car.

"Slow your roll fool before you run over my friend!" says my BFF.

I slide out the passenger side and step up to her door. TiAnna reaches out the window and gives me a hug.

"Smooches behave," I say in her ear.

"Smooches maybe," she says with a girlishcious smile.

I wave until they're out of sight. Hm? A dark blue Ford pulls up right behind 'em and turns the corner when they do.

Ok. Cut the paranoia. I need except for I can't help but feel something's getting ready to go down.

6

My BFF

8:00 p.m.
In bed already

Chillaxin watching The Game on BET. I like Jason and Brandy as a couple. They're opposites like Jeremy and me. Jeremy is more like Brandy; he's immersed himself amongst the black urban culture. Me, I use to be like Jason, learning to fit in. I am also articulate like him, proper talking like some black folks say.

In Stone Mountain, I'm around more black people unlike Druid Hills. Here I don't attend private school but public school. Luanne chose to live here. What's good about it is she no longer gets to play matriarch of mama's Druid Hills home. Mama's parents bought the estate for her and daddy when they got married. Daddy recently sold mama's big beautiful house back to my grandparents for the full price of $20 mil. Someone else is living there now I hear.

"Hell, they can afford it," daddy says.

Maybe so but wrong nonetheless. As I say, my daddy is mean.

Luanne wants her brats living near the amusement park. Such a silly reason for buying a home. She also had daddy buy her mama a house in Conyers. Daddy doesn't like nor want her mama around the brats 'cause she was Don Juan's whore. Dad has forbidden her to drop by whenever, so Luanne visits her in Conyers and rarely takes the kids.

My high school is located on the dividing line between the middle-class and upper-class neighborhoods. Stone Mountain High is diverse with African American students making up 45 percent, Latinos 10 percent, Asians less than 3 percent and white students, the rest.

Black kids at Stone Mountain speak mostly urban slang and I've picked up some. I can even talk ghetto but TiAnna and Jeremy laugh at me. They say I can't help but sound like a southern black, white girl. How I speak comes from mama and gramma. Daddy is also articulate. Mama and gramma say, "It's better to speak with grace and elegance rather than like uneducated black people."

Earlier on

While living in Atlanta I attended a private grade school with other wealthy kids. The majority were African American. The head master, staff and teachers regularly taught us values like respect for others and ourselves. We didn't have issues with bullying or fighting.

But then we moved here

And daddy enrolled me in Stone Mountain elementary, comprised of middle-and upper-class students. The environment was much different. Some students were rebel rousers and others were cliquish.

The black kids made fun of me – the way I talked – and my fancy clothes mama bought me. I did my own hair sometimes keeping it in a ponytail with matching barrettes and bows. Unc Rae-Rae would send over his girlfriend Sadie once a week to take me to the beauty salon for my hair and nails.

The first time I chose a fuchsia nail polish daddy made me take off. Said I'm too young to be wearing nail polish. Shoot. He needs to worry about how Luanne's nails look. The only color polish she wears is black. She's a demon child. Next time Sadie took me, we had my nails painted white. Daddy didn't notice.

I'm grateful to my uncle and Sadie. Daddy's wifey doesn't know how to take care of a black girl's hair. I mean, her being biracial doesn't help squat. She's lucky her hair is wavier than nappy. But poor Brittany. Her hair use to look tore-up-from-the-floor-up. Daddy finally told Luanne, "Do something with that girl's damn hair!" Now Luanne takes Brittany to a salon regularly.

In grade school, the kids mistook my shyness as conceit.

"You stuck up witch. You act like you better than us," they'd say.

My attitude stemmed from recently losing a mama, daddy remarrying someone who hated me and then stealing me away from a familiar home, family and friends.

Things changed when I met TiAnna. She was also new to Stone Mountain Elementary and in my homeroom. She stopped a group of kids from picking on me. Told them her daddy worked as a secret operative for the CIA and could have them sent away to a rat-infested foreign prison. They'd just disappear one-by-one and no one would come looking.

I don't know if they believed her, but they left us alone.

"Don't worry girl they just hatin'," says TiAnna. "You wanna be friends? We both look good."

I laugh and say, "Ok."

We've been tight ever since. I started dressing differently so I could fit. Unc Rae-Rae let Sadie take me shopping. I took TiAnna with me and bought her a new wardrobe too.

My BFF ain't changed much

And she still has me rollin'. In high school chemistry class, the other day a foul odor arose and dissipated. Nothin' unusual for chemistry, but it did smell like fart. What did TiAnna do? She got so mad she stood up, right in the middle of the teacher's lecture. With her hands on her hips she says, "Hm stank! Whoever farted needs to eat more veggies. You smelling ain't the truth. I mean dang!"

What now

BFF. She's calling me, so I put my DVR on pause. "Hey girl"

TiAnna interrupts. She's talking fast, yelling and crying all at the same time. I can barely get a word in edge wise.

"Say what! Ooo snap!" I'm finally able to say.

She says the police busted Virgil for drugs shortly after they dropped me off. She was with him.

"Damn Tip. Everybody was lookin'. How embarrassing," she says sniffling. "I tried to cover my face. Didn't want anyone to see me."

TiAnna doesn't like to be made a fool. I can tell you Virgil's 2nd chance with Princess T is gone.

"That damn fool had dope underneath the carpet in the trunk. They could legally search his car 'cause they saw him selling to folks at the mall. They tailed him out of the mall and followed us."

"Ooo for real?" I say.

"Yeah. No shit. The cops made us get out with our hands up. Like I'm some damn criminal!"

"Wow T!"

"Virgil told 'em I didn't know nothin' but arrested me anyway."

"Shame!" I try to act surprised, but I'm not. Of course, they took her downtown. I feel bad for her. And I thought I was being paranoid.

"I was over at juvie where they finally released me. I had to call daddy to come sign me out. Lucky for me, they won't press charges."

"I know your daddy is maaaaad."

"No shit! I'm probably grounded, 'till the cows come home. I left mama downstairs still yelling after she took my cell phone. JR let me use his to call you."

I want to tell TiAnna how I really feel about Mr. Bad News Virgil but I don't. My BFF's gonna hurt for a while. Her man is going down.

7

Who da Man?

May 29, 2012
Before school starts

I look for TiAnna like I usually do. Today is the day her and me find out if we made the Stone Mountain senior cheerleading squad. I didn't want to try out, but TiAnna talked me into it.

Jeremy will be off at college next year and I don't want to cheer for the other jocks. My appreciation for sports is because of him. When he plays, I cheer until I'm hoarse. I also watch games with him at his house or at Stone Rec.

TiAnna isn't at our normal meeting spot, so I'm guessing she stayed home. Our spot is 1 of 5 chat-and-chews here. The school has 3 others on the 2nd floor and one near the main gym. The chat-and-chews have comfy chairs and round tables where kids kick-back, eat, talk or meet up between periods. This ain't the place for students who want peace and quiet or space to get some studying done.

This chat-and-chew is the most popular 'cause it's close to the cafeteria, centrally located near the school's main hall. The hall goes right by the main office, the north and south stairwells and front and back exits. This spot gets crazy crowded during class changes.

Okay morning bell. Time to…

"Ohhh heyyyy!" My boo is coming this way, grinning showing off his dimples and pretty white teeth. He stops when he gets a few feet from me, takes one step back and looks at me like "Girl you look damn good." Then he hunches over, charges me as if he's quarter-backing on the field – gently of course – grabs, and slowly kisses me, sliding his tongue back and forth in my mouth. I'm giving him tongue action too. Afterwards we hug.

"I missed you beautiful."

"I missed you too. We doing lunch later?"

Jeremy thinks for a moment then says, "Naw. Let's meet afterschool. We gotta run through the graduation ceremony. Be here at 3:30."

"Yeah okay." I'd forgotten senior graduation is Friday night. I'll be there.

We kiss again and quickly suck each other's tongue, which makes us giggle. We then go our separate ways.

Jeremy is my thick cuddly teddy bear. At 6'10, he weighs 220 pounds. Good thing he's a quarterback. He has to stay in shape. Last summer I got after him for gaining weight. He had a belly mostly 'cause he likes to drink beer. Jeremy shaves his head bald. He has the perfect round face and wears tiny diamond earrings in his ears. His eyes remind me of a Basset Hound. I often tell him to smile otherwise he looks sad.

My Jeremy is the best and my first real boo. We haven't had sex even though we've been together for over a year. He was a junior and I was a sophomore when we hooked up at a jock party. Before then we only passed each other in the halls. He'd smile and wink and I'd smile and give him one of my shy girl waves, waving with your fingers.

I support Jeremy's love of football. Except I use to get annoyed with the girls always in his face. I had to set them straight and let them know I ain't having it. Before we became an item, I use to see him with this one white girl. She's a cheerleader one of those Taylor Swift looking types. I recall being a little jealous thinking, "Another future pro ball player with a white girl."

Shoot. White girls only want black athletes for their money and the damn fools hand it right over to 'em. They should know white girls won't give them the time of day, if they are broke. Except, of course, if they're one of those trailer park white girls. It's sad. Our black men are caught up in "I gotta have me a white girl" even if it means dissing' black women.

Some of those athletes had black girlfriends or wives once. Unfortunately, their exes are ruint. I meeean dang black women. We gotta maintain ourselves. We got too much competition.

Remember when they came out with the story about one former athlete's high school sweetheart? I meeean she ain't cute. Paleeze. If I looked like her, I would've got a quick facelift or makeover before they put me on blast. I meeean, embarrassing for the rest of us hotties.

Lucky for me Jeremy and Ms. Swift weren't together even though she tried to get with him. Jeremy says she offered to go down on him right outside the locker room after a game. He called her all kind of crazy nymph hoes. She avoids him now.

Jeremy says, "White girls scare me. They'll get you killed; scream rape without blinking an eye. I ain't going out like dat."

Instead, he is content with having a sane girl, like me. Some of us can be crazy too.

Jeremy sweats how I look. I'm tall, curvy and toned with a tiny waist. Not skin and bones. He likes to play with my 36B breasts. TiAnna hates on mine 'cause she has small ones. She may have me on the booty though. Hers is bigger and rounder. Jeremy says I have a badunkadunk. Yep. Boo agrees I'm girlishcious as long as I don't cuss around him. Damn, it's hard.

Jeremy's been patient about us not having sex, but we do go down on each other. We started down that road around the holidays last year. I bet y'all dying to know what happened. Ok I'll tell.

We were at his house. His parents were out for the weekend. We got to kissing, which led to us kissing each other's bodies and then our privates. He does me first. Having a wet mouth all over my twot-twot doesn't take long for me to enjoy. I mean I get to hollering. This is the first time I experience this funny sensation coming down through my vagina leaving me all wet and sticky. Now my turn to do him. Jeremy school's me the first time, which makes me nervous. His thang-thang is quite big and long. I remember the penis head hitting the back of my throat, making me feel like I'm gonna choke. Jeremy got so excited he pushed and pushed until bam! This warm liquid starts down my throat. I gag not caring for the salty sour taste. Poor Jeremy. He says, "Sorry," with those sad looking eyes.

Some girls told me drinking sperm can cause a stomach infection. So, I'm careful. Huh. How would I explain something like this to my daddy? Sorry daddy but rather than let Jeremy bust my cherry I sucked his thang-thang and accidentally swallowed his sperm. That would be the last time. I'd end up dying from grief. He would've killed Jeremy.

I don't believe my boo is a virgin, but I trust him. He's been faithful since he's been with me. Jeremy knows I'm not after his future money. I got my own. The money hungry girls at Stone Mountain sitting on the sidelines hope we break up. They want a shot at being the first Mrs. Jeremy Simms. Not gonna happen. I'm his queen.

At lunch time

I run into Tommy Crumbs with his skinny self. He walks towards me holding his head high as usual. He has his nose pointed upwards – snobbish like – mouth squinted to one side like he's saying, "Hmmm," while rolling his eyes at folks he selects. No one in particular Tommy just likes to gossip and can find something wrong with anyone. He walks slowly, sliding his feet and switching his ass. He also waves by letting his hand go limp, flapping it up and down, thinking that's cute.

Tommy is one of those boys my daddy doesn't mind me hanging with. He's a closet homosexual and everyone knows. I don't think he'll come out while he's living at home. His daddy's a deacon and his mama is extremely religious. She practically damns you to hell without a reason. I personally can't stand the woman. To this day, she can't figure out why Tommy and me ain't together.

This one-time Tommy came over, we were in my room talking about anything and everything.

Out of nowhere Tommy says, "I'm a virgin." Then he says something stupid, "I want you to bust my cherry girrrl."

I fell out laughing. Cherry means a girl's virginity and he sounded so gay. Tommy ignored my laugh and jumped on top of me! He kissed me all over my face with god awful wet kisses! I couldn't stop laughing. Then he rubbed on my breasts — all hard — and I shoved him away. I told him daddy would be surprised at how he was acting. Maybe I should make Jeremy play as if he's gay. Then we could do-the-do right under daddy's nose.

What I said made Tommy drop tears. I've seen him cry before 'cause he's so damn sensitive. Except I hit a nerve. He admitted he's gay and has a boo. He wouldn't tell me who and I didn't push. I got the impression the person was much older. The few boys that attend All Saints Baptist Church stay clear of Tommy.

Tommy says TiAnna and me made the cheerleading squad. He also heard about T and Virgil.

"Shucks. Tried to tell girlfriend about Latin Mandingo," says Tommy. "Can't say nada about her man."

He's right but I say, "I think it's pretty clear now."

"Good," he says jerking his head back. Pivots, walks off down the hall like a runway model looking for someone else to gossip with.

8

My Boo is All That

3:45 p.m.
Playtime

For Jeremy and me. We head over to Stone Rec about a mile from school. The center is for high school students only. All the athletes hang here and you gotta have student ID. This keeps out the younger kids, those damn pedophiles and rapists lurking around.

Before mandatory identification, a pedophile raped a girl and killed her right in the place. We called this place the Hall back then. A pedophile stalked the sophomore and made his move while she was in the girl's bathroom alone. Followed her into the bathroom and bolted the door; raped her, slit her throat and slipped out the back door without anyone noticing him.

The city forced the owners to shut down until they put in safeguards. Stone Rec reopens a year later under new management, with onsite security and requires photo ID.

Stone Rec is famous for its pool hall, famous burgers and fries. The burgers are real nasty juicy with pepper bacon, hotlinks, fried egg, if you want, and all the trimmings – like pickle, onion, cheese, lettuce

— and the Rec's special burger and fry sauce. The sauce is a mixture of mayo, ketchup and hot sauce, making you wanna holla. It's spicy good.

The Rec is already crowded. We squeeze our way to the pool tables in back. Some of Jeremy's jock buddies saved us seats at a booth near 1 of the tables. I slide in next to Damon, and Jeremy, next to me.

Also, here from the football team is Leonardo who we call Lenny for short and Chris whose nickname is Casper because he's so damn white, almost ghostly. His eyes stay red, probably 'cause he's high. He should keep some eye drops in 'em for real. Those bloodshot eyes and white skin make him look like Edward on Twilight. I know girls think he's cute, but I don't. I'm not into white boys, but I've seen some fine ones. Mr. Twilight and Casper ain't among 'em.

Damon, who plays the team's linebacker, is here with Delinda his crazy ghetto ass girlfriend. She's a junior and goes to the school across town in the hood. It ain't nothing like the hood in east ATL though. You can at least go to this one after dark but have to be careful.

Granddaddy and gramma Oliver would say, "Lots of poor black folks living in one area means trouble."

You do hear about more black crime. Daddy says it's because the white news media over reports black crime.

Damon is curious about Jeremy's trip to Miami. Jeremy gives a full report; the same thing he told me. He accepted the University's offer, will get a scholarship and a chance to play starting quarterback. If he does well he could go pro in a couple of years.

"Ain't no big deal. I'mo handle bitness," says confident Jeremy.

Damon says he's still exploring options. He'll be meeting with Philly U next week and L.A. U the following week.

Lenny doesn't know if football is his thing and Casper is a junior. Jeremy told me in private they aren't golden boys like he and Damon. Yet, they're better than most of their other teammates.

"So you gonna leave your girl eh," says Lenny with a wide grin. "The hounds are waiting."

Jeremy looks at me, smiles and says, "Baby and me gone be together. Distance ain't nothing. My girl plans to make a move next year, right babe?"

"Yeah," I say, smiling. Out the corner of my eye, I see Delinda turning up the side of her mouth. Her and me ain't never been friendly and don't speak other than say "hey." Delinda's way to street for me. Daddy may want me to stay grounded, but I draw the line when it comes to hoochie or ghetto mamas. Daddy agrees.

I wonder if Damon plans to take her with him. I'm inclined to believe Jeremy. She's Damon's "I can get some anytime girl" with no strings. I suspect Delinda has a crazy side, so she may force him to take her. She did go off on Damon one time in the parking lot. He calmed her down by threatening to make her walk home. Delinda has a gang member brother. I don't think she needs his help to get at Damon.

Anyhoo. Not my concern. We can be cool as long as ghetto stays away from my block.

9

Mama Knows

May 30, 2012
After school

I have Jeremy drop me at Dr. Anderson's office. She's my psychiatrist. Dr. Evelyn Anderson, who's African American and the best in her field, is nationally recognized. She's counseled me since mama's been gone and has helped me quite a bit. I'm impressed by her candor. She reminds me of gramma Oliver. At 56, this woman looks good and healthy. She's articulate, except when she likes to refer to my family as "y'alls," which is kind of funny.

I love coming here, the ambiance relaxes me. I suspect the warm pastel walls help. Dr. Anderson has a beautiful African art collection of wall paintings, tribal masks and clay figurines. The one painting with a young African American girl, running carefree through a field of lavender with her hands in the air, eyes closed and a big smile on her face touches me.

Her other pieces include the 8-inch-tall figurine on the corner table, catty-corner from her desk on the left side of the room next to the door. The statued man dressed in a gold headdress with a blue-gold ankle length dashiki, stands next to a woman holding a nude baby boy in her arms. An ornamental scarf wrapped around her head, adorned in orange and gold ankle length dress. You can imagine what this family scene does to me.

The other one sits on the coffee table sandwiched between the brown leather recliner – where I'm sitting – and the couch. The statue is a 5-inch tall African woman in a purple flowered dress, kneeling with a basket on top of her head.

I'm laying back in the recliner. Today we plan to talk about what happened to mama. Dr. Anderson walks with me down this road often to jog my memory. Little by little, I remember bits and pieces but not enough to satisfy me. I want to know what happened that night.

Dr. Anderson comes in and takes her seat across from me. She makes sure I feel comfortable before we begin.

Someone murdered mama 9 years ago right before my birthday on June 8, 2002. I was 7 when I found her body. I may have walked in on the killer but don't remember. Daddy wasn't home but thanks to him, I'm alive.

What I remember was

Daddy came home earlier than expected. The killer must've run off when she heard him come through the front door. When he came into the room where mama and me were, he saw mama slumped across the couch, lying sideways with her legs and feet hanging off the side. Covered in blood from multiple stab wounds. I was kneeling beside her with my head on her bloody stomach. I shook mama, trying to wake her, but she wouldn't move.

Mama's barely alive when the medics arrived. Daddy was holding me while the medics work on her. He keeps me from looking while the police asks me questions. He wanted to take me from the room but I threw a fit.

Daddy called mama's parents who planned to meet them at the hospital. Before he went, he took me to gramma Ellis's. He wouldn't take me with him and Luanne was visiting her mother.

When daddy arrived at the hospital, my grandparents informed the staff not to let him see mama. My gramma and granddaddy Oliver were responsible. They assumed he was guilty and obtained a "no contact order."

Unc Rae-Rae later broke the news to Daddy. Mama died that night at 8:45. Unc Rae-Rae also told daddy the coroner discovered a bruise and laceration on mama's forehead. They believed the killer knocked mama out with a blunt object before stabbing her. They found no signs of a struggle or the murder weapon.

A couple of days later, mama's family held a memorial service for her and barred daddy from attending, so my uncle took me.

At the church, purple flowers and a beautiful photo of her surrounded mama's closed casket. Gramma Oliver said damages to her body prevented an open casket.

"I want to see mama anyway," I said. But they wouldn't let me. All I could do was lay my head on her casket and cry. The same way I did the night, I found her.

Nearly a year went by before the police no longer suspected daddy. This made my grandparents angry because they still think he's guilty. So do other family members. The rumor is daddy killed mama or had someone do it 'cause she was having an affair.

I may not remember the killer, but it wasn't daddy. So I continue having nightmares and learn to deal in my sessions. The nightmare is the same and brings me closer to the truth. It's only a matter of time before I know who killed her.

I don't tell daddy about what I learn in my sessions with Dr. Anderson. He's not the loving daddy who kept me sane for the first years. I'm afraid he'd tell Luanne and the thought makes me nervous.

10

I Get No Respect

June 8, 2012
8:15 a.m. Breakfast is ruined

Thanks to daddy. He makes an announcement that catches me off guard but Luanne and her brats aren't surprised. Daddy says we're moving to Portland, Oregon sometime next month. Apparently, the time is right to open up a west coast headquarters. I didn't realize daddy planned to expand so soon. The last I heard he was still trying to raise $90 mil. I wonder where he got the money all of sudden.

I guess I'm to suck it up, forget doing my senior year at Stone Mountain and move to white-ass Portland. I've already gotten the low down from Tommy Crumbs when I mentioned this possibility months ago. I didn't care at the time. I thought daddy had set the move for after I was long gone.

"I ain't going," I say.

"You don't have a choice in the matter," that man says, looking over his black reading glasses at me. Although I'm angry, I want to laugh. He looks like a damn fool in those big round plastic things.

Luanne got those for him. Thought he'd look younger or cool. She also buys younger style clothes for him like jeans with holes in 'em and Snoop Dog hoodies. Daddy is a 48-year old, grown-ass man with a 16-year-old daughter! That's what he gets for marrying a woman half his age.

The nerve. On top of the "we're moving to Portland bullshit," he ignores me when I ask him to go to mama's grave with me. That's when I throw my full plate of food against the wall. "Woohoo!"

Then he grabs and holds me. The fool. I'm not going to make it easy for him! I'm struggling and kicking so much I manage to make my way, pulling daddy into our front entryway. Brittany and Jayden skedaddle.

"LaTonya! Cool it!"

He's calling me by my real name, showing me he's mad. Boo on him. I ain't letting up this time.

"Tell your wifey to cool it!"

"You're acting like a child."

"Naw babe, she's bein' diz-ra-spec-ful," says Luanne.

"Who you calling disrespectful? You don't deserve respect!" I say, defending myself. Daddy's such a wimp.

"LaTonya, I'm done talkin'."

I meeean, he must think I'm scared of his little warning. "I don't care. You always take her side."

"I'm not taking anyone's side."

"Scuse you? You gown let her towk to me like dat?"

Ooo! Damn wifey again.

"Luanne chill. I'll handle this."

Uh what? Daddy talked back. I'm sc-a-r-e-da him. "Yeah, keep quiet L-u-u-a-n-n-e-e-y."

"What ya need is a slap silly," says Luanne.

Oh no wifey didn't try to get bad ass. "I dare you skank!"

"Dammit LaTonya!"

Ooo daddy cussed at me. Bad daddy. Time to go in for the gut. "Don't LaTonya me! Today's the anniversary of mama's death and I don't get a damn bit of compassion from you and nothing but grief from your bee-atch!"

Yep. I said it really ghetto. TiAnna would've been proud. Ha. My daddy ain't the only one mad. I want to snatch Luanne's dirty blonde hair off. Her skinny ass face would look better. Ooo she's fugly. How could daddy marry her?

Daddy and Luanne make a funny looking couple. Luanne towers above daddy and she has the nerve to wear heels. She's a damn Amazon. Mm, mm, mm. Pitiful. The way she walks, tall lanky legs like an ostrich.

"Let go of me daddy. I'm whooping' her ass!"

"Settle down girl!"

"Back up off me daddy you're hurting me. I'll call 9-1-1."

"Naw I'll cowl 9-1-1. You need to be locked up."

Daddy's wifey is talking again. I scowl at her. Bitch can't even talk.

"Call 'em, so they'll have somethin' to take me to jail for after I whoop your ass!"

Daddy is holding onto me tight around my waist, pinning my arms. I feel like he's crushing me. Damn I wish he'd let go. He's struggling to keep me like this 'cause I'm giving him a run for his money like mama use too. Glad we're in the front foyer. Luanne bought lots of tasteless crap I can throw – since I can't grab a knife.

"Luanne! Get the hell out of here! I'll handle this!"

Ooo. Daddy cussed again. I'll give him half an award for being a no-wimp daddy.

"Let me go daddy!"

"Not until you calm down."

Shoot. Let me stop struggling. I'm getting nauseous from being so angry.

Phew. He finally let go but it doesn't matter. I have the last word.

"Go to hell!" I walk out the front door; slam it in his face.

"I'll leave you alone!" I hear him say through the door.

Good idea, I'm thinking. I lost my mama again today. He and wifey better stay clear.

11

In Mama's Honor

8:45 a.m.

The best part

Of this place are these hard ass steps – not good. Luanne made daddy buy a house in this upscale area where neighbors won't give her the time a day. Folks with lots of money can spot low class; they know Luanne is among the lowest.

She tried to make friends with the Brandon's across the street. Their kids are around the same ages as the twins. One day she took the Brandon's a store-bought Sweet Potato Pie. Mrs. Brandon hasn't invited her back and the brats didn't even get a play date. Luanne figures they're racists. As white as she looks, I don't think they thought about race. I imagine they were just turned off by her. Especially after she had the outside of this house painted purple!

This house is new and didn't need painting. At least not, purple. Who does that? Soooo tacky. Now we have pissed-off neighbors. The homeowner's association asked daddy to repaint the exterior back to the original color. According to covenant rules, owners can only use neutral colors. Daddy said he'd do it but Luanne threw a hissy fit – the house is still purple.

She even made the inside tacky. Calls herself trying to decorate. Luanne loves to watch home and garden shows but I'm not sure which one she watches. Must be something called "Remodeling tips for the tacky wacky." Luanne hired an interior designer to help. A longhaired hippy looking white guy I believe she found in the Nickel Ads. He was so fake he smelled funky. I mean, like a wet dog. Luanne thought he was attractive. Like she did with daddy, she flirted with him so much, she made him uncomfortable. Huh. She's so stupid. The guy was gay. I know a gay boy when I see one. Thanks to the fool she hired, and her tacky sense of style, we end up with different colored walls everywhere. Luanne claims this is an international theme. The kitchen is burgundy and the rest of the house is done up in gold, green, yellow and blue. The front foyer color is dark gold and splashed with green blotches. Makes me want to throw up. She claims the color palette represents royal serenity. What the hell!

She also bought mismatched furniture – modern to Victorian – and had nerve to put wicker in one of the sitting rooms. What! I had to beg daddy to let me redo my room. It was horrid. At first, I thought it was for Brittany. She may have liked the Pepto-Bismol walls; white shag throw carpet and get this: a black brass day bed. Who does that? I think she did it on purpose. I meeean, the wooden chest-of-drawers and night stand didn't match. She claims the wooden furniture was the in thing. I held back from saying, "Put the damn shit in your room!"

My room looks hella good now but living here is wearing on my nerves. Gramma and granddaddy Oliver, Unc Rae-Rae and daddy's own mama hit the ceiling about daddy's marriage to Luanne.

Right after mama died my grandparents tried to get custody of me. I wish they would've succeeded but Daddy was a step ahead this time. Before he announced his marriage to Luanne, he secured his rights and a no-contact order against my grandparents and mama's family. They could no longer contact me. Daddy's attorney convinced the judge it was for my emotional wellbeing. The judge was friends with daddy's good buddy, Judge Simms, who for many years would help daddy cause problems for me.

His attitude and how he treats me, makes me wonder what attracted mama too him.

My parents met at Emory University in Atlanta – mama was 25 and daddy 31 – and where mama graduated Suma Cum Laude with both a Bachelor's and Master's Degree in Teaching. Daddy attended Georgia Tech and graduated Magna Cum Laude with a Bachelor's and Master's in Building Construction and Architectural Engineering and a Ph.D. in Environmental Engineering.

They dated secretly for about a year – mama's parents wouldn't have approved. They wanted her to marry Atlanta United States Senator Stanley Rutherford, a conservative Republican.

Mama never put her teaching degrees to use. She married daddy instead and was pregnant with me at the time. She also did this against her parent's wishes. According to them, she married down. Mama also changed her party affiliation to Democrat and invested over $10 mil into daddy's start-up company. Her parents saw this as the ultimate betrayal.

The man who treats
Me better than daddy

Unc Rae-Rae just drove up in his blue Prius. "Heyyy Unc Rae-Rae. You must've been feeling' me."

Unc Rae-Rae is 4 years younger than daddy is. He's so fine with his sly grin and golden-brown eyes. I hear he's really charming and a ladies' man; the Atlanta women love him.

My uncle is taller than daddy is. He's 5'10 with an athletic physique. He also has a nice ass and walks like Denzel Washington. Too bad he's my uncle y'all. Naw, I'm just playin'. But for real, I can't help but say mm, mm, mm.

His friends call him Ray and I call him Unc Rae-Rae. Me, Jeremy and TiAnna got to go to his birthday party this year – he turned 44.

"I see you got a fresh fade sporting your RAE, Mr. Raymond Anthony Ellis," I say, admiring my uncle.

In the streets, they call him a player. He has 2 or 3 girlfriends, is as cool as they come. The blue Prius he's driving doesn't match his personality. He likes classic cars but chooses to drive conservative ones. He just bought a Toyota Camry to drive along with his Chevy Tahoe and Honda Accord.

Tommy Crumbs, who prides himself on knowing everybody's business, says Unc Rae-Rae doesn't want to draw attention— keep the cops away. It's rumored he smuggled big drugs when he worked on ships and he made lots of money.

Unc Rae-Rae does dress in designer clothes and sweats. He jogs 5 miles a day, pumps weights at a gym and plays neighborhood hoop. You wouldn't think it, but he's half vegetarian and the only meat he eats is fish. My uncle is leery about food. He's read several articles and has seen disturbing documentaries about how processed foods, oils and meats give us cancer and slowly poison us.

"But it's legal 'cause it's all about the money," Unc Rae-Rae says. "I ain't payin' them to kill my ass."

Unc Rae-Rae is taking me to visit mama's gravesite. No need to ask daddy. For some reason when he comes around, daddy straightens up. Treats me a little better for a while after Unc Rae-Rae leaves.

One time I overheard Unc Rae-Rae and daddy having a heated conversation about me. "If you don't treat my baby girl right, all bets are off," says Unc Rae-Rae.

"She's my daughter and don't you forget it," says Daddy.

"All bets will be off," my uncle says again.

I wonder what he means, but it shut daddy up.

Yippee, I'm sprung

And I'm smiling again. As Unc Rae-Rae backs out the driveway, Luanne's brats stare at us from their upstairs window. Brittany doesn't talk to me at all. Jayden talks to me like his mama snooty and mean.

We stop at a flower shop to pick up purple roses – mama's favorite – for her grave located in the family mausoleum at Druid Hills Mortuary. From the flower shop to the gravesite it takes 2 hours because of the heavy Atlanta traffic.

My grandparents told me my crypt is in the family mausoleum. Hopefully, I won't have to use it anytime soon. At one point though, I wouldn't have minded joining mama. Dr. Anderson helped me through those dark days, which stirred up the strangest dream, I only dreamt once. Unlike my nightmare, this one left me at peace.

I'm standing on a porch trying to get into a locked screen door. Standing behind it is a woman. Her dark face is almost skeleton like encircled by a soft golden hue with her head wrapped in a white scarf. She's holding white prayer beads. Even though she looks like this, I'm not afraid of her. I asked her to let me come-in.

"It's not your time," she says – I immediately woke up.

Right before noon

We arrive at the site. Judging by the enormous number of purple roses, lots of people have been by to visit. What an awesome sight. I bet the flower shops mark this annual event on their calendars as a special mama's day.

I move some of the roses out of the way so I can sit closer to mama's crypt which says:

In loving memory of God's child
Loretta Lynn Oliver-Ellis 1969-2002

Mama was so young. She barely had a chance to live life. Whoever murdered her deprived all of us of her beautiful soul.

Unc Rae-Rae is standing behind me. He's quietly feeling the loss of mama as much as I do.

"I'm sorry baby girl," he says.

I look over my shoulder at my uncle; his eyes are wet.

"You don't have anything to be sorry for," I say. "I'm okay."

Unc Rae-Rae drops his head, looks down to avoid eye contact.

"Yeah? I'm glad. One day… well, I'm hoping soon, this will be behind us," Unc Rae-Rae says.

He's holding something back and it saddens me a little. He'll tell me when he's ready. Hopefully he won't make me wait too long.

"Hey suga," I hear a familiar voice say.

"OMG! Granddaddy Oliver!"

I jump up, grab him and give him a big hug. Unc Rae-Rae told him I'd be here. Gramma never got over mama's death so she refused to come.

"I miss you and gramma."

"We think about you all the time Puddin'," says granddaddy. "Boy ain't you looking more like your mama every day." He steps back to admire my beauty.

"Don't she though," says Unc Rae-Rae. "Lookin' good as a bowl of Collard Greens on a Sunday."

I must've gotten some of my good looks from my granddaddy too. He's extremely handsome and the same height as Unc Rae-Rae; He also stays in good shape for a man who recently turned 62.

Granddaddy Oliver stands with his hands in his pant pockets and speaks while rocking back and forth on his feet – heel, toe – and bounces up and down when he laughs.

Granddaddy's face is smooth with no wrinkles; he's got bushy, tamed brows and carries a permanent grin. His eyes remind me of Gizmo the Gremlin. Mama gets her complexion from him – high-yellow. His hair has turned gray since I last saw him, but it's still wavy – he's got white in him.

A little bit of history

My granddaddy, Franklin Theodore Oliver V, is a 4th generation mogul with major holdings in steel, real estate, commercial, farm land and an assortment of investments overseas. He's the current President and CEO of F.T. Oliver, Inc. worth $25 Billion.

The Oliver family records date back to the 1700s. Granddaddy Oliver's grandfather, Oliver III (my great, great granddaddy), who was born in 1837, is where the Oliver's African American bloodline starts. Oliver III was the son of a slave woman named Magda the 16-year-old concubine of Oliver II.

Oliver II created the family fortune. The south knew him as the largest crop and landowner throughout Georgia, Alabama and Mississippi. Legal or not, he had 3 wives: 2 of them resided at their own estates, apart from the Master and his 3rd wife Clarice, the youngest at age 28. She and Oliver II stayed on the estate in Georgia.

Clarice gave birth to a boy 10 years earlier and the first named Theodore Franklin Oliver III. Shortly following the boys 10th birthday, Oliver II disowned him and stripped him of his name. He found out a poor, young white farmer named Ben actually fathered the boy – he and Clarice had an affair. I meeean, Master Oliver was old as Methuselah. You know the dude in the bible related to Noah who lived to be 1000 years old.

Folks say Oliver II was a cold-blooded, mean man – sounds like daddy. He forced Ben to sign over his farmland in exchange for sparing Clarice and the boy's life. To avoid further embarrassment, Master Oliver banned them to Europe. He didn't allow Ben to go but he did disappear a few months later. No one knows if he fled to Europe on his own, or if Oliver II had him killed.

Around the time, Clarice gave birth, 15-year-old Magda bore a son and named him Tangee. Everyone knew Tangee was Master Oliver's but a Mandingo claimed him. Tangee looked more like Oliver II as he grew older. He was so light-skinned he could've passed for white.

In 1858, Master Oliver died of pneumonia at age 84, 7 years before Abe Lincoln abolished slavery. Before he passed away, he willed his entire estate (land and assets) to 20-year-old Tangee, who legally became Theodore Franklin Oliver III.

The Oliver name and wealth came with another condition: Young Oliver III had to denounce his black mother publicly and pretend his mother was an unnamed white woman, who died in childbirth. Oliver cared for Magda and the remaining slaves, who stayed on at the Oliver estate while he was away and up until his mother's death in 1888. The US also had abolished slavery. Right before Magda died Oliver III acknowledged her in the family record as his real mother.

Young Oliver attended Harvard University and at age 27, earned a BA and MBA and a JD, passing the bar at 34. After leaving school, he travelled Europe. In Sweden, he met a wealthy mogul who taught him about the steel industry. Oliver purchased the mogul's company, merged it with the Oliver holdings and turned the entire company into a multinational corporation within the first 10 years. Oliver soon relocated F.T. Oliver, Inc. headquarters to Atlanta, leaving a branch office in Sweden where it exists today.

Back to history in the making

Unc Rae-Rae and granddaddy are close, unlike my daddy, who doesn't get along with mama's parents and now my uncle.

"Tell you what poppa Oliver, I'll bring Tippy by on her birthday."

"Sho nuff? Mama sure would like to see her." Granddaddy calls my gramma, mama.

Between now and then I'm guessing I won't see him, so I'm taking advantage of the bear hug he's giving me.

"Alright then. Time to take our girl home," says granddaddy. "Don't want brother Ellis calling the posse."

"Not a chance," says my uncle. "We got a un-da-standin."

"Let's hope," granddaddy says. "I'm going to pray for you all."

12

Whose Truth?

June 9, 2012
It's my 17th Birthday

And I wish I felt as good as I look. I'm standing in the mirror admiring myself. I'm definitely girlishcious! My black friends tell me I got "good hair." Like mama's, my hair is long and thick and rarely needs a flat iron. Except when I choose not to wrap it after it's washed. Instead, I let my hair drip dry into boof and curls, which only requires me applying a little oil and conditioner each day.

You know what? I do resemble mama more and don't see any of daddy in me. My complexion is copper-toned, but I have mama's oval face, nose and full lips. I also have strong cheek bones but not as distinct as hers. I'm 5'8 like her, a little taller than daddy is. I'm shapely with almost a perfect score for measurements.

People say I got Unc Rae-Rae's heavy-lidded, sultry, bedroom eyes and broad smile. He doesn't look much like daddy either. Probably 'cause they're actually cousins. Gramma Ellis raised him from the time he was 5. His mother – her sister – died of breast cancer and he doesn't know his father.

In case you're interested, the closest to a father my uncle had was granddaddy Ellis who took-off with another woman. Daddy was 9.

Daddy was 16 when he saw him again. Ran into him accident at Underground Atlanta. Granddaddy Ellis recognized him. I'm guessing a parent would never forget what their child looked like. Daddy says he was with his woman and a young girl. He suspected she must've been his daughter.

He said, "She looked like his sorry ass. Had the same wide-ass nose and big-ass lips."

You mean like you have daddy, I'm thinking. Daddy also said granddaddy had the nerve to come up to him and say, "Hello son."

"Can you imagine?" says daddy. "Huh. Like he ain't never left. I tell you, I was mad and shocked at the same time. I couldn't even say what I had planned to all those years. I wanted to call him all kinds of SOBs for leaving us and then whoop his ass! When I finally got up enough nerve to speak, I said "Pardon me. You have the wrong son."

He said, "Naw you Robert Ellis Jr. You got my name."

I said, "You partially right. My name is Robert Ellis. The asshole who gave me his name no longer exists and hasn't since he left mama and me 7 years ago. He's dead to me!"

Daddy says he didn't give granddaddy a chance to respond. He turned and walked away. When he got home, no one was around – my uncle was in the streets and gramma Ellis was at work – so he let loose and cried 'till he hurt. He decided then he'd never let anyone make him feel pain again. Maybe because of what happened with his father, he grew up to be heartless. I mean, daddy should've gotten over it by now. At least stop taking it out on my uncle and me.

A couple of years ago daddy's sister, who he still refers to as "that girl," sent him a letter. He believed she wanted some money. RJ Designs was turning huge profits. Daddy had his attorney respond with a formal letter, warning her to never to contact him again, or she'd be facing a harassment charge.

Daddy won't introduce me to granddaddy Ellis who's living in North Carolina with the mistress, whom he married after gramma Ellis died. Gramma Ellis had refused to give him a divorce, knowing granddaddy's woman was pregnant. Mama said she wanted his child to be born a bastard as payback.

Check this shit out

Unc Rae-Rae told granddaddy Oliver he'd bring me by to see him and gramma today. But daddy grounded me! Yeah y'all. On my birthday. After I got home from visiting mama's grave, the devil reared its ugly head. I told the devil when daddy shows up tell him I plan to get emancipated.

What's so stupid?

Is this shit started last week! Daddy's been holding a grudge since.

Luanne had the nerve to ask me to babysit her twin brats because their regular babysitter got sick. She and daddy had plans. I told her flat out no! Heck, the chubby-ass twins are 8 years old and think they are grown-ups. They need to go on a diet. Maybe their mama is trying to make sure they don't end up anorexic like her.

I did also say to her, "I won't watch your damn brats!" Yep, sure did. Didn't matter though. She demanded I cancel my plans, which pissed me off. She said it with her hands on her hips, pointing at me with her boney-ass finger – in my face! The nerve!

The bitch then says, "I'm your mother whether you like it or not! You'd better do what I say!"

I called my BFF later to tell her what went down. "No she didn't," says TiAnna. I explained how I got so mad I cried mad tears. I let her know I had one mama and she could "go to hell!"

Daddy, of course, came to his wifey's rescue. Said she's been like a mother to me since I was 8. He even dared to say Luanne had been sort of a mom to me while mama was alive. He crossed the line. I told him I hated his ass and how dare he disrespect my mama!

"Your wifey is the product of a pimp and a ho," I say.

You know he hauled off and slapped me across the face! Daddy's never ever hit me – not even spanked me. I swear the devil was in him. I think he knew too, so he took off like a damn fool. I was going to knock his ass out. I sure wasn't crying and I don't remember any pain only being mad, mad, mad!

My Birthday isn't over after all

Thanks to my Unc Rae-Rae who's standing outside my bedroom door. Ooo I'm hugging him tight. Mr. Fine smells so good. Down Tippy. Down.

"Happy Birthday," he says to me. I start crying. This is the first happy birthday I've gotten today.

Unc Rae-Rae tells me get ready while he talks to daddy. I keep my happy smile to myself and change into the outfit TiAnna bought.

I've been flunking my "be cool and smile." Unc Rae-Rae's advice would be, "Do like the Japanese do and never let 'em see you sweat. Be more strategic," says Unc Rae-Rae. My uncle saying those words make me wanna laugh. Sounds funny from someone who's so cool.

Unc Rae-Rae says he learned this from reading Asian Mind Game and another book by the same author called Thick Face Black Heart. He says the lessons in those books help him maintain his cool. Especially when cops harass him, which they love to do.

I think Unc Rae-Rae's planned a surprise party for me. TiAnna's been dropping subtle hints. She has a hard time keeping secrets. Of course, I couldn't get anything out of Jeremy. He knows how to keep a secret.

First, we stop

At my grandparents' house. When gramma Oliver sees me, she breaks down. It's been way too long.

This house brings back memories. Those were happy times. Mama, gramma and me did a lot of singing and dancing together in the large family room. Mama's college graduation portrait is still hanging above the fireplace. My grandparents had commissioned a relatively new, but up-and-coming artist to paint it. Thanks to them, Pasqual Ibam is famous today. His art is in major galleries around the world.

Pasqual really captured mama's beauty. She's sitting majestically hands folded in her lap, looking like an Egyptian queen with strong jaw lines, high cheek bones and large beautiful eyes.

Mama's wearing a soft yellow silk dress draped below the knees and a purple rose pinned above her left breasts with short sleeves, a curved neckline and wasted sash. Around her slender neck, a diamond choker with matching hoop earrings, hair pulled back behind her ears, hangs to one side and drops down the front of her right shoulder.

Mama always sits with her legs crossed to the side and one foot behind the other. She says this is how real ladies sit – they don't cross their legs unless they're trying to attract attention – which is a lesson we learned from Ms. Denorsha.

Gramma and me leave Unc Rae-Rae and granddaddy in the family room and head upstairs. She walks with such style and grace. At 5'7 and shapely, her soft-skin, medium brown face, full lips and large light brown deep-set eyes, requires no make-up. She wears a little when she's out in public.

We're in my grandparent's bedroom and it still looks the same. It's huge but not as big as it looked when I was a kid. The main area is gramma's private boudoir, elegant and refined like her. This room is equipped with an antique sofa and loveseat with red cedar, antique end tables and coffee table.

Behind the couch is a tall solid gold hanging lamp, which reminds me of a weeping willow with 8 branches. Each branch blooms with a pink tulip style light bulb. The fireplace is to the left with a big screen television hanging from the wall.

On the right is a large floor length mirror, covering the entire right wall and stops at the entryway, leading to the bedroom. The big brass bed is set back against the far wall, near the big glass doors, opening onto the deck. I've never been in their bedroom – not allowed.

Left of the entry is a 3 by 5 red cedar antique jewelry case, where Gramma keeps expensive costume jewelry. Her good stuff – diamonds, rubies and emeralds she locks away in a safe.

My grandparent's walk-in closets are through the entry on the left near the floor length windows, covering the back wall. They have so many clothes, shoes and accessories, the closets look like mini department stores.

A door leads out to another deck, overlooking the 500-acre property of beautiful old growth trees. In the distance, the lake is where mama and me took walks and had picnics. I remember Unc Rae-Rae going with us. The first time he saved us from this big old' rattlesnake. Ooo. It was scary. We screamed and ran all the way back to the house. Unc Rae-Rae finally showed up and was laughing big time.

"Women," he says. "Looks like I'm gonna have to escort y'all from now on." And he did anytime we wanted to go. Mama told me not to tell daddy.

Gramma opens the top drawer of her chest, takes out a purple satin box about the size of a clutch purse and hands it to me. On the box are the initials LLO in gold letters, Loretta Lynn Oliver. Inside the box, a beautiful rose diamond ring I remember mama wearing. I pick up an old black and white photo of a beautiful black woman I also remember. The woman in the photo is a spitting image of mama but it's actually a picture of my great, great gramma Shelondra Oliver. Great, great granddaddy Oliver met and married her while visiting France. She was French African. Said to be one of the most beautiful women in southern France. Another photo in the box shows me at 5 years old with mama and Unc Rae-Rae huddled around the fireplace. My gramma says to keep this one close to my heart and don't show daddy. "We don't want to upset him," she says.

Hm? Another secret involving Unc Rae-Rae.

13

Tired of Goodbyes

3 hours later

We're in the car, waving good-bye to my grandparents. Before we pull out of the driveway, I quickly show my uncle what gramma gave me. He smiles at the picture of the 3 of us. His eyes get wet.

"I remember this," says Unc Rae-Rae. "I went with' y'all to one of those pageants my bro… your daddy hates. You took 1st place. You were 5."

"Oh yeah. I remember. I won and thought I was all that."

"Yeah and you still do. But then, so do I – think you're all that," says Unc Rae-Rae.

I can't help but blush.

Then he says, "I'm not a fan of pageants either. I asked yo' mama to take-off yo' make-up so there wouldn't be any mistake about who the woman was in this photo."

"Ha. Now you sound like daddy."

It's night time now and

Unc Rae-Rae says he's taking me to dinner and TiAnna, Jeremy and Tommy will be joining us. We stop at his house first because he forgot my gift — so he says. He also wants me to go in with him, claiming I won't be safe in the car alone even though he's running in and out. He also tells me to bring my gift, he'll put it in a safe place and we'll stop back by on the way to my house.

Once out the car my uncle picks up pace. I have to run to catch up. He's halfway up the walkway, when I catch him. I put my arm through his, playing as if I'm his girlfriend, all show for his nosey neighbor Ms. Minnie. Unc Rae-Rae says she's a recluse — been living in the same house for 30 years — and is always peeping out the window at folks, especially him. She doesn't realize I'm his niece. I can imagine what she's thinkin'.

Once at the door, he pauses to tell me daddy says I can spend the night. I smile and say, "You the man."

Inside, the lights are off and all is quiet. I'm gearing up for a surprise and better be ready to go into acting mode. I hold onto Unc Rae-Rae as we head left to the living room; he flips the switch and "SURPRISE!" It's my birthday party with 20 of my friends from Stone Mountain High and a few from the Rec. Jeremy and TiAnna hug me first. Jeremy kisses me quickly on the lips while looking at Unc Rae-Rae from the corner of his eye. He's wrinkling his brows, giving Jeremy a silent warning. Unc Rae-Rae is cool but doesn't play about me drinking, doing drugs or having sex.

TiAnna places a party hat on my head with the words "Happy Birthday Queen Nerd," written across the front. She gave me the nickname in grade school, because I always make the honor roll.

Unc Rae-Rae excuses himself and heads upstairs. He trusts me to keep my friends in line. He also probably has one of his girlfriends upstairs. I wonder whom? Maybe Sadie? She's my favorite.

An hour before midnight

The noise has gotten louder and I'm having a hard time focusing. I tap Jeremy on the shoulder. "Shia, whas frong wit me," I say.

I meeean. I can't even talk. I hope my uncle doesn't come downstairs. I think Jeremy says he overheard someone say Bobby

Franklin spiked the punch. This girl Shelly offered to be on punch duty; she's made several bowls and I had several glasses. Ugh. I'm nauseous and giddish at the same time, laughing' and tickling Jeremy. I grab him and give him a big long wet kiss. Hmmm. Jeremy's not a punch drinker and he's not smiling.

"Hm. Whas his proflem."

Jeremy walks over to the table grabs the punch bowl, goes into the kitchen and pours out the rest. He comes back out to where I'm standing and shakes his head.

"Y'all crazy drunk!" he says.

"Oh?" I say. My nausea is worse and I no longer wanna laugh. This drinking ain't the truth. Shit. The room is spinning.

"Whaa tha hao," I try to say.

Crash! Shit! A boy shoved this other boy into Unc Rae-Rae's stereo. Who the hell invited them! Damn! Unc Rae-Rae is running down the stairs with his glock. Mona, his other girlfriend is with him. She's one of those mean girls who looks like she's ready to whoop ass.

Unc Rae-Rae runs over to the 2 boys fighting, grabs 1 of 'em around the neck and points the gun at the other. Mona's yelling at everyone to "shut the fuck up!" The noise and rowdy behavior doesn't stop until Unc Rae-Rae fires his gun into the ceiling – everyone stops! No moving, no talking.

TiAnna is standing next to me and she smells like weed. Damn. My uncle's gonna send me up shit creek thanks to all this drinking and smoking in his house.

Unc Rae-Rae's yells at everyone to sit down and don't move unless they want an ass whooping. Mona's standing next to him, hands on her hips, nodding her head. Unc Rae-Rae orders Jeremy to go peruse the backyard for stragglers then check the rooms. A sense of sadness comes over me when he walks away.

It must be a full moon

Oh, shit! The doorbell rings. I hope it's not the police. Ahhhh naw. Bobby Franklin's ass opens the door and in comes daddy! What?

His eyes go straight to Unc Rae-Rae holding the gun. I'm managing to stand but rocking back and forth. TiAnna's head drops to my shoulder.

"Ain't this a bitch," Unc Rae-Rae says.

Daddy grabs my arm. Wow! How did he get over here so fast? He yanks me toward the door. Poor TiAnna falls. On the way out, Daddy yells at Unc Rae-Rae and he yells back at daddy.

"You motherfucking coward!" says Unc Rae-Rae. "Bet's off!"

I guess I'm gonna finally find out what he means.

The finale is not so grand

I'm in daddy's car. I think I hear police sirens but my head hurts too bad to care. And he's making it worse by yelling at me. I think I hear daddy say, "I can kiss my friends and Unc Rae-Rae good-bye." I try to get out of the car but daddy has a firm grip on my arm and I'm too drunk to fight back. He straps me in, puts the car in gear and drives off – fast. Ooh. I'm getting nauseous. I want daddy to slow down. "Da... Dada," I try to say, but throw up all over the front of the dashboard and floor – I black out.

When I wake up, I'm in a room and it's not mine.

14

On Lockdown

June 10, 2012
Early afternoon

My eyes open to a familiar voice.

"Uh-huh. You did it this time!"

Oh hell no. Please not Jayden. He's making my head throb. I turn my head towards the horrible squeaking noise. Sure enough, Jayden the brat is in my face, looking like his damn mama.

"Daddy's been here all night. Mommy, Brittany and me just got here. They at the cafe downstairs."

Now I know where I am. In a hospital room with an IV sticking out of my right arm. Before that, I was... I was at Unc Rae-Rae's. My birthday. Somebody spiked the punch.

"You got alcohol poisoning," says Jayden. "Daddy is really worried."

"Yeah I bet," I say softly. But Jayden heard me.

"You ungrateful," he says, sounding like that damn woman. I close my eyes hoping he thinks I've fallen asleep, but keeps on talking.

"Your uncle went to jaaaail," the brat says.

Like his mama, he hates Unc Rae-Rae and always refers to him as "your uncle." I wanna go find him and make sure everything is okay. Instead, I keep my eyes closed. Ooo. My head hurts.

"Daddy told mommy he's gonna make sure he do time. He's getting a restrain order too. So huh! You can't see him noooo more."

Okay. Enough of Jayden's mouth. I should slap the shit out of him. Owe. Hurts when I move. If I can ma...

"Hey! What you doing!" says Jayden as I pull out my IV.

At least he shut up. He runs out of the room screaming "Where's my daddy? My sister's trying to run away!"

Wow! He referred to me as his sister. Whatever. I'm on a mission. Daddy better not have hurt my uncle or else he'll be sorry.

I hurry to the closet for my clothes, right when daddy comes barreling through the door with Luanne, Brittany, Jayden and a nurse.

"What do you think you're doing," says Daddy, using his bouncer stance. "You need to get your ass back in bed."

I ignore him and start taking off my gown.

"Ooo showing your titties. You nasty," says Jayden.

"Luanne get them kids outta here!" says daddy.

The room's spinning, I'm flushed but don't care, not staying here. I'm scared and don't feel safe. Something's getting ready to go down.

"Where's Unc Rae-Rae? I hear you're pulling' some shit!"

"Look Tippy. You need to do as you're told or else."

"Or else what?"

The nurse touches my arm and says, "You need to rest."

"No. I'm leaving'. Something's not right."

Through the door first, come 2 men dressed in all white, then more nurses, and orderlies, making me nervous.

This time daddy threatens me, "You will do as you are told or face the consequences," he says.

"Where's my uncle?" I've forgotten I'm only in my underwear.

"In jail. Keep this up, you'll be joining him."

He's not bluffing. I bet he called his friend Judge Simms. "You would, wouldn't you?" I say.

The pain running through my head and body is nothing like the anger I have right now. "You're a mean man! I get you hate me! The feeling is mutual!"

"You've gotten away with too much thanks to your uncle. Now he's giving you alcohol and drugs."

"You a damn lie," I say while crying mad tears. "You want him gone. He's the only one left who loves me. You already took my grandparents away."

"Well I hope y'all had a nice chat. Won't happen again."

"You, you're following me?"

"I keep my eye on you to keep you safe LaTonya"

"Bullshit daddy! You don't give a damn about me!"

"Tippy they broke the protective order, broke the rules. period!"

"Call the police put the handcuffs on me then. I'd rather be in jail than be with you anymore."

"Yeah. Yeah. Frankly, I'm tired of your mouth, your behavior and thinking you grown. I'm sick of your damn uncle always getting in the way, believing he's in charge. Well he's not in charge, dammit!"

"You..." I start to say.

"Uh. Not another word. Here are the rules. Your behavior will change starting now. You will stop using foul language."

Ha, laughable. I picked up shit language from him.

Daddy continues, "Your disrespect for the family stops now. You will do as I tell you too. No friends, no nothing until you change your ways. I hope I made myself clear. If not, we can make other arrangements I guarantee you won't like. Here's the agreement in writing. Sign."

Daddy hands me a pen. Rather than sign right away, I contemplate gutting him with my fist. I mean, I'd have to run out with no clothes on. Maybe I could hit him twice, and then grab my clothes. I know Karate thanks to him. He taught me to defend myself. From what I learned, I may be able to take him. I'd have to deal with these big old' white dudes too. And this damn nurse would probably call security. What about Unc Rae-Rae and my grandparents? I don't want them to suffer because daddy loathes me. I snatch the pen from him and sign the agreement even though something's telling me this was wrong.

Put me out of my misery

So, daddy won't have too. I know he wants me dead or drive me crazy. He already took away mama's family. Now he's gotten rid of my friends and my uncle. They helped me survive the turmoil. I hope the drugs they gave me will put me to sleep forever. At least I'd be gone from daddy, Luanne and this mean cruel world.

I think I'm asleep 'cause

Unc Rae-Rae is speaking to me. He says, "Hang in. Things will change he promises. Mama will be home soon. Meanwhile play along with daddy and avoid Luanne. Daddy's in trouble financially and Luanne's blackmailing him. I'll hold onto your gifts. Remember your daddy loves you."

"I love you too daddy, I say."

Now I'm awake 'cause

The night nurse wakes me in the morning around 5 to do lab work. She says, "My shift is ending. I want to make sure you understand it's our secret, right.

"Huh? Uhhh. Okay." I nod. Good, I wasn't dreaming. I did speak with Unc Rae-Rae on the phone. Watch out daddy. Change is coming.

July 15, 2012

Daddy and me haven't spoken since leaving the hospital. He has me under lock and key – took my cellphone – until we move to Portland. I said good-bye to Chester and Eloise. They retired and stayed in Stone Mountain. Daddy wouldn't allow me to say good-bye to my friends, not even Jeremy. I don't understand why he's being so hateful. He's using what happened at my party as an excuse. None of my friends or Jeremy ever disrespected him. Jeremy, especially, tried extra hard 'cause he knew how daddy was.

All I know is Unc Rae-Rae's is in jail – still. They won't let him post bail which is unusual. The DA is claiming he's a flight risk. I don't know what happened to Jeremy or TiAnna.

The reality is, I'm daddy's prisoner – for now.

15

P Town, I've Arrived

August 26, 2012
Portland, Oregon

Dear Mom:

We went to church in northeast Portland. The congregation is predominately black, which was quite a shock since I heard Portland didn't have black folks. Luanne chose the church because a friend of hers at All Saint's Baptist knows a deacon here who said this church is the one to attend. Many of Portland's high-profile black folks attend.

After the sermon, members of the congregation greeted us. They're so damn pretentious. Some of them were rolling their eyes. Near the bathroom this old fat lady with a too tight pink dress for her fat ass — oops sorry mama — was whispering to this other lady who was just as big as she was. She wore a bright yellow Sunday suit that at least fit. Both of them had on big wide hats. I almost laughed. Didn't anyone tell them the 80s are over?

The lady in the tight pink dress said "folks from Atlanta think they are the blacks of all blacks." Her friend in the yellow said "mm mm mm. Why they come here then?" They saw me, changed the subject, and gave me one of those phony smiles. I rolled my eyes like they did. Her grammar was horrible mama. You would've been upset.

Unc Rae-Rae is in county lockup. Daddy put a restraining order against him; he can't come near me. Jeremy's gone to Miami U. I don't hear from him anymore. And TiAnna not as much.

I'll be starting a new high school next week, some place downtown called Abraham Lincoln. The school is predominately white and remains the top in the school district. I'm a TAG student, of course, and the school has a strong science program, which would be good for me getting into engineering school. Regardless, I don't wanna go, but Unc Rae-Rae says hold on. I will for now.

Will write soon,

Love Tippy

Living in Portland's so-called upscale neighborhood is much different from Stone Mountain and especially Druid Hills. We live in Council Crest perceived to be one of Portland's finest. Our small 7500 square foot home hides among several old growth trees nestled behind an iron locked gate with a "private property" warning sign.

We have 7 bedrooms, each with a bathroom, a family game area, a small movie theatre, dining area and a master kitchen. Luanne's planning to hire a nanny and chef. Hm. More of the same.

I'm still not speaking to daddy, so we don't argue. I think the devil says hello or good-morning, which is usually in the kitchen while I'm getting my rations. I ignore him – pretend he's invisible.

In my head, I'm saying what he said to his daddy, "The man who gave me this name is dead to me and has been since he left me and mama. I prefer he stay dead!"

Sept. 10, 2012
7:30 a.m.

Daddy hired Benny, an old white man, as the family driver. I'm only using him until I get use to this city.

On the first day of school, I avoid daddy, so I can start the day half ass okay. Benny drives the brats and me and drops me off last, giving me more time to think. This new school shit is for the birds.

We pull up in front of Abraham Lincoln High. Benny puts the car in park and waits for me to get out. My hand is on the door knob, but I'm glad we can afford the gas. I may be sitting here awhile.

I have yet to speak to Benny. He did converse with the twins — asking if they were excited about school — and Jayden took over the conversation running his mouth as usual.

Staring out the window, I see lots of white kids huddled in groups, standing alone, pacing. Some are walking to the back of the school — in 1s, 2s and 3s — toward a courtyard with more white students and a stadium way in the back.

Here come more white kids, arriving on foot and on bikes. Across the street, a red convertible pulls into the parking lot fast, skids on the brakes almost hitting a white boy. The driver has the gall to flip him off, puts the car in gear and speeds off through the lot. The driver is one of those Portland black people.

My BFF would shake her head and say, "Shameful! Why do ignorant black people have to show out in front of white folks?"

I told her once she sounded like my grandparents and their black Republican friends. TiAnna hates when I compare her to Republicans. She'd rant like daddy saying, "Those damn black Republican uncle Tom sell outs!"

"Well here I go," I say, opening the car door.

"You'll do fine," says Benny, finally speaking. "What time shall I pick you up?"

"Uh? I'll call you."

I'm standing outside thinking more about what Tommy Crumbs says about Portland. We should be extra careful while living here. The white folks are racists and black folks are wacked. He says gangs shoot at someone every day. These gang members are the black kids who migrated to Portland with their families from economically depressed areas affected by natural disasters.

"Those kinda Negroes are psycho," says Tommy. "They shoot people for no reason and got nerve to say they're gang members. Real gang members have a product. These wannabes are ignorant."

Tommy has never been to Portland, but he watches a lot of TV and swears by what he's saying. Portland and the northwest is the breeding ground for Nazi Skinheads. I personally know of a case from back in the 80s about an Ethiopian murdered by the skinheads. I tell Tommy, a lawyer for the family sued the skinhead leadership residing in Orange Country, took all their money, running them out. I also remind Tommy racism is alive in America.

Well will you looky here. I see an Asian, a couple of Latinos and a slightly plump black girl who's waving. Look like she's coming my way. Shoot. I wasn't planning on making any friends here. I'm planning a possible escape back to Atlanta, knowing daddy would track me down and put me away.

"Hey girl! I'm Shonny Washington," says the plump black girl. "Most everyone calls me Shonny."

"I'm LaTonya Ellis."

"Where you from LaTonya?"

"Atlanta."

"No kidding! Atlanta's where mom wants to live. She can't stand Portland even though she's been here most of her life."

Shonny is speaking with a northwestern accent. More proper talking than me.

There goes the bell. Shonny walks in with me. Tells me we only need to confirm or change our classes today.

"Do you have plans later LaTonya?"

"Um not really."

"Wanna hang out? You can ride with me. Great day to drop the drop."

I hope she's not the one with the red convertible.

"Cousin Jerome is having a gathering at his house. He's 21 and in his 2nd year at Portland Community College."

Shonny notices me hesitating.

"Jerome's cool," she says. "He keeps his nose clean, unlike his younger brother who stays in trouble. No need to worry about him. We ain't seen him in years since he took off to California with one of his gang buddies. Jerome surrounds himself with friends who are doing something with their lives, on the straight and narrow. They go to school, work."

Damn. She sure is running her mouth, putting Jerome all on blast. And talks fast as T does when she gets excited. I'm having a hard time keeping up but T would say, "You're listening too slowly."

We're standing in a long line near the cafeteria where the seniors check in. Shonny says we're to find our locker and classrooms and be ready for tomorrow. The student union is also hosting a welcome assembly at 9:30.

"Girl he cute too," Shonny says nudging me. I assume she's still talking about her cousin.

"Jerome lives by himself in his family's house. His daddy died of prostate cancer right before he graduated high school 3 years back. His mom passed on earlier this summer. Jerome believes she accidentally overdosed on sleeping pills. Giiiiirrrl. Folks can be cruel. His mom's so-called friends claim she killed herself because she couldn't deal with his daddy's death."

Shonny pauses briefly then says, "Their deaths almost broke him. He's managed to pull through the depression an all. Both his parents left him money and the house is paid for."

"Hm," I say. I wish she'd shut up though so I can get going. But here she goes again.

"Thought you might like to meet some quality black folks. I guess you heard a few negative stories about P Town."

I nod and say, "Maybe I'll hang out. I'll let you know."

We exchange cell numbers and plan to meet back here after the assembly. I finally got my phone back from daddy after 2 months. Yeah. That long. He's a mean man.

Planning my escape

By the time Shonny and me meet up, I decide to hang out. I'm not ready to go home. Come to think of it, this may be the perfect time for me to escape.

16

Shonny

Wouldn't you know

Shonny does own the red convertible. We get in and drop the top, inviting in the warm September day. She puts the car in gear, steps on the accelerator and drives fast out the parking lot like she did this morning. Here goes roadrunner.

We speed through downtown Portland – down Market to Broadway and pass a building with a big neon Portland sign. Shonny says this is where they hold white folks' concerts.

"Black people rarely come downtown anymore," she says. "My mom told me years ago downtown and northeast Portland use to be hoppin'. The place with the Portland sign once bore the name, Paramount. The previous owner brought in topnotch black entertainers like Barry White, Patty LaBelle, Gladys Knight, Charlie Wilson, Earth Wind and Fire. The city wanted the Paramount bad, so they designated the building a historic landmark. The City of Portland forced the owner out under the guise of historical preservation. Huh. The government can steal your property and you can't stop them."

Then Shonny says, "Once they took possession, no more black concerts. Next, stop northeast Portland. They used gentrification to shut down prosperous black businesses, black-owned entertainment and property by introducing crack cocaine, which sped up the process."

"Wow," I say. "Do you at least have department stores in this little old downtown with tiny little buildings?"

"Ha! This downtown is nothing like downtown Atlanta with the underground and stuff," says Shonny. "We just have a Nordstrom and Sacs. The malls are where the bulk of the stores are. You don't see many blacks there either. They usually get kicked out – the black kids."

"Dang," I say, avoiding my favorite cuss word. "I heard they don't like black folks here?"

"Yes and no," says Shonny. "Our small black community means less power. What's worse, black gatekeepers get paid to keep money out of the hands of the larger community."

"My daddy says we got black gatekeepers everywhere."

"I'm sure your daddy's right. Shame."

We're heading over the Broadway Bridge crossing the Willamette with lots of iddy-biddy boats and medium-sized ferries traveling up and down the river. We don't see this in Atlanta – bridges, rivers and boats – only bricks and mortar.

The closest I came to this kind of scene was when Jeremy and me visited New York Times Square. The city has all kinds of people making the energy off the hizzle. Much different from Portland which so far feels like an old folks' home where you go to die.

We've landed on the other side of the river and Shonny takes me on a brief tour of northeast. We pass the coliseum and Rose Quarter the new home for the Portland basketball team.

"Most of the team is black like any other city," Shonny says. "I was told they're not allowed to hang around black people here. Most come here alone and grab a white woman. You know how they do."

"Yeah," I say. "My friend says Portland is the place for interracial dating, especially, black men with white women. Black women in Atlanta date other races now too."

"Well good. Single black women should expand their dating choices. Otherwise, they'd be dateless. But don't get me wrong LaTonya. There are a lot of black couples here – mostly old school. But I bet Portland's worse when it comes to the black men white girl thing. Black men come here for a white woman and hide with 'em out in Lake Oswego and West Linn. When some of the other basketball teams play here, they go white girl crazy too. One retired famous black basketball player from 1 of the east coast teams and married to a black woman at the time, got wit' a Portland white girl. She has pictures I'm surprised she didn't sell."

"Hm," I say. "Glad I gotta boo. His name is Jeremy. This is his 1st year playing football for Miami U. He's expected to go pro in a couple of years."

"For real?" Shonny says. "Got you a college boy. Too bad. My cousin would like you."

I ignore the comment since I'm not interested in meeting anybody new. My hope is Jeremy and me will be together as we plan once we get back in touch.

"We also have pro soccer and hockey," Shonny says.

Figures. Something for white folks. They sure don't want black folks getting too comfortable. I keep this thought to myself.

Shonny shows me the Lloyd Center Mall, some quaint little restaurants and a place called the Dollar Store. What can you buy for a dollar? Strange.

We're on Martin Luther King Jr. Blvd. – at least they got one– where Shonny nods at one of the beauty supply stores.

"Asian-owned," says Shonny.

"No different than anywhere else," I say.

Shonny jumps into another long-winded explanation.

"My mom says MLK, once called Union Avenue and this other street called Williams Avenue, had black-owned nightclubs up and down. Like the Table of Square, Cotton Club, Geneva's, Lou's Higher Ground, Gas Room and Upstairs/Downstairs. People from Seattle and L.A. use to come here to party. There was even a 24/7 FM black radio station named KQIV run by a young dude in his 20's."

"Then like they did in San Francisco back in the 60s when they brought in Heroine to the black community, they brought in crack cocaine here. Blacks lost businesses, all the clubs' shutdown and their homes or black owners sold them for nothin'. The community never recovered. The white folks took over northeast."

Shonny doesn't take time to breath. She keeps on talking, "Back in 1943, Blacks were confined to a place called Vanport where Delta Park is today. A flood destroyed Vanport. You should read the history about Vanport and Portland's early black pioneers. Actually, it's quite interesting. Looking at the way things are today, you'd never know blacks have a long history here and some did quite well."

Shonny finally pauses so I take this opportunity to run my mouth.

"My daddy told me powerful people usually like to destroy vibrant black communities to keep blacks oppressed and for economic reasons as well. As long as the communities remain ghettos run by gangs and drug dealers all killing each other, they leave 'em be. Unless of course they want the community for their purposes. Like here I'm guessing."

"My daddy also says black folks can't blame anybody but themselves. No one forced the drugs down their throats, put the guns in their hands and made 'em sell drugs. We chose to carry out the racist agenda – destroy ourselves. We beg for crumbs thinkin' the churches self-appointed black leaders and the government will make life better for us. Like the government finally giving us 40-acres and a mule, they promised. They compensated the Native Americans and Japanese."

"Your daddy sounds smart like my mom," says Shonny. "Mom says each one of us must take responsibility. Especially adults must become empowered, so they can teach the next generation how to fish.

Right now, we are too self-absorbed, living for the day rather than plan for the future. She says she's concerned about our black youth. How's your mom and dad adjusting?"

Ooo. She would ask about mama. Shonny must've seen me flinch.

"Sorry for being nosey."

"Mama died when I was 7," I find myself saying. "I live with my daddy and his new wifey who I can't stand and their 2 bratty 8-year-old twins."

"Ooo girl tough deal. My mom threw my daddy out a couple of months ago after finding out he's having an affair with' a white woman. I was the one who found out and about his 2-year-old boy."

"Ooo shame!" I could top her story with Luanne and daddy's bullshit. But Shonny has more to say.

"Every night for the past 3 years he left home around 8 and wouldn't come home most times until in the morning, right before he had to go to work. I can't believe my mom put up with his crap all these years. She was a Christian. Her brother, who's a pastor here, would come over and pray wit' her. Saying God will work things out."

"1 night me and my friend followed dad to a house in Gresham. He pulled into a driveway and a half-breed comes running out saying, "Hi daddy!" Girl, I cried." Shonny's voice cracks.

"Did he see you?"

"No. I waited 'til I calmed down and got my big behind out the car and walked right up to the house. My friend tried to stop me. A white chick about my mom's age opened the door. She looked like the back of my butt, which ain't lookin' good, considering I could stand to lose some pounds, Ha!"

"Dang, tellin' your mama must've been awful."

"Yeah," says Shonny. "At first though I waited, giving my dad a chance to man-up. Huh. He chose not to come home that night or the next. Had my mom worrying. He finally called her and told her he was going through a tough time and needed some space. Pissed me off! So I told her what the real deal was. She packed his stuff and we drove over to where he was. Girl she threw his clothes in the middle of the white woman's yard and yelled, "Marvin bring your black funky behind out here right now!"

"Girl, all he did was peek out the window like a scared fool. I know mom wanted to whoop his butt. We figured the cops would end up comin, so we left."

"Did he ever come home?"

"He tried, girl. But mom had already changed the locks. Shortly after, she filed for divorce. It'll be final soon."

"Do you ever talk to him?"

"Girl no! Not interested. He can be with his new family. Mom and me will be okay."

Everybody's got troubles I'm thinking. I misjudged Shonny. I'm glad I decided to hang out with her. We both needed to vent.

"My friends call me Tippy."

"Tippy? Okay. You can call me Shonny if you want."

She's smiling now. This is good.

We stop at Christopher's Gourmet Restaurant on MLK and Shaver. Shonny had pre-ordered 5 slabs of ribs for Jerome. I hand her $50 to help pay for the food and gas for her car.

"Thanks," she says.

Inside Chris's, a steady flow of black people come in to pick up orders or eat in. White people stop in too – they love our cooking. The tables quickly fill up seating about 15 to 20 people. A young black dude is cashier and waiter. He brings our order and I tip him $10.

Once we're back in the car

Shonny says, "Girl, you must be ballin'. You made his day."

I smile.

"Too bad the white developers are planning to tear the place down," Sonny says her face turning to a frown. "Christopher's is one of the last few black businesses in this area. Along with his cafe, they are tearing down the remaining black businesses on MLK. Once that happens, they will have succeeded with making what we use to know as the black community, a community designed primarily for white-owned businesses for the white residents moving in."

"Another reason I want out of this place," I say. "No culture here it at all."

"You got that right," Shonny responds.

She then puts the mustang in gear and drives fast up Skidmore; crosses 7th; turns right on 15th; left on Prescott; and right on, 21st. Jerome's is the 3rd one from the corner on the left. Earlier Shonny described this as a huge 2-story house with four bedrooms and 2 bathrooms. She sure exaggerates. No offense, but his home is about the size of my grandparents' garage and the carport at my mama's house in Druid Hills.

All the houses on the block boast cement stairs connected to a walkway, leading to the front entrance. Jerome's got a front porch with wicker furniture, making the setting look kind of old-school. Must've belonged to his parents. I hope he's cooler than that.

I hear music playin' from inside – Anthony Hamilton is doing the honors. Shonny knocks on the door twice before we walk into a softly lit entryway. The music gets louder further down the hall and the different aromas get stronger with amazing smells of soul food and lighted lavender scented candles in holders along the walls and on top of wall side tables.

I also absorb the variety of family photos filled with happy people, mingling among the candles. The same boy is in most of them starting from a baby to young adulthood. Must be Jerome. I'll say. He's a cutie. The photo at the end of the wall shows him in a high school cap and gown. Written across the bottom are the words, "Congratulations my handsome young man. We will always be with you." He has his arm around an older woman. Probably his mother.

Uhhh. I wonder where Shonny is. I just now notice she's disappeared.

The music switches up.

"Heeeey. Usher's Climaxin." I snap my fingers, swaying my hips from side to side. "Shoot. I need to get my groove on."

I turn left and head towards the music; dancing and bopping my head up and down with my eyes closed. "Go Ush… oh shit! Who…"

I run face first into someone's chest. Stepping back, I look up and Ooo holla! Staring down at me with a big grin is one of the most handsome faces I've seen since I left what's his name in Atlanta.

17

Pretty White Teeth

He makes me speechless

With his wide smile showing off pretty white teeth.

"You must be Miss LaTonya," he says still grinning with his fine ass. "I'm Jerome."

He extends his hand. I grab the tips of his fingers, staring and drooling. I must look like a fool, but I can't help myself. Usually I'm not attracted to darker skinned dudes. This one is an exception – mm, mm, mm – reminds me of Morris Chestnut. He's also got perfectly straight pretty white teeth like my man Morris.

TiAnna and me met Morris Chestnut last year at the ATL Soul Fest. I thought I had died and gone to heaven. He gave us his autograph and took a picture with us. I keep Morris's picture close and dream he'll be mine one day. Only if Jeremy and me don't make it.

Jerome's at least 6 feet and slender built, but not thin. He's wearing a short sleeved yellow polo shirt showing off his muscles. Ooo, I bet he's got a firm ass too.

"Shonny told me to come find you," he says.

Ooo. Girls, his voice is low and sexy. He's definitely got swag.

"Shy huh," he says, touching my left arm. "No worries. You'll be safe with me."

I follow Jerome out back. There's a small gathering of close a dozen or so people – the ratio of ladies to gents is about the same. Shonny is sitting across the way at a table playing dominos with 3 guys. She sees me and waves.

Jerome introduces me around. First to 2 couples – a black athletic looking guy named Ray and his I'm assuming, skinny and blonde white girlfriend Kelly. She snuggled really close to him when she saw me. Then there's Lester, another black guy; he has a belly and got nerve to be drinking beer. Sitting right next to him is his brunette, fat, fat, fat white girl Sheila.

Ray gets up and greets me with a hug; Lester nods while taking a swig of beer. Their girls give me a half smile, looking at me like, "we know you look good, but leave our black men alone."

Jerome then introduces me to 3 other ladies – Lucinda, she's Latino, and 2 black girls, Debra and Jalinda. They are huddled around one lone white boy who they call AJ aka DaMenace. He's telling his groupies he's producing another rap album. A guy named Buster shouts at him from the domino table.

"You wannabe Eminem. The white boy rapper position is already filled," he says.

"Aw you just mad cuzz you sound like Latoya Jackson," says AJ DaMenace.

"Ooo shame," says Shonny.

DaMenace's groupies laugh. Ya know, Buster's voice is high-pitched like Pharrell's. Funny, it doesn't go with his bald head and big burly physique. He's dark-skinned and about 350 pounds of pure fat. Round face with big full cheeks, big old' lips and wide eyes; they make him look like he's scared. His complexion is uneven and spotted with black freckles. Buster talks, slowing some of his words and adding to other words. Sounds silly.

"Don't know whaaat you talkin' 'bout. Maaannnn I flows. I a ra bet I goes plaatinum befo' you."

"In the rap world we call Buster, The Messiah," Jerome says, chuckling as I follow him over to the domino table. "In case you haven't heard, everybody and they mama in Portland thinks they're rappers. We've got a lotta white boy rappers here. Much different from ATL no doubt. DaMenace has some phat lyrics though. Be bustin' on some beats."

Shonny told him where I'm from. Hope she didn't put me on blast like she did him.

Jerome leans over and whispers in my ear, "Messiah's damn good too! I joke with him most of the time. Been thinkin' about his offer to invest in his work." He then says out loud, "Don't quit y'all day jobs!"

"Sheeeit! Messiah? A a a job? Ni, nigga ain't finished high school. He betta hope somethin jumps off," says a boy named Roscoe sitting to Shonny's left. He talks fast and stutters a little. I can tell he's short even though he's not standing. I suspect he's a Blazer fan 'cause he has on a team jacket and one of their caps with the lip turned to the side. He's also wearing Jordan's with the laces untied.

"Niiiiggaaa you a lie. Me annnn yo mama walked hand-in-hand down the aisle together," says Messiah.

"Na, na, now you lying'," says Roscoe. "My mom's ain't finished high school ne, neither. And sh, she sho ain't got no job. Always asking' me fo' money."

More laughs. Huh! I thought Ms. Shonny said all Jerome's friends had it going' on. So far, I've met wannabe rappers, nigga's ain't got jobs, ain't finished high school and their mamas beg 'em for money. Oh and white girls with bad hairdos, who probably give money to the "ain't got no job" and wannabe rappers.

I wonder about the groupies? What's their story? Maybe they think DaMenace will make it big, hoping to be the first in line to get his money. He's lucky he's cute for a white boy. Looks better than Robin Thicke, even though Robin's not half bad himself. What messes Robin up is he turns red too quick when he's singing? Lookin' like he's constipated, tryin' to take a shit.

"You hungry?" says Jerome.

I shrug since my voice won't work, which he's finding amusing.

"Come on Miss LaTonya. Let me feed you some of my good cooking. Maybe I can get a smile."

You mean I'm not smiling. Well let me start then. My smile is girlishcious. Ooo and he cooks. I follow him to the table under a tent, laid out like a soul food smorgasbord with Shonny's ribs and me; mac and cheese; collard greens; yams; red beans and rice; and store-bought potato and macaroni salads, still in plastic containers, the white girls must've brought. The white folks I knew couldn't make potato salad.

The one time I tasted a white person's potato salad, I almost threw up. German Potato salad a white lady, Maggie, made for the Church on the Way annual Sunday picnic. She coated the half-raw potatoes with vinegar, mixed in bacon bits, chives and eggs. Ick! Horrible?

Jerome says he did the greens, mac and cheese and red beans and rice. He learned from his mama.

"Mama knew how to throw-down," he says, looking sad for a moment. "I also did these master pieces right here – sweet potato pies, the red velvet and lemon cakes. Yep."

"You did?" I say, with one of my best smiles. Shish. I finally spoke.

"Aw. I got you to smile. You should smile more often," says Mr. Pretty White Teeth. "Wait 'till you try a slice, or 2, or 3. You certainly don't have to worry about your figure."

Jerome's admiring me, leaning his head back a little, looks me up and down.

"Can you burn?"

"Yeah. I mostly bake."

"Ohhh reeeally," Jerome says, handing me a plate. "We should have a bake off."

We fill our plates and head to an empty table over by the fountain not too far – but far enough – for a private conversation. The fountain we're sitting next to is actually quite beautiful. Made out of white marble, the entire piece stands about 5-foot and spouting water from the top of the pillar down into a large round attached bowl. An angelic figure with wings is kneeling inside the bowl, holding a smaller one in both hands.

Jerome says his aunt – his dad's sister – made the piece for his parents after they purchased this house 15 years ago. The smaller bowl is a bird feeder and represents the gift of offering. Jerome says his aunt is talented and his family wishes she'd do this fulltime.

"Aunt NeNe only does this as a hobby."

"How long?" I say.

"10 years. I offered to help her out, but she's not interested in doing this as a business."

"Oh yeah?" I say.

"Yeah," he pauses, takes a bite of his food, chews and takes a big gulp of his lemonade. He then says, "So tell me about Miss LaTonya."

First, I tell about how I miss Atlanta and my friends without going into details about what went down. Then I tell him Tippy's my nickname and my parents named me. I skip over the part about murdered mama. With both our mama's gone, I don't want to ruin this wonderful moment.

Turns out Jerome's a real jokester and he's having me rollin'.

"You sneak up on people, eh Tippy?"

"Ha. Not on purpose. Folks should be more careful."

"That they should. That they should."

He pauses to give me one of his charming smiles then says, "Can I call you LaTonya? Rhymes with beautiful." He winks.

I blush, lower my head and play shy girl. They I say, using my soft voice, "Okay."

"Ok then beautiful LaTonya."

Out of the corner of my eye, I notice Messiah over by the fence. He's on the phone, looking over at me and Jerome with his hand cupped over the cell's mouth piece. I wonder whom he's talkin' too.

I'm starting to feel bad but trying not to let it affect my mood. It gets worse though when Messiah comes over to where we are. He leans over Jerome and speaks into his ear but loud enough so I can hear.

"Say maaan, I need a favor," he says. "Caaaan you run me to the corner sto'? My baby mama neeeeed some a change. I'd go myyyyself, but uhhh had tooooo much to drink. So 'ave them other niggas," he says, swaying as if he's tipsy.

Jerome nods agreeing to take him but I'm thinking it's a bad idea.

Jerome invites me to go along. My gut says stop! But my heart says, "Tippy you gotta go!"

"We'll be right back!" Jerome says to his guest. "Be good kids. Don't want trouble with the neighbors!"

"You got homeowner's insurance?" says Lester.

"Ha! Ha! Don't count on a pay day from me," says Jerome.

The Messiah is a few steps ahead of us. When we get to the front door, he says, "I gotta piss. Meeeeet y'all out uh front."

Meeting Jerome makes me think Portland could be bearable. He'd be a nice distraction and could help me keep my mind off Jeremy.

Jerome puts his arm around me, walks with me over to his Rav 4 parked in the driveway. Rather than get in, he turns and faces me. He stares off into the distance and I follow his gaze to Prescott where it's calm and quiet but eerie.

"Did I tell you mom died?" he's looking at me now. "Dad died before she did, not long ago."

"Mine too," I say. "My mama." Damn. I tried to avoid this. Happy Jerome and LaTonya turn to sad Jerome and LaTonya.

I reach up and touch the side of his cheek, which feels like he's losing life's battle. His beautiful dark skin turns to a field of gray. Warmness arises releasing a hue of bluish gold gently hovering above and circling his glorious crown.

Jerome's smiling, melding his wonderful grin into my heart. He's talking in slow motion, "I... wiiissh... weeee... haaad... aaaa... chance... t..."

Then screeeeechhhh! A rusty brown Chevy turns the corner at Prescott. When it reaches us, it slows down passing in front of us, allowing time for a masked gunman to appear from the back window. Gunfire erupts! Jerome grabs me, throws me down and jumps on top of me.

All's quiet on the block

No speeding car and no movement from Jerome. I turn my face towards his. His face is close to mine, his eyes closed and his breath hardly there.

I'm reliving my nightmare and daddy can't wake me from this 1. The last of Jerome's life leaves his body. Like when mama died, there's nothing I could've done to save him.

18

Missed Me Again

On the same block

Too many voices.

"Help! Someone got shot! Call 9-1-1!"

"Who got shot?"

"Call the police!"

"Are they dead?"

"Who shot 'em?"

"Wait! We know them!"

"Stay back!"

"Too much blood!"

"Stay back! This is a crime scene!"

"Oh Jesus Lord! They dead!"

Am I? Jerome is. Is he at peace? I'm not. This is hell all over again. Thank you, Big G., You did it to me again!

"You step over this yellow tape you will be arrested. Do I make myself clear?"

"You racist ass police! If they were white, you wouldn't let 'em lay out there like dat."

"Yeah, yeah, prejudice or not stay the hell back!"

"This one's breathing. No pulse on the other one. Where's the coroner? We need to move his body and get this lady out of here. Can anyone give an ID?!"

"Me! I tried to tell this damn cop to let me through!"

"Officer! Please let the young lady through."

"Oh god! My cousin Jerome! Is he dead? That's LaTonya Ellis is she...?"

"Miss what is your name?

"Shonny."

"Hello Shonny. I'm Jay Dobbs, the lead paramedic. Ma'am, I know this is hard, but please focus. This young lady is in shock and we need to take her in. I'm sorry. It's too late for the gentleman."

"Oh God! Not him too. This ain't right."

I think I said goodbye

When they moved Jerome's body after Coroner Jonathan Davis pronounced him dead at 4:30 p.m. on September 10, 2012. Please pronounce me dead too.

"Here's her purse and cellphone. I believe this is her daddy's number."

"What's his name?"

"Robert Ellis. He owns RJ Designs here in Portland."

Dobb's dials the number. When Robert Ellis picks up, he immediately begins to explain.

"Yes sir. We understand it was a drive-by. No, no sir. She's alive but in shock? How old is she? 17? Okay sir. We understand. We plan to take her to Legacy Emanuel Hospital right now. Do you know where it is? Yes. Yes. The police are here. They can give you more details. Yes, media is here too. Okay I understand. We can't release her name anyway sir without your permission. Sir, would you like to speak with the police?"

Early evening in Atlanta

My BFF and her mama are at it again.

"Mama. Why do you have to make a big deal out of nothing?"

"Look TiAnna. You don't need to be going anywhere especially with some boy."

"Excuse you? I'm 17; not a kid."

"17 sure didn't stop you from getting busted with that raggedy ass Mexican boy. Getting drunk at a party!"

"Wow! For real? You ain't gonna let up, is you?"

"You and your friend caused enough trouble. Good, she's gone."

"Leave Tippy out of this! You don't give a damn about... Owe! What was that for?!"

"I'll slap you again. Keep talkin'!"

"Screw you mama!"

"Come back here girl!"

"I'm not comin' back this time mama! Go to hell!"

I storm outta the house and soon end up on Livingston Street, heading toward downtown. I keep walking but I ain't gonna walk the 3 miles it takes to get there.

Dang, I should've grabbed a coat. It's cold as hell. Glad I got on sweats. Shoot. The moon is half full and there's hardly no light in the sky. Sho am grateful for the street lights and my safe neighborhood. No crime here really except for the damn kids who vandalize cars.

"Ooo I can't stand that woman! Shoot. Let me call my girl."

Come on pick-up. Shoot I hate voicemail.

"Tippy answer the phone. Girl where you at? Make room for me in Portland. I'm coming! I ain't taking this shit no more. My mom done lost it! Call me back as soon as you get this! I plan to be on the next train smoking. You gonna have to send me some money though."

Sept. 12, 2012

I'm having a tough time adjusting to my new psychiatrist Dr. Sheila Ryan. Not because she's white but because she's nothing like Dr. Anderson, who highly recommended her.

Dr. Ryan told daddy to be easy on me. She also recommends I do my studies at home for at least a week, which is why daddy hasn't scolded me for what happened. He's following Dr. Ryan's advice and dares Luanne, Jayden or Brittany to say anything.

The police haven't found Jerome's murderer but allege a possible gang shooting. Portland gangs have been involved in several shootings – 5 since we've moved here 2 months ago. The news reports the drive-by as gang related but no gang affiliation with the victim. I'm glad they don't trash Jerome's memory. Media loves to stereotype black men, making them out to be criminals or gang members.

The newscaster doesn't mention my namel. The judge granted daddy a legal injunction, stopping the media from accosting my family and me. The injunction is for my protection. The ATL police still haven't found mama's killer.

Daddy hired Nurse Stone, who happens to be black, to keep an eye on me. I guess in case I wanna kill myself or do something crazy. Can't allow that to happen. Daddy won't have anyone to torture.

I'm so depressed I don't want to answer my phone, which keeps ringing from a private number. When it rings for the 3rd time, I punch answer and yell into the receiver, "What do you want!"

"Hey baby girl."

"Unc Rae-Rae?"

"Yeah. I called to check on you. Are you all right?"

"No. Where are you?"

"At the big house."

"I want you to come and get me. I don't like it here."

"I know. I know. I'mo make it right. Promise."

"When?"

"Soon baby girl. But look here, you got to stay down. No more of this almost getting killed shit. My heart can't take it. Un-da-stand?"

How did he find out? Daddy didn't tell him. But then again, my uncle has ways.

"Sorry I made you worry Unc Rae-Rae. I'll be more careful. Promise."

"Good den aw'ight. Remember your daddy loves you."

My mood is much better

Sense talkin' to Unc Rae-Rae.

When the phone rings this time, I answer without hesitating.

"Hi," I say as cheerfully as I can, given the circumstances.

"Hi Tippy this is Shonny. How are you?"

"Hangin' in."

"How are you, your mom and everybody?"

"Girl it's tough. I'm at a loss for words."

"Yeah me too. Seems like all the good people go too quickly."

"You ain't never lied, girl. All I can say is Jerome is with his mom and dad. He really missed them."

Rather than respond I get quiet. It's hard for me to find anything else to say.

"Tippy, I wanted you to know we're holding Jerome's funeral tomorrow morning at New Life Church on Williams and Killingsworth. Service starts at 11:00. I'll text you the address. If you want, you can write something about Jerome and post it on the Facegram page we created to honor his memory. I'll email you."

"That sounds cool. Thanks for offering Shonny."

After I hang up from Shonny, I go look for daddy. Nurse Stone says he's working from home. I put on my fuchsia robe and go down to daddy's office. When I find him, he's with Luanne.

"Good morning Tip," says daddy and hugs me tight.

Hm. What's he up too.

"Hi," I say. "I'm going to Jerome's funeral tomorrow. Thought I'd let you know."

"Oh? Are you up for that?"

"Yeah I guess."

"Well alright. How about we go together?"

Whaaat? I'm shocked. Then damn Luanne opens her big mouth. No surprise.

"You're lettin' huh go to dat gang member funeral," she says to daddy but looking at me.

I'm about ready to jump the bitch when daddy gently touches my arm. Then he faces his wifey.

"This is between my daughter and me," he says. "An A and B conversation, C fit to shut the hell up!"

Luanne puts her hands on her hips, leans back and rolls her eyes trying to do "ghetto sister style." Paleeze.

"Oh, she's yo daughter na?" she says.

"Don't start," daddy warns her. "I guarantee you won't win."

Luanne puts her forefinger to her mouth like she's saying shush. She's got the biggest smirk on her face too. She knows a secret and I bet it has something to do with me.

19

He's Back

September 13, 2012
10:45 a.m.

People are waiting outside at the church when daddy and me arrive. We'd planned to join the folks at the end of the line until we spot Shonny near the front, motioning for us to join her. She's standing with a lady who looks just like her – probably her mama. She's also slightly plumb, short about 5'2 with medium brown skin. Both she and Shonny are wearing long French Braids.

"Pardon me," daddy says to the lady we cut in front of. She nods.

"Hi I'm Shonny. Mr. Ellis I'm assuming?"

"Yes. Pleased to meet you," says daddy.

"This is my mother Carole. Mom this is Tippy and her dad Mr. Ellis."

"Thank you for coming," Carole says. She shakes daddy's hand then hugs me and whispers, "I know my nephew is smiling."

It's no secret I was the last 1 to see Jerome alive. The memory of those last moments with him, I'll hold in my heart forever.

Inside the church, the décor is dated and looks nothing like the other church, which is upscale in comparison. The walls are a faded burgundy color and the 3 sections all have long dark wooden benches with no cushions. The usher seats us in the middle section, 3 rows from the front. We have a clear view of Jerome's shiny redwood casket surrounded by beautiful flowers.

"You okay," daddy says squeezing my hand.

I nod and pull out some tissue from inside my clutch. In the middle of blowing my nose, the soloist begins to sing, accompanied by an organist and guitarist. She has a beautiful strong alto voice.

"In times like theeeseee, yooouu neeeed a saaviorrr. Be very suuuuree. Beeeee veeeerrry suuure your anchor hooolds. And grip that soliiiid and grip that solid rock."

Shonny, who's sitting on my left, leans over and whispers, "That's Yolanda. She had the biggest crush on Jerome; he paid her no attention."

So what! I wanna say. She's getting ready to say something else but the pastor saves me from her mouth.

"Welcome to New Life Church. I'm Pastor John Jackson. Today we are celebrating the life of Jerome Jackson."

Aw naw, here goes Miss Big Mouth again.

"The pastor's me and Jerome's uncle. My mom's brother. Jerome's daddy was his and mom's baby brother."

"Please stand and join me in prayer," says Pastor Jackson.

Boy he ain't wasting any time

The pastor jumps right into his sermon. Black preachers love to talk and this 1 is no different. He spoke about everything from the negative political climate to Jesus' crucifixion, managing to parlay back to Jerome without taking a breath. He talks about his passing and his newfound attitude towards life, which included attending church regularly. He also spoke about Jerome's kind heart, how he served others and the Lord. Pastor Jackson also commends Jerome for his efforts to accept and connect with his half-brother despite people's ungodly attitudes.

"Jerome did not judge. He left the judging to the Lord almighty!" says Pastor Jackson, raising his voice a few octaves.

Several people lower their heads, as if guilty, except for Shonny, who nudges my arm with her elbow. I glance at her out of the corner of my eye in time to see her curling up the left side of her mouth. She's starting to annoy me.

Pastor Jackson ends his sermon with another prayer and then invites Jerome's family and friends to come up to the podium to offer testimony. One-by-one folks go up and testify. Each person tells a story about how wonderful and kind Jerome was. Some stories are funny and others are serious. All of Jerome's friends from his backyard gathering speak except for Buster. Where is Buster anyway? Hm? I can't believe he didn't show up to his own friend's funeral. To think Jerome was thinking about giving him money for his rap career.

"What an asshole," I say under my breath.

Over the next hour, we hear more Jerome stories. Shonny and her mother go up together.

"Is there anyone else who wishes to speak?" says the pastor.

I turn around to see if anyone else is making a move. Way in back, a handsome young black dude stands up.

"May I speak?" He asks with a deep booming voice grabbing everyone's attention especially Shonny, who says, "Wow! That's Jerome's half-brother Darius. What the hell is he doing here?"

20

Big G's Other Victim

September 13, 2012
Stone Mountain. My BFF's in trouble

"Where you taking me?" Ooo. I'm dizzy. "Whas happening?"

I remember walking... I stopped to call Tippy... Got her voicemail... Thought about going home 'cause I got nervous about a strange car I saw. I started walkin' fast thinking how glad I was the car is on the other side of street. I thought I could run to a neighbor's house if something crazy jumps...

Awwwwwk! They grabbed me from behind, put a smelly cloth over my nose and mouth.

When did they tie me up? How did I get back here? I can hear them whispering. Are they male or female? I hope not sex predators.

Huh. We're leaving town; the traffic noise is fading. Stay awake TiAnna. Stay awake. Where are they taking me — north or south, east or west — which direction? God I'm so damn stupid. I should've trained like Tippy, instead of tryin' to be cute. Didn't wanna break a naaail. Now look at me. I'm probably gonna die!

Stop and pay attention girl! The car you're in has tinted windows. Can't see out. No street lights. No sounds of passing cars, only the road – swish, swish.

Um yeah. I remember the parked car was burgundy. It reminded me of daddy's friend, Jerry's car. A Lincoln MKS with a sunroof like this one only I don't see any stars; only black angels. I should've followed my gut. Too late TiAnna.

We're slowing down going over a bump then we go left and stop. Must be a garage door I hear. We creep forward and stop again. Engine goes off; the garage door closes.

I don't know what happened

But he won't stop yelling.

"Dammit! What the fuck! I ought'a make you lick-it-up," he says.

Can't help but throw up. At least I'm awake. How long have I been laying here? He brought me in and threw me on the bed – slapped me a couple of times. Then I passed out.

"It's da chloroform you gave 'er," she says.

"Aw hell. Get this shit cleaned up!" he says.

I hear him leave the room. Ooo. Why did he have to slam the door? I'm feeling sick again.

"Uh, um, ca can gets sa wader," I say.

"Mm hmm. I'll get you some water alright," she says.

"Owe." Why did she grab my hair?

"In you go!" She shoves me into the bathtub, then turns on the cold water. "Dat ought'ta wake yo' ass up."

"Awk ugh sto' ugh drown ugh awk please turn off uh ca ca ca cold," I try to say.

"Take those wet clothes off, put this on. You should be grateful for dis towel I'm givin' ya. Maybe next time I'll make you drip dry."

God can I get some help? If I could call you a bitch I would. Standing their wit yo boney ass. Talkin' smack.

"Hm. You don't look nothin' like me but we sissy's aw'ight."

Uh, what? I don't think so. You skinny white bitch wit' yo bleached blonde, stringy long hair. I don't do sissy shit wit' white girls.

"I'm your sissy Chelsea. Mummy threw me away. Least she don't do dat to you."

"Don Juan is my saving grace, my God." She leans her neck back flicking her hair from side-to-side. "We got lots a time to get acquainted. But don't be tryin' ta steal my man. Just do as you're told, so you can stay alive! C'mon, let's go call mummy."

Ring a ling

"TiAnna is that you?!" says Mrs. Johnson answering her cell phone. "I hear you breathing. Please stop playin and bring your tail…"

"Ha! Ha! My, my mummy dearest. What a temper. This is yo other daughter Chelsea. Remember me?

Lydia's stunned and doesn't know what to think.

"C'mon mummy. Cat got your tongue?" says Chelsea, using a fake British accent.

Chelsea picked up the accent from a British john she dated and adopted it as part of her MO.

"Chelsea?" Lydia says. "No. This can't be."

"Oh, but it's me mummy," Chelsea continues to tease. "You tossed me away and forgot me eh? Well here I am! Me and sissy are getting acquainted."

Lydia clasps her hand to her chest, wondering if the person on the other end of the phone is Chelsea or someone playing a cruel joke.

March 1, 1988
Early Atlanta

Lydia is Sheila and Bode Young's only child. At 14, she'd grown into a fully developed beautiful young girl. Her dark skin glistened with oil and she stood about 4'6 with big brown round eyes that bugged out like a Chihuahua.

Lydia started her period nearly a year ago, putting her mother on guard watch. Mama Young didn't miss a chance to tell Lydia, "Stay away from those nasty boys!"

Much to Mama Young's happiness, Lydia and her friends loved to hang around the Young home. And Sheila and Bode loved the distraction. They found it challenging to keep their only child busy – the child they gave birth to while in their late 30's and despite Sheila Young's attempts to self-abort. The Young's didn't want children.

School's out early

And Lydia arrived home around 1:00. Her parents are at work, so no friends allowed in the house without adult supervision. Lydia skipped up the sidewalk, leading to the family's yellow 2-story home and waved to Joshua – a landscaper – her father hired 6 months earlier.

17-year-old Joshua was pruning the rose bushes. He waved back and smiled, exposing his cigarette stained teeth. Today was the 1st time Lydia's home alone while he's there and he couldn't be more pleased.

About Joshua

Who lived with his pregnant older sister and her man wasn't happy about it. Joshua's glad he was out of the house for most of the fireworks. His sister and her man argued regularly.

Joshua would like nothing better than to "beat the shit out of him," he told his sister several times. Each time she begged him not to. Said they needed his help.

"Huh what help? You the one working even while you're pregnant," Joshua said to his sister one day. "He's a fucking asshole!"

Joshua loved his sister and did what she wanted. She's his only family since leaving Aunt Jessie's in upstate New York.

Their father's sister, Aunt Jessie took them in after their parents were killed in a plane crash, returning home from an anniversary trip. Joshua was in 8th grade; his sister 9th grade.

Aunt Jessie, a widow, owned a dairy farm she ran along with several ranch hands. Joshua and his sister were welcomed into the farm labor team. They had no friends and Aunt Jessie home-schooled them.

As members of the team they worked most all day and then on occasion became the ranch hands favorite pass time. Aunt Jessie condoned the ranchers sexually-abusing them. Using her nephew and niece to satisfy the workers was much cheaper than giving out raises. She could barely afford to pay them base pay.

Less than 3 months later, 13-year-old Joshua purposely hung himself from the barn loft. One of the ranchers found him alive. His aunt showed no mercy; she beat him with a cord until he bled.

Joshua remembered his sister holding him after the beating. He tried hard not to cry. Aunt Jessie threatened him, "No crying unless you want more!"

I swear I'm gonna get us out of this," she says while bandaging his bloody welts. "I promise.

Around 2:00 in the morning, Joshua's sister wakes him. She said, "Get dressed. We're leaving now!"

He got dressed, grabbed a few things and crept down the hall behind his sister. Nearing their aunt's room, Joshua stops and starts shaking! His sister grabbed his hand, pulled him along past Jessie's room. Joshua glanced in quickly, "Glad she's sleeping." They hurried down the stairs, out the front door and hopped into Aunt Jessie's old Ford Truck.

Joshua's sister's drove them the hell out of there and didn't stop until they reached Pennsylvania where they ditched the car. They took a bus to Savannah, Georgia. Joshua's sister wanted to go there after seeing this beautiful coastal city in movies.

A year had gone by but Joshua couldn't stop looking over his shoulder expecting the police, or worse, Aunt Jessie to show up and drag them back into hell. He closed the door on that chapter after watching his favorite TV show on cold cases. The featured case was about Aunt Jessie. Her body was found the morning after he and his sister ran away. She died from asphyxiation and her death was labeled suspicious. There was no mention of Joshua or his sister.

For a while they lived off the money his sister stole from their aunt. When money got scarce his sister would do anything to keep food on the table. She was 16 when she met Don Juan.

Back at Lydia's

Joshua knocked on the Young's front door. Lydia opened the door, leaving it latched and peeked through the small opening.

"Hey little sis. Mind if I use the bathroom?"

"My parents aren't home."

"Oh. Okay, I'll go pee in one of the bushes."

"What! In front of the neighbors!"

"Well sis when you gotta go, you go," Joshua said, rocking back and forth.

"Okay. But hurry up. My parents will get mad if they catch you."

"Sure thing little sis. Wouldn't want no trouble."

Once inside Lydia points to the main floor bathroom.

"There you go. And go right out when you're done."

"Will do little sis."

Joshua's eyes follow Lydia as she heads upstairs. "Nice," he said under his breath.

Upstairs

Lydia's room door is open and she's standing near the bed. Her eyes widened when Joshua showed up outside her doorway.

"What do you want? You gotta leave. My mom will be here soon," said Lydia, trying to sound tough but scared as hell.

"Well I guess we shouldn't waste any time little sis."

"You gotta go now! I'll scream."

Joshua was right up on her before she got the words out. She tried to scream, but he picked her up, threw her down on the bed and held her arms down with his knees.

"Help, Hel..!"

"Shut the fuck up," said Joshua quickly placing his hand over her mouth. With the other, he slapped her across the face 3 times. "Scream again and I'll kill you!"

"Mmm hmm," Lydia whimpered, "Ummmm."

"All you gotta to do is play nice and I'll let you live."

"Mmm hmm," Lydia continued.

"Oh stop the damn crying. You're gonna love this. I promise."

Joshua kept one hand over her mouth while he ripped off her top and bra with the other. He became vividly excited as the frightened Lydia squirmed beneath him trying to get loose. He dropped his head, attempting to kiss her but Lydia spit in his face.

"That does it! No more nice guy!" Joshua slapped Lydia's face several more times until her nose bled.

"Ahhhhhh!"

"Shut the fuck up," said Joshua with both his hands around her neck, choking her.

"Ugh, awk, gak..."

Lydia fights the darkness surrounding her nakedness. No choice but to surrender to an unfamiliar touch of force and pain. The grinding motion quickly builds to a foul release... ahhhhh... into the darkened vessel creating hate and shame. All silent – for now.

Mama Young is home

And started yelling for Lydia.

"Lydia! Lydia! Girl you better be home."

Mama Young hung up her coat and goes upstairs to Lydia's room.

"Oh Jesus!"

The past is alive

Exposing Chelsea as Lydia's first born conceived through rape 27 years ago. A secret she and her parents hoped to take to their graves.

"Why so quiet mummy," says Chelsea.

"I don't believe this is Chelsea!" Lydia says.

"Oh now mummy don't play stupid. Tell you what. Say hello to my sissy."

"Ma....ma..." the voice stutters. "Please help. He got..."

The line goes dead.

"TiAnna!"

Lydia hangs up and dials *69 but the number is blocked. She then dials TiAnna's cell and gets voicemail. She throws the phone down and drops to her knees, holding her head in the palm of her hands.

"Dear God help my baby!"

21

Big G Ain't Here

September 13, 2012
11:30 a.m. at the church

Shonny's in good company. These folks don't like Mr. Darius either. They're staring and whispering. No respect for Jerome. None!

"Quiet," says the pastor. "Young man, please come forward."

Darius scans the crowd.

"Paleeze," says Shonny under her breath.

Shonny's buggin' and I plan to put a stop to her mouth. I lean over and whisper, "Y'all ain't right. This is about Jerome, not you."

I hope she shuts up.

Darius steps out from the back row and walks down the aisle toward the front, swag-striding like President Obama. His heads up, face forward and he looks mighty damn proud.

I get a good look at him when he passes. He's mixed, but a shade darker than daddy's wifey. His curly brown hair is cut into a box and faded on all sides. Darius is tall like Jerome, a tad-bit heavier but built fine. I smile when I imagine him with tattoos on his body – his chest, arms and thighs – done tastefully.

Ahhh. He stops and touches Jerome's casket, pulling me right there with him. "R.I.P. Jerome. We love you."

Darius takes the stage
And nods at Pastor Jackson – the boy's got manners.
"Go ahead son."

Darius steps behind the podium; taps the mike and clears his throat. Whew! Feedback. He adjusts the mic and looks out into the crowd – right to left – then back to center where he rests his eyes on me. I ain't one of them Darius I wanna yell! Um. He read my mind. He's smiling with his Chris Brown fine looking self. He's got them green eyes too and I'm loving how he looks in his baby blue suit.

"My brother yo… I uhhhh."

He stops to clear his throat, blinks his moist eyes to stop the tears.

Darius shouldn't hold back. He should cry and so should all men – cry sometimes – not just the Tommies. Stop acting so damn macho like daddy. He should cry too. Look at him sitting there all quiet. Probably wishing this would be over. I'm gonna have to thank him for being a good sport.

"My brother Jerome was the only real friend I had in dis world. He accepted me regardless of how I came about even though my own pops denied me. I grew up in Portland and got bullied by all the neighbor kids. Around town they called my mama "poor white trash who seduced a good decent black man." Don't matter what people think. I shouldn't have been blamed for "their" mistake.

Orreeeeeek!

These noisy benches. Shame. They need to do something about 'em. I glance at Shonny. She's got the same frown on her lip. At least she's not nudging me.

"When I was 7, Jerome stops dis 11-year-old kid from beatin' the crap out of me. Jerome was 8. We didn't live far from each other and attended the same school. Jerome took me aside one day and says we make a pack. We will always have each other's back — we was brothers. I didn't know he knew about me but he had heard. Portland's small ya know. Jerome taught me to defend myself. When I turned 12, I took defending myself to a whole new level."

Wow. I know how he feels. Like TiAnna coming to my defense when the kids picked on me.

"I joined my first gang after pops found me and Jerome hangin' together. We was playin' hoop over at Irving Park our favorite after school pastime. We planned to try out for the NBA and talked about teams we would shoot for — Bulls, Lakers, Miami, and Blazers."

"I remember the day well. Mama was in the hospital with pneumonia. She took ill due to her MS. Her immune system was challenged and she had a tough time fighting the pneumonia. I had gone to visit her earlier; Jerome went with me."

"Imagine bein' 12 years old and the doctor tellin' you your mom's dying. Then dey says I'd be getting' a visit from a social worker, who'd talk with me about my options after she passed. They already wrote my mama off. Too dem she was nothin' but a welfare case. She could barely take care of me. Refused to beg my biological pop for a dime."

Uh-oh! Darius got his lips tightened. He wants to whoop somebody's ass. These fakers better watch out. Glad I'm not on his shit list.

"Jerome pulls me out of there and we went over to the park. We walked all the way from Emanuel Hospital, talkin'. He was there for me. But when pop found us together, he made his hate for me known. He told Jerome, "Go get in the car! Time to go home!" Jerome refused and started an argument with pops. I pleaded with Jerome to just let it go. Finally, he did; he gave me a hug and walked away. Pops succeeded in putting an end to our relationship for a while anyway."

"Once he was gone pop says somethin' I won't forget. He says he won't acknowledge me as his son. I was a mistake, a cruel joke and he wanted me die or somethin'."

"You and your whore mama stay away from me and mine," that's what he said to me.

Ooo. Shame. Make Mr. Ellis look like a saint.

"Not the day to disrespect my mama yo. He turned and walked away. I picked up a rock, ran up on him and hit him in the back of da head. He fell. I tried to hit him again but he shielded himself. Good thing. I would've ended up in jail for murder instead of assault."

There he goes. Let the tears fall. You still the man Darius. The pastor hands him some tissue.

Darius wipes his eyes, takes in a deep breath before he speaks.

"Thank you, pastor. I'll keep this right here, if you don't mind. Many of you know I went to Juvie for 2 years. Pop's made sure of it. Mama got better. She was with me through it all. Jerome stays in touch through mama. Even when I left town. I may be a wretch in y'alls eyes but my brother loved me no matter what. Nobody can take that away from me."

Ahhhh. You got me crying Darius.

"Let's us pray," says Pastor Jackson standing next to Darius.

Everyone is bowing their heads but I think I'll opt out like Darius. He's looking at me too. I wonder what he's thinking. You probably understand like I do huh Darius? The Big G who so loved the world and gave his only begotten son loves to play cruel jokes on young souls like me and you. Yep, we're the Big G's number 1 victims.

Special Note to Mama

Dear mama, I haven't heard from TiAnna and I am worried. She said she wants to come to Portland. Her and her mama probably got into a fight again. I tried to return her call several times and got voicemail. Today it's disconnected. I called her parents and left a message but they haven't called me back. I got a hold of some of our old friends and they say she hasn't been in school for over 3 weeks and no one knows why.

I need to speak to Unc Rae-Rae because he'd be able to find out for me. He hasn't called in a while. Sadie phoned to let me know he got put in the hole for knocking one of the inmates out.

And Jeremy, I guess he's forgotten about me because he still hasn't returned my calls and I stopped trying last week after I left him a nasty message. I even cussed 'cause he don't like me too. I have to tell you what I said even though it ain't nice. I said, "You asshole. I should've expected you to throw me to the curb. I'm glad my party got turned out when it did cause I was gonna give you some. I plan to find someone else and screw the hell out of him. I may make a tape and send it to you. Go to hell!"

I am glad Unc Rae-Rae warned me about giving up my "sweetness" too soon. Just think if I would have did the-do with him he'd be off claiming victory leaving me to sulk. Speaking of giving up my twot-twot, I wish we could talk for real. These urges I'm having are killing me. The other thing me and Jeremy was doing was good but I really want to experience doing-the-do. I need a female perspective not Unc Rae-Rae's and daddy's. They're always going to insist I stay a virgin forever. Then I can stay their little girl — at least Unc Rae-Rae's. Anyway, the way things are going, I won't have to worry about losing my virginity anytime soon.

Daddy is behaving by keeping Luanne off my back. He's been a real comfort since the funeral. The funeral was tough. I couldn't bring myself to go to the repast. I did speak to Darius, Jerome's brother though. We said we'd keep in touch. Apparently, he'll be around town for a while. Jerome left him the family home and he's staying there. He deserves it after being denied his rights all of those years. Shonny had something negative to say about Darius but I shut her down. I told her I didn't want to hear it anymore.

Mama, please talk to the Big G for me about my BFF. He doesn't listen to me. T is in serious trouble. I'd pray for her but I don't trust the Big G to do the right thing. If you ask maybe, he'll do something.

Love always,

LaTonya

22

Devil's on Holiday

September 23, 2012
Early at breakfast

Daddy's reading the Portland newspaper.

"The Portland mayor's race is heating up," he says. "One candidate wants to be mayor so he can fix potholes."

My daddy prefers to get his daily dose of news the old-fashioned way. He even has Bennie pick up an Atlanta Journal Constitution from a downtown newsstand, which carries newspapers and magazines from around the county. If you happen to be in the same room with him while he's reading, he'll comment about a story and it doesn't matter if you're listening. He sometimes laughs out loud and says, "Ain't that some pitiful shit?" I usually say yeah although I pay him no attention."

Speaking of news, the police have no leads on Jerome's killing. His family keeps pressure on them by holding vigils in front of the Prescott house where people have been leaving flowers. I saw Darius standing on the porch a few times looking like the uninvited guest. Jerome's damn family is still treating him like shit.

An anti-gang activist was interviewed by TV media at one vigil. He says Portland gangs are on the rise again and more African American kids are falling prey to the lifestyle.

"These kids have nowhere to go and have to be 18 to get a job here," he says. "We're not doing right by our kids. Instead we help the state fill up the prison beds. Black youth make up nearly 47 percent of kids incarcerated in Oregon's juvenile system. This is in a state where we are less than 2 percent of the population."

Daddy says kids should be kept busy doing something constructive – keeps them out of trouble. Juvenile crime is rising around the country especially among boys who tend to get in more trouble when they hit puberty.

Daddy grew up poor
But stayed out of trouble because of his mentor.

Daddy was 10 years old when he met Mr. Thomas, a billionaire, on the day he got caught stealing some bread and peanut butter from the corner store. He had no food at home. Gramma Ellis was having a tough time taking care of things after his daddy walked out on them. She worked part-time cleaning houses and refused to ask for help from anybody, including welfare.

"Your gramma was too damn proud," says daddy. "Some days we went without food."

Mr. Thomas stopped the store manager from calling the police on daddy by offering to pay for the stolen items. The manager would've preferred daddy go to jail. Daddy says the manager said "they should all be locked up," meaning black people.

"Asshole. He was black as they come!" Daddy says. "He must've been one of those black Republicans!"

Daddy found out later Mr. Thomas was the owner. He built the store in the community to provide an affordable place for folks to shop. Daddy did say it had the cheapest prices in south Atlanta; one of few that took food stamps and allowed credit.

Mr. Thomas would secretly shop the store to make sure his workers were treating everyone with respect. Daddy says gramma Ellis always had good things to say about Mr. Thomas.

"Mr. Thomas sho a good white man," she'd say. "He lets me take a grocery cart home – say he'd tell the owner he'd pay for it."

Mr. Thomas fired the manager the same day and later brought in another black manager, who according to daddy must've been a Democrat. He was much more understanding.

Mr. Thomas drove daddy home after letting him gather up several bags of groceries. Daddy said it was like Christmas. He got ice cream and candy, a luxury item for his family. I guess gramma Ellis was hesitant about taking the food, but Mr. Thomas insisted and said daddy could pay him back by working for him on weekends. He'd pick up daddy and bring him home. Gramma Ellis agreed. Mr. Thomas paid daddy anyway – $200 a week – which daddy used to help gramma Ellis.

Mr. Thomas lived in a mansion all by himself. The same one where he and his deceased wife raised their 4 kids. Daddy says the place had 15 rooms: a huge indoor swimming pool, gym and horse stables up the road. Mr. Thomas bred racehorses he entered in all the big races around the country.

Mr. Thomas talked to daddy about making the right choices and choosing the right career path. He encouraged daddy to "be a leader rather than a follower, a giver rather than a taker, who owned the store rather than work in it."

Mr. Thomas paid for daddy's college education and Unc Rae-Rae's. Yep my uncle has a Bachelor's degree in Social Work. He says it was the easiest one to get.

"My brother chooses to hustle instead of using his degree and paying taxes," says daddy.

Daddy said gramma Ellis had given him a real good whooping the day he stole from the store regardless of why. She then warned him never to steal again.

"No sons a mine is gwine up like thieves," she'd say.

Gramma Ellis always lectured daddy before he went to Mr. Thomas's "not to steal from that nice white man." She also told him rich white folks purposely leave money around to see if you'll steal.

"They do dat to me up at dem rich white folks' houses I clean for. I don't touch nothin," gramma Ellis said.

Daddy says Mr. Thomas did leave small amounts of money– a dollar or $2, sometimes $5, and always some loose change around and in places where daddy could see it. Daddy says he never stole from Mr. Thomas – ever! Even though Mr. Thomas's oldest daughter tried to set him up.

"She even tried to get Mr. Thomas to fire me, a 10-year-old!" says daddy. "Some money came up missing. Mr. Thomas knew it wasn't me. I didn't take the money he had left out on purpose."

Daddy overheard Mr. Thomas and his daughter arguing about the missing money. Mr. Thomas told her to go straight "to hell!"

Daddy says, "Mr. Thomas loved to use the cuss words shit, damn, hell and ass. I never heard the "F" word out of his mouth, only from your uncle who got his foul mouth from the neighborhood thugs he ran with."

Now I know why daddy uses those four cuss words. Our words got roots.

"Mr. Thomas's daughter is how those rich ass Republicans act," says daddy. "Mr. Thomas was a Democrat though."

Daddy did say someone told him Mr. Thomas was a moderate Republican but swears it was a lie.

Then he says it again, "There's no way in hell Republicans are nice except for Collin Powell. Now he's okay. The general stood up to "W" and also voted for Obama, so he knows what's right."

I need daddy's attention so

I say, "Daddy. Can I ask you somethin'?"

"What's on your mind Tip?"

"Do you think I'm bad luck?" I got daddy's attention.

"Girl, what the hell kind of question is that?"

"Weeell, mama died. Then Jerome gets killed. Then something happened to my BFF. Somethin' happens to everyone I care about. Daddy you sent Unc Rae-Rae and Jeremy away. So I'm thinkin' I'm nutso and you won't tell me. Maybe I'm cursed or got the plague or somethin'. I don't care if Luanne doesn't like me for whatever reason. But you're my daddy and you hate me – for whatever reason. So, I must be getting punished for something. Did I have something to do with mama getting killed? Maybe I'm a child serial killer and you're trying to protect everyone from me."

Daddy lifts his brows, his eyes widening lookin' at me like I'm from outer space or somethin'.

"Girl is you crazy!"

"That's what I'm asking you daddy?"

"Girl sometimes I can't believe you're 17. When did you last see Dr. Ryan?"

"You're doing it again daddy. Avoiding my questions. Are you going to answer me this time?"

"What the hell am I to say?"

"How about the truth. Or Tippy you're okay. Tippy I love you, or..."

Daddy sets his paper down and looks at me, his face softening.

"Tippy I love you. You're my daughter. My first born. You'll always have a special place in my heart no matter what. You're not to blame for your mother or anything else bad that has happened. Shit happens. I'm sorry you've been in the middle. You don't deserve the pain. Life can be cruel sometimes. But you've got to be brave. Keep a stiff upper lip. Tell the devil to kiss your ass! You can do it because you've got my genes. I hope we're clear. I don't ever want to hear you talk like this again!"

This makes me cry a little but I quickly wipe my eyes. Daddy's avoiding my question about Unc Rae-Rae and Jeremy. I don't think he'll ever admit to anything. My daddy says he doesn't hate me and the first he's told me he loved me in a long time. And hey, considering he's the devil, he did give me permission to tell him to kiss my ass! I guess I should take what he says and run. No tellin' how long this sympathetic daddy's gonna last.

23

An OK White Girl

October 1, 2012
Before school at Abe Lincoln

I look for Shonny but don't see her. She's not in 3rd period either so she must be out today. I haven't spoken to her since Jerome's funeral. I wonder if she's pissed at me for shutting her down about Darius. If she is, oh well.

Lunch time came around quickly and it's a good thing. My stomach is talking to me. In the school cafeteria I buy a chicken salad and a Diet Snapple Peach Ice Tea, one of my favorite diet drinks. I had to slow down on how much I was drinking. One day I had so many – OMG – I had a stomachache for days.

I take my tray over to the comfy chairs, grouped in 2s and 3s, around the corner from the main lunch area. This area is less crowded and less noisy with only a few students huddled together whispering, reading and eating. There's an empty chair next to a white girl with her bare feet propped up on the small table in front of her. She peers over her book and smiles.

"There's enough room for your tray if you want," she says with her mouth full of food.

I put my tray on my lap opting not to set it near her bare feet.

"Naw. I'm fine." I say.

Hm. She needs a pedicure. Chipped polish and crusty heels is tacky. Shame. She doesn't look bad for a white girl. She got those big blue eyes white boys like. At least they did at Stone Hill. I'd hear the jocks babbling about this 1 white girl Lisa who led the Stonetts Dance Team. "Baby got those fine blue eyes making me all horny and shit," they'd say.

Nuh-uh. This salad ain't good. I may start leaving campus for lunch like some of the other kids.

"Hi, I'm Julie. You're new?"

"Yeah. I'm LaTonya."

"You use to hang with Shonny. Too bad she transferred."

"For real?" I say.

"Oh, you didn't know?"

"Naw."

"Hm," says Julie. "She's going to Benson now. Shonny says she's much to ghetto for this school. Ha!"

I ain't laughing. I'm offended Shonny would say something so damn stupid and to a white girl. Why do we do this to ourselves?

Instead I say, "You must know Shonny pretty well."

"We talked but never hung together," says Julie. "I do know she was getting tired of being here. The lack of diversity really got to her this year. I think she also has a new love interest. She kinda hinted around but didn't mention any names."

"Hm," I say.

"I don't know how much you know about things here but happy to help," says Julie.

"Oh okay," I say.

"Oh and in case you're interested, there's a party coming up on the 19th. A lot of the seniors from here will be going. Shonny knows too. Maybe she'll show up with her new love."

A white folk's party? Doesn't sound like my thing even though I like all kinds of music. I prefer pop over hip hop.

"Thanks for the invite I'll let you know."

Julie gives me her cell number. "See ya round," she says. She grabs her tray and books, sticks her feet back into her black flats and heads off down the hall, waving.

This is good all nice and quiet. Gives me a few moments to myself. I'm done picking at my food, put my tray on the table and scoot down in my chair. I'm tempted to put my feet up except someone may come along and I wouldn't want them to feel like I did. Except, if I had my shoes off, you'd see my nice toes with a fuchsia French tip; matches my nails. I got a fill and a pedicure the other day at an Asian nail shop near here. You can always find 1. They're like black churches, 1 on every other corner almost.

An image of my BFF flashes in my head; she's crying and screaming for help. Again, I feel helpless like when something happened to mama and Jerome. I want with all my heart for my BFF to be okay. But she's not and I gotta help her somehow.

At the Atlanta jailhouse

Unc Rae-Rae is on the phone with one of his girls.

"What have you heard Mona?"

"Not much, Ray."

"Okay baby here's what I need you to do. Call Lonnie and ask him to sniff around some of the "ho's on Preston Street. See what he can find out."

"Ooo Ray. You think she may be out there?"

"I hope not. It'd be hard to deal with some of the pimps down there from in here. They'll murder a nigga over their girls, especially those they grab without pulling 'em."

"Okay den. I'll check with Lonnie when I hang up."

"Uhhh another thing. Check-in with Sadie to see if any movement on the other end. She's got to come home. Tippy needs her."

May 20, 2000
Where's my happy place

Where's daddy? Where's Luanne? Mama's screaming! I'm scared. Please help… "Don't move you little bitch. Don't move!"

Huh, huh, huh, huh… gotta calm down… huh, huh, huh, huh … I can do this. Dr. Ryan would say, "Lean back, close your eyes and think happy thoughts." Then she'd say, "Now breeeeeathe… in and out. Now breathe in and hold. And release, haaaaaaaaaa."

I'm imagining me and mama at gramma Oliver's and this silly song is playin' over and over, the 1 mama sings when she's mad at Luanne. "Flat foot floozy with the floy, floy, flat foot floozy with the floy, floy, flat foot floozy with the floy, floy, floy, floy." Mama and gramma start hop-dancing and singing. I jump in hop-dancing and singing. Mama grabs my hands and we dance. She then leans down and says, "You can only sing this with me and gramma. This is our secret."

Yes. I took charge. Another nightmare gone and I'm no longer afraid. I'm ready to remember.

24

My BFF is No Whore

October 2, 2012
Outside Stone Mountain

My BFF gets no mercy.

"It hurts, it hurts! Please stop!"

Don Juan did what he wanted to me over the next several hours while Chelsea sat and watched. He even brought in several other guys who also had their way with me. This is not now how I imagined sex would be. This wasn't love, they were malicious and brutal. They don't care about my feelings and neither does Chelsea, who claims she's my sister. How could a sister sit and watch; be so heartless and cold?

When it was over, she has the nerve to come and sit next to me, talk to me like she's concerned. "Go ahead and cry. You'll be fine," she says. "Least you'll be ready. These johns are getting kinkier by the day. They want some of everything."

The dreams I talked about with Tippy are gone. I can't even remember what they were 'cause now I'm on the ho stroll. Don Juan must've pegged me the day me and Tippy saw him on the black college tour. What did he do? Stock me? Did he know Chelsea was my so-called sister back then?

"Owe!" What did she stick me with? Whatever it was, makes me not care. Even though the pain is all over my body. They tore me up and I'm bleeding.

"You should feel betta," says Chelsea.

The bitch is stroking the back of my hair.

"It does the trick for me. Pretty soon you'll do whatever it takes for the next hit."

Chelsea bends over and begins to kiss me, starting from the back of my neck down. I guess I know what's coming next. The boys are done so now her turn.

I'm surprised she did anything

But last month, Lydia reported TiAnna as a runaway rather than tell the truth about her possible whereabouts. She has no intention of telling Randall either.

"I get sick when I think of what might be happening to you TiAnna. Maybe it's not as bad. Maybe you've accepted Chelsea as your sister and you're staying away to punish me. God, let this be true. I should be punished. I'm so sorry my secret has come straight from hell to haunt us both."

Visiting Mama Young

Who says truth will set you free?

"Time, we face the past Lydia. No matter how painful. God has a way of showing' us what needs to come to light," says Mama Young.

Lydia is visiting her mother, who's dying from stomach cancer, in a hospice facility. The first round of chemotherapy didn't work and Mama Young refused further treatment months ago. The doctor gave her less than 6 months to live. Mama Young says she's ready to join Papa Young in heaven, who died a few years ago.

"Mama I can't. Randall would never understand."

"What do you mean? That man has already stood by you once before. He's been a good father to TiAnna. He didn't have to accept her, but he did."

"Oh mama. What have I done?"

"You did nothing. The devil was hanging around our home and we should've known. I knew somethin' was off about that boy. Yo papa wanted to give him a chance. I should've followed my gut."

Lydia's home

And alone in her sewing room. She closes her eyes and decides to pray. Something she hasn't done in 9 years. Mama Young died today while she was visiting, taking with her their secret. Lydia will miss mama, but she's relieved.

"No one can find out about Chelsea. TiAnna will be okay, she'll come home."

God please don't let TiAnna pay for my mistakes. I didn't mean to hurt anybody. All I wanted to do was talk and all she did was laugh in my face. Says I could never have him because he was hers. God, she took him from me and my child. She already hurt a man who truly loved her. It didn't matter. All I heard was an evil laugh. She had no shame. She wasn't the angel everybody thought she was. God I was wrong and will accept my punishment. I'm prepared to burn in hell for relieving you of 1 less godless child.

Oct. 18, 2012

It's early evening at the Johnson's

Mr. Johnson signs for the UPS package addressed to him. He opens the letter inside and begins to read:

What's up step-daddy this is Chili remember me?

Lydia gets home, after making arrangements to have Mama Young cremated, and goes directly to the TV room. As usual, Randall's sitting in the recliner but doesn't acknowledge her presence with his usual "Hey darling, how was your day?" Lydia suspects he's asleep.

She tiptoes over to the left side of his chair, gently places her hand on his shoulder and leans over.

"Oh! I thought you were asleep."

He doesn't speak or look at her.

"What's the matter? Looks like you've been crying. Have you heard from TiAnna?"

Randall pushes her hand from his shoulder and stands up. He turns toward the entryway; still ignoring her, he freezes in place like he's in a trance - then leaves the room and out of the front door.

"What the hell!" Lydia says out loud.

She plops down in Randall's chair, leans back until the foot rest pops out, lifting her legs into a resting position.

"I'm too exhausted to think but have to find my daughter?"

TiAnna's been gone for days and no leads. Right after Chelsea called Lydia phoned the convent where Mama Young says she took her baby. What she didn't say was she gave the child to a woman they met in the parking lot; not the nuns. So, they had no information but said they'd pray for the family.

Lydia pulls the back rest forward, letting the foot rest slide back beneath the seat. When she stands, she notices a crumpled piece of paper on the floor. She picks it up; straightens it out and reads the handwritten: What's up step-daddy this is Chili remember me?

"Oh lord," Lydia says, clasping her hand to her mouth.

I bet ya thinkin' I got some nerve sending a letter to your house. Hey pops I figure we close like dat. We've had some good times. Remember the last time? You talked a lot about your wife an all. How she wouldn't suck your dick and how she's so cold in bed. I bet you horny right now huh pops? Ya knows I can suck your dick real good. Have ya hollering'.

I hear you've been looking for me. Probably wanna tell me 'bout your troubles. I already know. You know how? Your wife knows. She's my mama. I'm your stepdaughter. Ooo kinky huh? My real name is Chelsea so surprise! And guess who's with me? My sissy. We're having a good ol' time. I'm teaching her to be just like me. Family is family right pops? You know I know betta than anybody how you nasty bastards like young pussy. This is good bye. Thanks for helping me find my family.

Chelsea your Chili

8:30p.m. times a ticking

And Lydia's in her room sitting on the bed. She's tired and feeling defeated but has one last thing to do. She takes out stationary and 2 envelopes from the nightstand. She addresses a letter to Randall and the other to TiAnna.

In her letter to Randall, she reveals everything about the rape, about Chelsea and what she did 9 years ago. A secret no one knows about except her and someone who will probably never remember.

Randall I'm so sorry. All I do is make things worse. This is my fault. Don't worry. I won't be around to mess up our boys lives. What you did with Chelsea, I forgive you. Be happy for our children's sakes...

She leans both letters against the night lamp. Randall will easily see them when he walks in.

Lydia forces herself up and goes into their ensuite bathroom to the medicine cabinet for her bottle of sedatives the doctor recently prescribed. She pours half the bottle of pills into her hand.

"I got to. This is the only way. No more pain, no more memories, the suffering ends now."

She's tosses the handful of pills into her mouth and forces them down with water.

"Okay god. Please bring TiAnna home now."

Lydia lies on the bed, folds her arms across her stomach and closes her eyes – slowly drifting away she takes with her the sound of Chelsea's voice, "Mummy why did you throw me away?"

"I'm sorry Chelsea but I can't love you. You were conceived in hate. When I'm gone, maybe you can learn how to love."

25

A Daddy's Truth

8:30 p.m.
At the same time

Randall Johnson drives around south Atlanta looking for Chili at her normal hangouts, but she hasn't been seen in a while. About an hour later, he parks outside the hotel where they use to rendezvous, hoping she'll show.

Chili was Randall's first experience with a prostitute he met at a club on Langley Street. He was alone and drank until he was drunk trying to forget an earlier argument, he and Lydia had had over something Randall thought was petty.

"Anything to piss me off. Huh. No fuckin' again tonight. I ain't had none in so long I lost the feelin' in my dick! I can't understand what's wrong with the woman! Don't she know I love her?"

8:40 p.m.

Outside of Stone Mountain

"We leave Sunday mornin'. Outta state," says Don Juan. "Gettin' too hot; people askin' questions."

"Who's askin'?" says Chelsea.

"Don' matta. We outta here before you go down," he says, pointing his finger. "I be damned if I'm going!"

"We in this together baby," says Chelsea. "Sissy doin' good by us. The mens, they like her."

"Yeah as long as she high she fine," says Don Juan. "She needs to be mo' serving to the customus."

"Mo' she on smack, she do anything," says Chelsea. "Done already happened."

Kill me now

Rather than leave me locked up – as if I can run. I'm too high. And Ooo I hurt bad. All night long. So many I lost count. I hope the next one's a serial killer. I'd say to him kill me please!

Owe, shit! I can't move. God please don't let me keep living. Spare me and anybody who comes near me is gonna pay. I'll make 'em suffer, especially mama and daddy. I'll kill 'em slowly, make 'em hurt like I do.

"Hey I need somethin' I don't feel good! Can you hear me dammit?"

Chelsea comes into the room. "Sure sissy. You finally awoke."

"Don't you fuckin' call me your sissy!"

"Tsk tsk. Sissy's ungrateful. After all me and Donny's done for yo ass. Tell ya what, I'll leave you alone to think about showin' mo respect."

Chelsea turns to walk away. TiAnna grabs her.

"I need somethin' now!"

"Well then say please sissy and thank you."

"No."

"Well then…"

"Okay. Okay. Please sissy! Thank you!"

"Dat's better. Now give sissy a hug."

10:00p.m.
Where's that whore

Randall's thinking while he waits outside another one of Chili's hangouts. It appears she's gone A.W.O.L so Randall contemplates his next move.

He decides to go see an old friend in the morning but first checks-in on the boys to let them know he won't be home. When he asks about Lydia, the boys say she's asleep.

"Good. Let her stay asleep. I'll see y'all tomorrow."

Randall pulls out a bottle of brandy he had locked away in the glove compartment – his emergency stash for nights like these. He downs half the pint in one long swig then leans back in his car seat to settle in for the night.

After finishing the pint, Randall can't help but feel the brandy's effects. "You're one of my favorite girls," he says and kisses the top of the empty bottle.

Randall doesn't want to miss Chili just in case she has the nerve to show. He forces his eyes to stay half open by watching the hookers and johns prance in and out of the motel across the street. He laughs when he sees a man yelling at a woman after leaving a hotel room.

"Ha. Must've been a one-night stands," Randall says out loud. Then he switches thoughts reflecting on his past.

Back in the day Randall was the man. He ran the streets and dared anyone to get in his way. To save his daughter, he knows the old Randall must be reborn.

"You gonna give me back my daughter, even if I have to kill you Chili, or Chelsea, whatever yo name is and yo damn pimp!"

Oct. 19, 2013
7:00 a.m.

The next morning the Johnson boys leave for school without stopping to check on their mother. They figure she's already left for work; she usually does around 5:00 a.m. to make the morning shift.

Randall calls in sick. Today he plans to visit an old buddy in county lock up and arrives a few minutes before the jail officially opens. Meanwhile his cell phone is vibrating with an incoming call from the post office.

"Damn, not now. I ain't ready."

Randall turns off his phone, ignoring the call he figures is Lydia.

10:00a.m.
Inside the DeKalb County jail

Randall follows a group of people through security, down a long hallway into a large room. He takes a seat near the back of the room. Once everybody is seated the guards open a big steel door at the other end of the room. Several prisoners come through first then a familiar face, showing off his signature grin, stepping and sliding, wearing an orange jumpsuit.

That Negro always manages to be cool even in prison garbs Randall says to himself.

"Hey whassup man? What brings you here?" says Raymond Ellis, extending his hand. Randall hesitates, remembering the rules against inmate-civilian contact.

"It's cool," says Ray.

Randall shakes Ray's hand and nods - Ray sits across from him.

"Man you look like shit. Clothes all wrinkled. When's the last time you slept?" Ray says.

"I need your help locating my daughter," says Randall. "You know the streets better than me. My hustling days ended with Lydia."

Ray keeps quiet about what he's found out about TiAnna. Don Juan has her but Randall already knows.

"How's Lydia holdin' up?" says Ray.

"Lydia your ex-wife is holdin' her own," says Randall.

"No one knows about me and Lydia's short hitch. I'd like to keep it on the DL," says Ray. "You've been good for her, man."

"Huh. Yeah right man," says Randall. "At least I kept my hands off another man's wife until you unhitched."

"Look man," Ray says "You're askin' for help while at the same time bringing up somethin' that ain't your concern. You have Lydia; y'all have a child…"

"When Lydia left you, she was already pregnant Ray."

"What are you sayin' man?"

"I'm sayin' is TiAnna is not my daughter. She's yours!"

26

Feelin' No Pain

Outside of Stone Mountain

"Heyyyy this is T yours to be so allow me to re-introduce myself … this is real as it gets… Go Jay Z, go Jeezy, go, go – sounding hot!

TiAnna's in the bedroom – locked in as usual – sitting in front of the mirror putting on makeup. She's preparing for another long night. High as hell, TiAnna's rapping her own words to the music, "Call me sissy for another long night. Done shot some smack, drank a pint of Hennessy and blew some coke now holla wit' your hands in the air."

"Hurry up sissy!" says Chelsea through the door. "Donny wants us out by 8:00. We gotta convention."

"Stop your fuckin' yellin' bitch! Too bad you can't hear me over this loud music. Maybe your Donny will follow through on his threat bitch. Beat me 'til I'm dead bitch. Then he can suck those nasty ass dicks himself – bee-atch."

TiAnna ignores Chelsea and keeps on rapping. "What you say Jay?" Damn, that's gotta be disgusting…

"Motherfuckas," says TiAnna. "Think they care if I'm 17? Being held against my will? Thought I could appeal to this one grandfather-lookin' man's sense of family. Maybe he had a granddaughter. Instead the son-of-bitch says, "Whores come in all ages, sizes and colors. I like 'em anyway I can get 'em." I told him to go to hell and he told Don Juan. Asshole. Don Juan came in the room and slapped me."

Then he says, "Next time I'mo give you a beatdown so bad you'd beg me to kill yo ass! And take back my initials. You lucky I let you wear 'em."

That slimy motherfucka. Had my wrists tattooed. My left one has a D, my right a J. Then he says, "You belong to me. But bitch if you get caught, you don't know my name. Yo so-called sista won't show you no mercy. You don't mean shit to her!"

"You got 10 minutes before I come put my foot in yo ass!" says Chelsea.

"Fuck you!" T says. "Go Jay, go Jeez rrraaahhh!"

"We've got breaking news," says the news anchor.

"Wa wait. That's not how it goes Jay."

"The body of a woman was found minutes ago in Stone Mountain."

"Wa is tha' 'bout? police, amblance, pe... whas tha' say? Let me go ove there. Uh-oh my two bros and dads... mama? Ma uh… where…?"

"The coroner believes the woman has been dead since last evening but no one found her until recently," the reporter says. "The reason for the suicide is unclear. We've been told the Johnson daughter is missing. Mr. Randall Johnson has been out looking for his missing daughter since yesterday afternoon. No word on her whereabouts."

T's confused by the announcement. With the drugs and alcohol messing with her head she can't tell what's real, including the voices she thinks she hears.

Hey! Hey! Ohh! Ohh! "Whaaaat? Awe naw. Ain't real. Wait. Now who dat? Huh? Mama is tha' you? Jay say you dead. Why you sad? Sorry we fought K?"

"TiAnna. Where are you? Come home. Come to mama. You'll be safe here," says mom's voice.

"Right here mama. Can't you see me?"

"Come home TiAnna. No more pain. I have no more pain."

"K mama. I'll come home. I get up now. Steady as she go…"

TiAnna gets up and stumbles over to the night stand. She reaches behind the mirror feeling around for Chelsea's private stash, which is taped to the back. Right here. These are the pills you use after Don Juan whoops yo ass. I have to watch. One time he whooped you so bad, you hollered for mercy. Then he makes me patch you up.

I can't feel sorry for you. You had yo nerve sayin', "You probably got a kick out me getting' beatdown. Watch yo step, sissy. Don't think you gone move me out da way. I see how he looks at you."

As if I give a shit! Having his sweaty paws all over me! So, I'm gonna take all of 'em leave you nothing sissy! Let you suffer sissy!

Back at the DeKalb jail

Ray's in the rec-room when he hears the news about Lydia. He's waiting for the prison guard to take him to use the phone in the Chaplin's office, which he uses regularly. Ray struck up a friendship with the Chaplin, hoping to gain some brownie points. Ray doesn't believe in God – but doesn't say this to the Chaplin – nor would he ever "believe in the bullshit." He told this to the minister of the holiness church on the corner from his house.

Back in the day

The church in Ray's neighborhood, where he's been living for 2 years, has a largely black congregation. The church was notorious for loud Sunday and Wednesday revivals that went until midnight – a few times they extended them to 2 in the morning. The minister ignored the neighbors' complaints, forcing them to report the church to the city's noise abatement office. The local police recommended they do this and stop calling 9-1-1.

The city issued the church several citations and hefty fines for continued noise violations. The minister still refused to comply and retaliated by heightening the PA system volume. He yelled into the microphone saying, "We won't let the devil stop us. The police can take me to jail. Until then, these people will hear the word of God."

"You defiant bastards!" Ray called 3 members who stopped by to invite him to church. "You people are full of shit!"

"You're going to hell if you don't get saved," says the elder.

"I'm looking forward to it," Ray said. "Hell's gotta be better than y'all bullshit!"

Ray snatched the bible out of the elders' hand, threw it across the wet grass and said, "Next time it's going up your ass!"

They stopped coming to Ray's door but saw him when he'd jog past the church on Sunday mornings – on purpose – and right when church ended. They'd look at him and shake their heads. Ray would laugh and say, "No more revivals thank you Jesus hallelujah. Hallelujah. Thank you, Jesus."

At the jailhouse again

The Chaplin senses that Ray's depressed and asks if they can pray together. Ray nods thinking to himself, "I'll play your game. I need to use the phone." While the Chaplin prays, Ray returns his mind to the conversation he had with Randall. "TiAnna is mine and Lydia's daughter? Shit. Now I got 2 of 'em, who don't know they're sisters. I'mo make this right when I get outta of here."

'Bout time he stopped praying

So, Ray is free to dial a number he hoped he'd never have to use. The line picks up.

"Uhhhh, say man, I'm the last person you wanna hear from, but I need your help."

"Ha! Tell me why I shouldn't hang up on your black ass brotha!"

27

Me and Julie

Council Crest

It's nice and quiet for a change. I'm in my room, the TV's off and the babysitter's downstairs with Jayden and Brittany. Daddy took Luanne out to a fundraiser for a nonprofit youth program for Portland's at-risk black youth. Myra Clark, a black woman, founded the nonprofit 20 years ago and is still at the helm. Folks say she'll stay there as long as her family and friends remain on the board of directors.

Daddy met this black businessman named Larry Hughes, who's originally from Philadelphia, at a recent gathering for Portland's black men. Larry Hughes, who invited daddy to the fundraiser, has been living here with his family for 3 years.

Larry Hughes knows everything there is to know about Portland. He told daddy about the 2 black-owned community newspapers, which is good but there's no black radio station, no black music and the only black broadcast news is on cable if you have it. He says there is a syndicated black radio station on A.M. – he thinks it still there – with a weak signal you can only hear if you turn sideways.

Shonny told me the same thing, but it doesn't matter to me. I watch video channels on cable and listen to internet and satellite radio – this is the thing to do in the information age.

Larry Hughes didn't have nice things to say about this nonprofit but he is going to the fundraiser anyway. "Gotta be seen," he told daddy. "Keep my eye on these folks." He also told daddy that Myra Clark continues to have the last word on a lot of the education programs targeting Portland's black youth even if hers has no affiliation. She wants to control things and keep others out so she can continue to sit on her imaginary throne, pulling in a $350,000 a year salary plus bonuses. Daddy says it's criminal but people support them anyway. He says you have to "learn the game and play it better." My daddy can play the game better than anybody.

Then there are the cutthroats here like anywhere else, including Atlanta. Sonny told me about her mother's friend, who was the first African-American executive director of a media organization, which had a black CFO, black board chair and black deputy director – and they were Democrats! They all turned on her and helped this white commissioner scapegoat her for the organization's financial problems that were brewing way before she took the position.

Apparently, the commissioner was friends with the previous director, who the board removed, so she had an ax to grind and didn't want a black woman upstaging her white male friend, who was part of the good old' boy network. She's also married to a black man so you know that white woman felt threatened by this black woman anyway. They set her up real good, and to this day, still manage to attack her through board meetings, in conversations with people and the media even though she's been gone for over 3 years.

The deputy, now the current boss, who succeeded in taking this woman's job and destroying her reputation still talks smack about her to cover up for the fact she's stealing the money. She'd already been fired from 2 previous jobs but this black woman hired her as the deputy anyway, wanted to give her a chance. She still regrets her decision and trusts no one especially people just because they are black. This woman ended up changing her party affiliation from Democrat to Independent to make a statement.

Shonny went on to say that this one biased newspaper reporter, who's known for sensationalizing news, didn't care about reporting the truth. This black woman has to keep an attorney on retainer to keep those people off of her back. She's been contemplating bringing another lawsuit to expose them, and this time, bring the house down. She's a highly educated black woman with a strong professional background who they've managed to black-ball!

"You know the bitch who took her job and stole the money is still there?" says Shonny. "Goes to show you. It's about who you know. You can commit a crime and get away with it in this town as long as you do their bidding. That's okay though because this woman they keep going after is deeply spiritual and has been on a spiritual journey for over 28 years. Karma is a bitch so they'll get their shit back a hundred-fold. Vengeance is mind sayeth the Lord."

Daddy isn't bothered by cut-throats. He deals with them every day. "I got mine," says daddy. "And I don't need their help."

Daddy's clientele are rich and he doesn't beg for little contracts and grants. His clients beg for his services. Daddy told Larry Hughes he'd attend the fundraiser and do like he does "Keep an eye on these black folks who are keeping an eye on him."

Spoke to soon 'cause

"Shit! Jenna the babysitter is yelling at Brittany and Jayden and I can hear her all the way up here. Those damn brats are always whining with their grown asses. How can Jenna stand them?"

Saved by the bell. I hope it's Julie. Yep. I'm going out with the white girl to the party she told me about. I need a distraction. No news about my BFF yet.

"Tippy!" Jenna yells.

"I'll be right down."

I jump up, put on my heels and grab my jacket.

Julie is standing in the entranceway. She doesn't look like she does at school. She's looking cute. Man, she's tall. I think about 5'11. She's wearing black cowboy boots. It's a good thing 'cause heels would make her look like a giant. She's wearing black skinny jeans with a black-laced T-top and a red leather jacket. Her hair is permed, putting life back into her bleached blonde hair and her make-up looks nice. Her eyelids are painted with different shades of blue accentuated by false eyelashes. Mm hm. Well done but she doesn't quite make the grade to girlishcious like me and T.

"You look droolworthy, heyyyy," I say, lean back admire her fully.

"You too," she says. "Where'd you get those jeans?"

I'm wearing a pair of my fuchsia jeans. The ones I have on fit me really good and show off my badunkadunk. My high heels are suede fuchsia with a peek-a-boo toe. I also have on a laced T but mine is gold and matches my French tipped gold nails. And of course, I have on a matching fuchsia jacket. Mm hm. I know I look tight!

Before we head out, I remember I left my phone upstairs and run up to get it. While I was downstairs daddy called. I'll call him later since I know he's just checking in.

I told daddy earlier I was going out with a white girl and would probably get bored and be home in an hour. I bet they'll be listening to rock and roll, standing in corners giggling and staring at me like they do at school.

28

Common Ground

9:00p.m.
The Ellis boys

Haven't spoken since the police busted Ray the night of Tippy's birthday party. Ray knows his brother was responsible, but he's got to be cool – for now. He needs his brother's help. Once TiAnna's safe, he'll deal with his brother and Don Juan.

"This call ain't about me man," says Ray. "TiAnna's in trouble and Randall asked for my help."

"Yeah Tippy tells me she's been missing," says Robert Ellis, "She's worried. Why did Randall come to you or should I be asking? Given you use to mess with Lydia."

Ray hesitates before answering, "Lydia committed suicide earlier this evening. Where's our girl? I wonder if she's heard."

"Oh man," Robert says. "No. Tippy hasn't heard. She would've said something."

"I should check in with..."

"Don't you worry. You seem to keep forgetting she's my daughter," Robert says.

"Look man, I told you years ago, even after Loretta died, I would honor my word unless you give me reason not to."

"Are you threatening me Mr. Billy Paul? Mrs. Jones is gone." Robert says.

"Say look here," says Ray slightly raising his voice "Even though you…" he stops short of browbeating his brother and says "This ain't about me. Are you gonna help or not?"

"Where can we find her? says Robert.

"I hear she's with Don Juan."

"Aw man, that crazy nigga Ray?"

"I'm afraid so man. Word on the street is he's planning to take her out of state soon."

"Well then Mr. Raymond, we better move fast then huh?"

"Yeah man. Otherwise she'll be gone for good. Uh say, he's got her hooked-on smack; she's messed up bad. I made a call to a place out in Lawrenceville. I had Sadie take 'em up some cash."

Once Ray and Robert finish their conversation, Robert Ellis phones Tippy but gets her voicemail.

"Uh, Tippy give me a call. You know who."

Then he phones his friend Gary Lambert, Atlanta's Chief of Police. Chief Lambert says he will send in one of his best undercover cops to a new location where Don Juan's been hanging.

"If she's there we'll get her," says the Chief. "Hopefully we won't be too late. Once they take 'em out of state, we've lost."

The chief knows some officers accept hush money to stay away from the motels frequented by regular prostitutes, which is why he hasn't been informed about this particular situation. The chief enforces clean-up when pimps bring in underage youth. The pimps working Chesler are brutal and "turnout" mostly runaways but periodically bring in out-of-state teens from suburban communities. They either trick them or take them against their will.

The chief has been with the force for 15 years. He made chief 5 years ago after gaining fame for busting up one of the biggest Human trafficking networks in Atlanta. The victims ranged from 5 to 16. During the raid he remembers finding 2 young girls – ages 5 and 6 – in one of the rooms, shot through the head. The murders happened minutes before the officers arrived. Lambert found out at least 1 officer alerted the group, despite the lead detectives keeping the bust under wrap for nearly a year. Lambert had to notify the parents of the murdered victims in person. He regularly reminds himself of the intense grief he felt and vowed to never let what happened to those kids happen again.

Robert phones Judge Simms and asks him to set up a private rehab stay in an undisclosed location despite his brother's arrangements. Robert likes control and does things his way most of the time; he certainly doesn't trust his brother's judgment.

Robert Ellis says the rehab facility must be lock proof. No need for any trouble from Don Juan and his people. Although a real possibility, Robert also knows his brother. Don Juan won't be an issue much longer.

Earlier in Atlanta

Jerry does his best to console his friend. Been there for Randall since TiAnna disappeared and Lydia's death. So far, Randall has said very little, which makes Jerry suspicious but he doesn't pry. He also feels it's best Randall doesn't know Don Juan brought in a new young black girl a few weeks back. Jerry is aware of the indirect relationship the Johnson's have with Don Juan. He's Luanne Ellis's father.

Unbeknownst to the Johnson's Jerry Lang works as the lead undercover on the "ho stroll," which he hasn't been assigned to lately. He's thinking about strolling through on his own even though he doubts the johns will talk. They usually keep quiet when they're cajoling an underage hooker.

Jerry Lang's cell phone rings.

"Jerry this is Chief Lambert. We have a delicate situation for you to handle tonight!"

29

Boy Got Swag

9:30 p.m. in Portland

Julie's a better driver than Shonny. We take the I-84 freeway, get off at the Sandy Blvd exit and head east to 220th. We turn left, drive down this long road with an empty field on the right, a park on the left and houses way off in the distance. Down on the right there are half dozen vacant commercial buildings on the other side of the field.

We pull up behind a row of cars set back a distance from the faint light ahead where Julie says the party is.

"We gotta 'bout a 5-minute walk. I hope your feet hold up in those heels," she says.

"I can hang," I say. "These shoes are comfy."

We get out the car and walk down the sidewalk toward the light, then up this short gravel road, leading to a lighted red house. We walk up a short flight of cement steps, holding on to a wobbly wooden railing.

"Careful," says Julie.

Music is blasting through the front door and it ain't rock and roll. These white folks are playing Snoop Lion or should I say Snoop Dog since they're playing the song Gin an' Juice.

Looks like I'll be meeting white boy rapper wanna-bes.

We open the door and a living room greets us. I do like Julie and scan the room – all eyes are on us – the white boys are cheesing and the white girls catch an attitude quick. Their smiles go straight to "You bee-atch."

Actually, this heightens my adrenalin. The excitement of being here is different than at school where I feel alone in a sea of white folks. Being the only black person, I see so far, makes me feel like the shit! Yep. This is confirmation. It's me these white girls either hate or the white boys want, bad. They love black women but are afraid to approach us so I hear. Some white boys and even black ones have said we're stuck up – Not – we're just proud and don't mind showing it.

Like TiAnna says, "We should act like Queens of Zamunda like we are." She got the name Zamunda from the Eddie Murphy movie Coming to America. T says, "The world started with us and it's about time Disney recognized. Now bring on a story about a black queen."

Thinking about my BFF is killing my mood so I return my attention back to the white folks. I follow Julie meandering through the crowd, saying hey to folks she's introducing me to. The house isn't big. Folks are leaning against walls, sitting on the only couch in here; some on the floor near the walls.

We push our way through the crowd of people, blocking the middle of the room. Everybody has a plastic cup and I'm guessing isn't punch. So far no weed smells. Good, 'cause I'd be nervous.

The rapper Common is doing his thing; I bop my head to the beat as we make our way down a hallway, leading out to a backyard. Out here there's more white kids drinking from plastic cups. Portland rains a lot but we luck out today even though it's cold as hell.

The music volume is lower than inside. Tents are up and huge trees intimately surround the yard draped by a string of dim white lights that hang across ropes on both sides. Beneath one tent is a table with chips, dips, cheese and crackers – no food.

Several guys are huddled in the other tent and they're looking at us. One has a huge grin on his face. He looks familiar but hey, white folks all look alike. Some tall white boy with curly blonde hair comes over grabs Julie, picks her up and swings her around. He sets her down and kisses her on the lips, tongue action an all.

"Hi babe," he says finally. "About time."

Julie has a big smile on her face, giggling and blushing.

"This is Jason my boo," she says.

He's okay for a white boy, tall and skinny, same height as Julie. They make a cute couple. Jason starts pulling Julie back towards the house. She peaks back at me briefly with a smile. Then she's gone. Should I follow? I don't appreciate being left by myself. How rude!

I watch Julie disappear into the house. Shit. Maybe I should leave. I'm pretty outgoing, but I don't know how to make friends with these white folks. I start to head back in when someone grabs my arm. Out of instinct I pull my arm away, turn around and prepare to give the person who touched me a "Got your damn nerve," look.

"What up girl. Ain't it past your bedtime?" What! It's the white boy rapper AJ DaMenace.

"Hey," I say smiling and give him a hug. I wanna say thanks for rescuing me but instead say, "What you doing hanging?"

"Dis my crib," AJ says. "I'm letting my little brother host his gathering here. Good thing I'm the only house at the end of the block. Police would have a field day. But then our dad works for the Portland PD."

"Your daddy's a cop?" I say, leaning my neck back lookin' at him.

"Ha! I'm lying," he says.

"You must be the one playin' the rap music," I say.

"Girl you'd be surprised how many white kids love hip hop," AJ says. "I'm sure you've already been schooled about Portland."

For the first time I notice his diction. Hm. A white boy trying to sound ghetto.

"Wanna dance?" says AJ.

The song playing is unfamiliar but good dancing music. "I can dance to that," I say. "Who's flowing?

He pulls me over to the side near one of the tents. He's still grinning, "A rap artist named DaMenace. Pretty swank huh?"

"Ooo bangin'" I say, leaning my head back.

AJ DaMenace starts dancing. I guess that's my cue. There's not much room so we're standing pretty close; close enough so we don't have to shout. This feels funny; I've never been this close to a white boy before. He smells good and he's not bad to look at.

He keeps his blonde hair cropped close to his head and he's damn cute when he smiles. His whole face widens, creating laugh lines around his smile which shows off his pretty white straight teeth. He has diamond earrings in his kinda large ears but the rest of his fineness overshadows them.

AJ's telling me about his career like why he took on the stage name DaMenace he pulled from the old' school Dennis the Menace show.

"Like Dennis the Menace I'm innocently sneaky but don't mean no harm," says DaMenace.

"I need to watch you then," I say teasingly.

"Girl you can watch me all you want," he says.

DaMenace graduated from Grant High School last year. His parents wanted him to go to college but stayed in the music business.

"They don't like hip hop. They're ultra conservative, big time Republicans who hate Obama," he says. "We sure don't see eye-to-eye on a lot of things."

AJ tells me his parents tolerated his friendship with Jerome.

"We were thick as thieves, inseparable," he explains. "Later they began to like him. He turned on the Jerome charm. Anyway, what's not to like, right?"

I nod and lower my head for a moment.

"What about you girl?"

"Huh would you believe, I got staunch Republicans on my mama's side?"

"Naw. For real?"

"Yeah but my daddy's as liberal as they come. So I get my ideals from him since he's my only parent now."

"Oh? Your parents not together?"

"Mama died when I was 7."

"Sorry 'bout dat. You lucky to have a liberal daddy doe."

The music is slowing down to a song called Emergency by Tank. AJ pulls me close without asking and begins swaying back and forth. Jeremy is the only boy I've slow danced with and it makes me nervous. But AJ is being cool wit' me.

I'd forgotten about Julie. She shows up out of nowhere, tapping me on my shoulder. I turn my head toward her. Her face is right up close to mine. Hm. Hope her breath don't stink.

"I see you're in good hands. Sorry I left you," she says, lowering her head a little.

Hm. A little late for sorry, I'm thinking. Anyway, I guess I'm in good hands. I got my arms around AJ's neck and he's got his around my waist. Looks like Julie's been in good hands too. Her hair is messy, make-up is almost gone and she and her boo are cheesing. They must've found some place to do-the-do. Ooo nasty. Doing it in someone else's house without permission.

Julie and Jason are going to another party and asked if I wanted to go. At least they asked this time.

"I'll make sure she gets home safely," says AJ. There he goes again not asking. But I don't wanna hang with Julie and Jason. I might get left again and not be as lucky.

Julie pooches her lips out, giving me, "Ooo girl." In return I give her the "cutesy-girl" wave using my right four fingers. Then she hugs me around the neck.

"Don't do anything I wouldn't do," she says in my ear. For a minute she sounded like my BFF.

Once they're gone

AJ says, "Hungry?"

"Naw," I say.

"Wanna go for a walk den beautiful?"

"Okay," I say blushing.

AJ takes my hand and we walk back into the house. On the way to the front door, he grabs his brother and makes him walk out with us. Barry looks like the guy Shonny almost ran over at school and flipped-off. Poor guy. Who'd name their kid Barry? My white math teacher back home name's Barry. He's got a corny sense of humor and laughs at his own jokes.

"Hey no fuck ups," says AJ.

"Yeah, yeah," says Barry.

"I'm leaving my boys in charge to keep the peace. Hey and watch the drinkin'!"

"Yeah yeah," says Barry, walking away waving his brother off.

"I ain't playin'. They'll kick all y'all out if you start any shit!" says AJ. His brother has made it back to the front door. He waves again like saying "Whatever."

Me and AJ walk down to the park. It's clean and well-maintained with a few park benches, tables and playground equipment like a big slide, swings, monkey bars and a seesaw. The park also has several tall iron lamp polls with lights bright enough to see in either direction. The dozen houses way in the distance all have their lights on, adding to the park's serene ambiance.

AJ says the houses were built within the past 2 years. This once was an industrial area. There are still some vacant buildings developers plan to take down next year.

We sit close to each other on one of the park benches and AJ puts his arm around my shoulders. "Cold?" he says.

"Naw," I say. Hm. DaMenace is bold. He don't know me like that. But I better be cool. He's my ride home.

"My house use to belong to the owners of an auto repair shop," says AJ. "I worked for the owner from the time I was 13 up to last year. Me and the owner's son are cool. That's how I learned to be a mechanic. I got my mechanic's certificate last year."

"Oh yeah?" I say. "Jack of all trades I see."

"It pays the bills for now," says AJ. "I can afford the payments on my house I got on a lease option."

I'm smiling. AJ's bragging trying to impress me.

"You know I've never told anyone else this but you," he says, hesitantly.

Now I'm thinking he's gonna say something swank like girl you fine and I wanna get wit' you. Hm, not sure about a white boy though. But ooo this white boy is fine, making me get those feelings again – like with Jeremy and with Jerome – all the way down to my twot-twot. Okay, girl. Get a grip!

"I think I know who killed my homeboy, or had somethin' to do wit' it," says AJ. "Buster. Buster had Jerome killed."

30

Gotchu Matha…!

9:00 p.m.
At the Belmont

Don Juan parks his Lincoln out front. The motel is located on the eastside off the main highway, surrounded by Yellow Buckeye and Trident Maple trees. This 75-year-old, 2-story motel is as seedy as they come – with the typical hos, johns and pimps, including occasional guests having affairs or one-night stands. The Belmont is where most of the pimps bring their underage packages and pay the owner top dollar to keep things guarded. They certainly don't pay for customer service.

The building's outside brick is badly in need of repair and the property is poorly maintained with outdated plumbing, noisy pipes, old leaky faucets and the toilets rarely work. The inside walls need painting and some of the mirrors are cracked.

"Now look here Li'l Candy," says Don Juan. "You need to get the fuck up!"

Don Juan gave TiAnna the street name Li'l Candy, a code word for underage prostitutes. Li'l Candy's not moving. Don Juan reaches over the seat and shakes her.

"What's wrong wit' ya. Get the fuck up!"

Chelsea's eyes widen, wondering what's wrong.

"What'd you give her!" he says. "You messin' wit' my money!"

"She ain't had dat much," says Chelsea. "I be watchin' her."

"Well she ain't movin'! Get yo ass back there, Chili an' check her. She's got somebody waiting."

In room 202

Jerry Lang is the one who's waiting. He's pacing back and forth nervously, hoping TiAnna comes in alone. If she doesn't, he hopes she'll play along and not let on they know each other. He's there to help her. But Don Juan has messed her head up pretty bad. No telling what her level of paranoia may be. She's been here long enough to be "broken-down."

"Shit. Where the hell is she?" Lang says out loud. "Damn, I hate this shit! This place is nastier than the others. Son-of-a-bitch has her flat backin' in a rat hole where they don't even change the damn sheets."

Lang looks at his watch. It's 9:00. She's a half hour late, which makes him worry. "I hope nothin' went down."

His phone rings. On the other line is his partner, the undercover who's also assigned to this case. He reminds Jerry Lang the captain has stressed, "Secure the target and remove the barrier, if necessary."

Lang knows this means Don Juan, who the ATL PD could care less about, except those he pays. They know him as someone who's classless and ruthless and who handles his business the way old street pimps do. They are the most dangerous.

His partner called to tell him something's going down, "Take a look outside," he says.

Jerry Lang peaks through the front window right into Don Juan's car. Chili is shaking someone who looks like TiAnna. The back of her head is slumped sideways. She still doesn't move even when Chili lays her down on the back seat. Chili then gets out of the car and heads for Lang's room.

"They're on the move," Lang's partner says. "I'm on it."

Lang watches as Don Juan drives out of the parking lot. His partner who has a GPS tracker on Don Juan's car stays back momentarily then follows.

Chili knocks twice on Lang's door and walks in. I wonder what bullshit she's got for me, he's thinking.

"Hey boy," she says, teasingly. "You got me. Much better choice. You know my spicy moves."

"What the fuck do you mean a better choice? I was told to wait for somethin' special! And you ain't it! I already had you!"

Chili has had enough of her sissy getting all the attention, causing problems between her and her Donny. But she may not have to worry about her sissy anymore.

She dismisses Lang's remarks and says, "I'mo try not to take it personal. How 'bout I make it extra special? Give you a break on the money? How 'bout half my usual?"

Chili pulls at Jerry's clothes, touching her body then his. But Jerry's not having it.

"Look. J promised me the hook-up. This is bullshit!" says Lang, who's playing the role of a pissed off john. I could win an Emmy Lang's thinking. "Tell J he's lost a good customer!" Then he storms out of the room.

Chili picks up the only glass ashtray from the round table next to the window and throws it against the wall.

"Can't even break a damn ashtray! I hope you're dead sissy! You can join mummy!"

Don Juan broke the news about Lydia to Chili and Li'l Candy before they left the house. But TiAnna already knew. In hindsight, Chili wonders why TiAnna was so calm. Did TiAnna get a hold of the Oxycontin she left behind the dresser?

Don Juan doesn't know about the pills. He likes to be in control and this is one secret she wants to herself. Especially since she's been in pain more days than not. The pain has nothing to do with Don

Juan's ass beatings. It's in her abdomen and getting worse. The pain pills help some. But she's going to have to check-in at the 24-hour clinic at some point and when she has time. She's busy all night; sleeps most of the day to get ready for the following night and works 7 days a week. Donny doesn't believe in breaks.

"If she got those pills Donny can't know. He'd kill me over his Li'l Candy."

Chili takes off her coat and stretches across the bed. She thinks about her life and blames Lydia. She did have dreams once. Now look at her.

"You got off easy mummy!"

July 30, 2003
Upstate, New York

Before Chelsea met Don Juan, she had a good home. The Kramer's, an interracial couple from Syracuse, New York, adopted her 3 weeks after she was born. They couldn't have children.

Chelsea remembers being spoiled rotten up until age 5. But then a miracle happened. Her adoptive mother got pregnant and gave birth to twins – a boy and girl. Chelsea had a difficult time adjusting to her new siblings and didn't like sharing her parents.

To top it off, she found out by accident she was adopted. Her parents were having a private discussion about her and how they needed to ensure she felt loved despite the twins. Chelsea never told her parents what she overheard. But when she turned 17, they told her the truth. So, Chelsea insisted on finding her birth parents which her parents told would be impossible. Although they knew the truth, they avoid telling her.

Chelsea became troubled during her senior year in high school and eventually dropped out. Soon to be 18, she ran off, without her parents knowing and taking the money she herself earned. She contacted her parents once she was far enough away – in New York City. They begged her to come but she refused.

Chelsea often wonders if she would've returned home, what her life would've been like. Maybe she'd be married by now. Or have the fashion career she'd always wanted. She loved clothes and had a pretty good eye for fashion. At age 12, she started educating herself about the industry.

When she was 14, her parents bought her the sewing machine she'd asked for. It was top of the line. She began toying with design ideas and ultimately turned those ideas into designing her own clothes. Eventually she designed clothes for friends and friends of her parents. She made good money.

Within Chelsea's 1st week in New York, she met Don Juan, who talked her into leaving with him – to Atlanta. He said he'd help her get a fresh start.

When she got to Atlanta, her dreams turned into a nightmare. Almost immediately Don Juan "turned her out." During the early days of learning the trade she felt ashamed and too embarrassed to call her parents. Besides Don Juan wasn't letting her go. She had become his new girl, replacing an old ho, he had had for years and who also had a daughter Chelsea's age.

The more Chelsea got into the trade, the more drugs she took which helped her to forget what could've been. She eventually stopped communicating with her parents – Don Juan insisted – so she hasn't spoken to them in years.

When she does speak about her dreams it's with Judge Simms. He listens and encourages her. He tells her when she's ready he'll arrange everything, including getting her away from Don Juan. It was the judge who helped Chelsea locate her mother but left the rest up to her. Chelsea's plan took shape when she met Randall Johnson by pure luck.

Tonight's operation take-out is in full swing

And Lang's partner is following Don Juan down a familiar deserted stretch of highway on the outskirts of downtown Atlanta. There's an old abandoned scrap yard out here where the dead bodies of 5 female prostitutes were found in the past 10 years.

Out here the night sky is hard to see, darkened by rows of thick tall trees on both sides of the street and no street lights. A mile ahead his GPS signal stops. Lucky for him the car is all-electric so the engine is quiet but he figures he'd better shut off the car's headlights.

"Don't want to be spotted. I'll use the moon as my strobe light to help me see," the partner says softly.

He's already signaled for backup which is close behind him. The GPS stopped ahead and he follows it through the trees and down a gravel road. He stops immediately when he sees the rear-end of a car sticking out from behind a group of trees on the right. Don Juan's. He shuts the car down, grabs his glock, goes the rest of the way on foot.

Creeping up to the group of trees, he leans out enough to see in front of him. The car appears empty. He steps out from behind the tree crouches down, walking on bended knees around the right side of the car. He stands up slowly until his eyes reach the window. He peeks in – no one's there – then crouches back down and walks forward. Once at the front of the car he sees Don Juan in the distance, carrying a wrapped blanket over his shoulder.

"Must be the girl," the undercover says under his breath.

He calls his back up again to update him. His back up is close behind him and will proceed with caution. The undercover chases after Don Juan through the trees, heading toward the hill. But Don Juan dropped out of sight. When he reaches the bottom of the hill, he drops on all fours and crawls up slowly. Reaching the top, he looks over. Still no Don Juan.

"Where the hell did the fuck go?"

"Bam motherfucka! Surprise!"

"Aw shit!" says the undercover. "Fucker hit me."

Blood's rushing down the side of his face. He tries to turn over on his back but is kicked in his side. As he reaches down to grab his glock he dropped, he's hit again. Don Juan stands above him laughing. He kicks the undercover in the groin, then with his right foot, stomps down on his back.

"Ha! Ha! Mothafucka!" says Don Juan. "Following me huh!" Don Juan puts his own gun back in his side jacket pocket, then cocks the trigger on the 1 he grabbed from the undercover, "Yeah I gotchu now mothafucka!"

"Thank again," says a voice coming from behind Don Juan. "Turn around punk! I wanna see your face when I clock yo ass."

Don Juan looks over his shoulder while holding the gun over the undercover, "Who dat?"

"I'm here to pay a debt," he says. "Pow mothafucka!"

"Ahhhhh!" Don Juan drops to his knees. Now it's the shooter's turn to make a stand.

"You?" Don Juan says, smiling. "I have to tell you yo Candy was real good and sweet."

"How sweet is this you son-of-a bitch!" Aiming at Don Juan's head, the shooter shoots him several times. He wipes the gun and tosses it over to the undercover.

"All yours," he says. "Thanks."

Then he turns and walks up over the top of the hill. He grabs the wrapped blanket a few yards away, opens it and looks inside; it's TiAnna, who looks like she's sleeping. He blinks back his tears; picks her up in his arms, walks back up and down the hill to where it all ended. The shooter takes one last look at Don Juan.

"He can't hurt you no mo," he says.

Without further hesitation, he hurries back to his parked car and places TiAnna in the back seat.

"Gotta get outta here. I hear 5-O!"

The shooter drives back to the main highway and drives in the opposite direction from the oncoming sirens to the agreed upon location.

In route he makes a call. The line picks up to silence on the other end.

"Mission accomplished!" the shooter says.

Both lines go dead.

31

Girly Girl

10:00 p.m.
In hindsight

The Messiah hasn't been seen since Jerome's and is a no show to the funeral. And now AJ's telling me he thinks Messiah had something to do with Jerome's murder.

AJ's holding my hand his light blue cat like eyes catching mine.

"Forget I said dat." AJ says. "I shouldn't put Buster on blast."

Oh no. I'm not letting this go that easy. I tell AJ what happened at Jerome's party... Messiah acting paranoid while talking on the phone... Messiah asking Jerome to take him to the store... How Messiah goes to the bathroom right before Jerome and I went out front... How we waited outside nearly 10 minutes and Messiah never showed...

"Huh," says AJ. "I can't shake this feelin' and I've been hearing things too. The hood's been buzzing and Messiah is definitely layin' low. He wasn't even at the last Hop Fest. He never misses dat."

AJ's talkin' about the Hop Fest held twice a year – spring and summer – in Tacoma, Washington up near Seattle. The Fest is where upcoming Hip Hop artists from around the county go to battle. AE's from major and small record companies attend and sometimes sign new artists.

"I saw Darius there," says AJ.

He's through talkin' about Messiah, so I'm gonna be cool too.

"Shonny was there with her new friend. She always picks the fine ones," says AJ.

"Julie told me she had a new boo. Funny you would be noticing her man. Do I need to worry about you?"

"Ha! Girl you don't know? Shonny's 06'n. She likes bootylicious, badunkadunks."

"For real AJ?"

"True dat. When you came with her to Jerome's I thought dang. I need to find out what she got dat I don't got. Ha!"

Whoa. I got nothin' against Lesbos. I just don't want 'em thinkin' I'm into it. Me and TiAnna call 'em girl-on-girls. We have them and gay boys at Stone Mountain High. They usually keep their bitness to themselves.

Speaking of Lesbians

A girl me and T know named Tanya surprised us. We saw her necking with one girl out back by the bleachers at a football game one night. I think she saw us because she later began avoiding us. Before what happened at the game, we'd usually see her with a white football jock named Peter Bailey. He either knows Tanya's M.O. and don't care, or don't know. Whatever. Wasn't our place to say.

Tanya is one of those really pretty black girls – half Asian and half black – with slanted deep brown colored eyes. Yep, you could say she is bootylicious with a shape to die for. I thought she could give me and T a run for the money But TiAnna didn't think so. She'd turn up her mouth and roll her eyes.

"Hm. Look at Miss Thang like her shit don't stank," TiAnna would say.

I'm not sure why TiAnna didn't like her. Maybe it's because this black boy Lonnie Lars on the varsity basketball team wanted to get with Tanya. TiAnna had a crush on Lonny but denied it. I saw her flirting with him. But Lonnie was too busy looking at Tanya who paid him no attention.

TiAnna has a lot of pride and I know her feelings were hurt even though she'd never admit it, not even to me. But even so, Tanya was always nice to us. Now I know why and kinda felt bad for her. She was in the closet and acting like she was really into Peter. Then again, she could be bicurious?

I want to make it clear

"It's not my thing AJ."

I bat my eyes to let him know I may be interested. I hope he takes the bait. Ooo. He's smiling and…

Ummmm. Here he goes. We're kissing. Yeah boy. In my head I'm saying it like Flava Flav. I'm definitely Girlishcious, droolworthy and all that.

Mm mm mm, his lips are soft and succulent. He's kissing me gently, keeping rhythm like mini waves you see at the beach. You're standing there in the sand when the water rolls in quickly, grabbing you softly around the ankles and feet. Then they move away slowly. Whoa, here comes the big one! Get ready! Kaplunk. Right down on your lips, swallowing them whole. Right down to the tongue action. It's divine.

Okay, here goes his hand. He's being shy – a gentleman. He gently rubs me up and down my right arm; then moves under it, rubs down and up, then back to my arm. But then we both stop abruptly when we hear sirens. Turning our attention toward Sandy, we see 3 police cars heading this way – lights flashing.

"Oh shit!" says AJ. "5-O!"

32

Boy Got Nerve

All's quiet at AJ's

And you'd never know there was a party going on. AJs buddies are standing with 2 police officers at the end of the driveway. A 3rd officer is hanging back, trying to inconspicuously scan the area. He stops us when he sees us walk up.

"I'm Andrew Justice the homeowner," AJ says, extending his hand to the officer who ignores it.

Andrew Justice is his surname, huh?

"What seems to be the problem officer?"

"Someone called 9-1-1 after spotting a naked girl running down Sandy about a mile from here," says the officer. "She's bruised up and drugged. A possible date rape."

The officer's looking directly in AJ's eyes.

"The young girl went to the hospital by ambulance. Told one of our officers she can't identify her assailants; alleges it happened here."

"Well, if something like that happened, I would have known about it," says AJ glancing over at his friends then back to the officer.

"You weren't here right?" says the officer.

AJ repeats himself, "I would've heard if something happened."

"Would you report it?" says the officer.

"Officer I'm an upstanding citizen who pays his taxes."

"Mind if we take a look inside?" says the officer.

"Yes, officer I do mind. If you don't have a search warrant, you're not welcomed."

"I see," says the officer squinting his eyes, "Well okay then. I guess we'll just have to bring back a warrant if necessary."

"Glad I could be of service," AJ says with a smile.

Good thing he's a white boy. If he was black, they would've bashed in the door, search warrant or not, and hauled his ass in.

The officer hands AJ his card. He motions for his fellow officers; together they turn and leave.

As they walk away, I hear one of 'em say, "Bullshit! All these parked cars and they think we're dumb fuck pigs!"

Me and AJ watch until they get into their cars, drive off and until they turn off onto Sandy. Then we join his 2 buddies, who are shaking their heads and shrugging their shoulders. They say Jones, who's standing guard up near Sandy, alerted them to 5-O, giving 'em time to tidy up things.

"Did Jonesy see some girl running outta here buck naked?" says AJ. "Because if she did, she didn't pass us. We were down at the park."

"Naw man don't know what happened," says the one named Jake.

"This is some shit," says AJ. "This ain't what I need now. Let me find out from Barry what da fuck happened!"

We head to the house with no one saying a word. AJ is still holding my hand and walking fast; I'm trying to keep up. Owe. My right baby toe is killing me. All of a sudden, these damn heels are hurting like hell!

Inside it's quiet with folks sprawled out everywhere with several on the stair steps slumped over – drunk – and in the hallway entrance. Barry is hiding behind some dude and his girl, trying to avoid his brother's beatdown. His face is flushed, running with sweat and his hair is all messed up. AJ lets go of my hand, pushes the couple aside and gets right up in Barry's face.

"I don't know what the fuck happened but your ass is mine you little shit!" AJ says.

The party is definitely over. AJ orders his buddies to corral the crowd and send them out in 2s and 3s, making sure no one's drunk. While this is happening, he has me sitting in his personal recording studio I think was once a garage. The studio has all these expensive gadgets, making me wanna sit really still so I won't break anything. And I don't wanna be noisy 'cause it ain't polite.

Shoooot. This may take a while. Let me take off these heels so I can massage my foot. Whoa. Much better. OMG! Now what? I'm getting bored.

With my bare feet I turn the seat of the swivel chair 1 way all the way around, then the other way. The 2nd time around, I can't help but be noisy. All this equipment, those wall posters and CD's sprawled out on the table across from me screaming, "Look at me please!" Like the eclectic mix of wall posters of concerts and festivals: Hop Fest, Popco and Soul Jam. I wonder if AJ performed at any of those festivals besides the Hop Fest. Popco features mostly pop artists and Soul Jam mostly R and B and jazz but have some hip-hop presence.

11: 30 p.m.
Still waiting

Hum? Who's the artist on the CD? I lean in closer to take a look, "Daaaa Meeenace Night Train. Oh, okay then. I'm scare-da you."

"Uh-huh. Why don't you get up and look? You know you wanna peep dat," says AJ. He just walked in.

I'm glad I was facing the door when he did. I would've pissed my pants. I don't like to be surprised. Ha. Like I surprise my daddy. I glance up at the wall clock near the door. It took about an hour to get everyone out.

"I got home training," I say.

"Yeah dat's right. I forget you refined and all. Definitely not hoochie." AJ reaches down picks up the CD and hands it to me. "This is my latest. It's got some of everything on it. A little hip hop some pop and soul."

"Oh what? You sing to?"

"I'm DaMenace of all trades. I'm versatile, making me a hot commodity."

"Okay Mr. Versatile, I can't wait to hear it."

AJ pulls a stool over and sits next to me.

"Sorry we got cut short," he says. "My brother left me a big mess to clean up. Can't afford no bad shit right now. I'm gettin' ready to release another album. And just the other day, my agent informs me that Boss Amanishakhete wants me to open up for her at a gig she's doing in LA. Anuff her producer will be there too. Being I'm a free agent, I wouldn't mind signin' wit' somebody like him. Gotta keep my shit clean doe."

"I don't know what's going on but whatever it is, won't it match your DaMenace profile?"

"Naw. Not dis shit," He says, then quickly changes his thought to get his flirt on, "You sho gotta pretty smile beautiful lady."

"Thanks," I say. I know he sees me blushing. "Boss Amanishakhete is tops in her game. She's a Word-Soul lyricist, a genre she created, right? I know my daddy likes her."

"Ha. Dat's cool too," says AJ. "But she appeals to a lot of young kids. Her new fresh taste and sound is different from all the same ol' commercial stuff, except for my stuff. I'm the shit."

"Okay, you the shit DaMenace."

"Yep. When it comes to Word-Soul doe, only Boss can give it justice. Others have tried but it ain't the same as how she says it's supposed to be "A cross between spoken word, hip hop and rap, with emphasis on the Word, underscored by jammin music."

"I heard her new single Murder 2012. It's pretty bangin'. It rose to the top of the charts in the first week. It's rumored she may take a Grammy in 2013," I say.

"Yep. Anuff is one of the top music producers," says AJ. "He does it all like hip hop, R and B, traditional soul and even released a Black Country and western singer earlier this year. Much better than Charlie Pride. Dis Black CW singer, Lamar Chapman, who's in his early 30s, has a single doing pretty good. It's in the top 10 on the CW charts. The CW genre is still pretty redneck doe. But da hicks are starting to take to 'im. Anuff is an artist too. Got some albums out. Uh you ready to go?'"

"Yeah. I better get goin'. Got some things to do in the morning," I say, lying.

When we walk back into the house, I notice AJ's s buddies have already started the clean-up. Man, they gotta lot to do. I'd offer to help but I gotta 12:00 curfew.

"You need to be helpin' bro," he says to Barry, who's sitting on the couch. He's lookin' pretty down. Bet AJ gave him a beatdown.

I notice it's after curfew

When we get in AJ's car and he tells me what happened. The girl the police picked up reported she was date raped.

"But no one knows where it happened. No one saw her here after a while. We're guessing it could've happened outside the house. There's a lot of vacant buildings around. If she was fool enough to go into one of those, not my problem," says AJ. "But these assholes may still try to hold me liable."

Now I'm no legal expert but date rape is serious stuff. If it's true, the DA will try to take everybody down. Most DA's are assholes. They just want to score points by putting someone away. Even if it means drumming up bullshit charges. Like the one who helped put my Unc Rae-Rae away for a year. The Atlanta DA is a known asshole who'll put anyone away, especially if they're black. Prejudice shit!

The drive home goes by faster than when me and Julie first drove here. It always happens when you want time to slow down.

"We're almost to my house," I say.

I wish he'd stop talkin' music. Maybe ask me out. I wouldn't mind. "This is me right here."

"Dang baby girl," says AJ. "Dis you? I guess people really live like dis, especially, y'all Atlantans. Ain't y'all all rich out d'air – Atlanta Housewives an all."

"Naw everybody ain't rich in Atlanta. There's a whole lotta brokees so I hear."

"Well broke ain't your middle name girl."

The gate opens and AJ pulls up to my doorway. He puts the car in park with it still running. I'm guessing he's planning to leave pretty quickly. He's got bitness to tend to back at his house.

"Well," I say with my hand on the door.

AJ rubs my left check with the back of his right hand. "You know I wanna see you again," he says.

Well it's about damn time! I'm thinking. "What do you have in mind?" I say.

"Darius invited me to an industry party on Saturday night. Wanna come?"

"Sure. Sounds nice," I say.

"Give me your digits," he says. We exchange numbers.

"Now this don't mean we can't talk before then. I'll call you tomorrow beautiful. You can call me too you know."

We kiss one last time, tongue action an all.

33

Ain't Misbehavin'

October 20, 2012
12:15 a.m.

The light is on in the family room. I hope daddy's not here. I peek in and oh shit! There he is. I hope he didn't hear me come in. I ain't that late but he'll give me shit anyway.

"Tippy is that you?" he says.

Damn door. Messing up my tippy action. Daddy ain't that good.

"LaTonya, you know I know it's you. Get in here tout de suite."

Hm. There he goes with that French shit I ain't heard in a while. I walk in with my coat still on, so he won't harass me about my blouse he'd call too grown. Daddy thanks I should be dressing like a nun in high necklines and turtlenecks. Haaaaaa. Here goes the tongue lashing.

"Sit over here where I can see you," daddy says, pointing to the twin recliner next to his. Ooo, where damn Luanne usually sits. I hope I don't catch fleas or lice or something.

I quickly scan the seat, making sure nothin' can attach to my clothes. Thank the Big G for leather. I look at daddy. Why he gotta look all concerned and stuff? Shoot. I didn't do anything besides be a few minutes late. Then again, I hope it's not news about my BFF. Or

Unc Rae-Rae? Those Atlanta jails can be crazy. But my uncle can handle himself.

"I got some news. We found TiAnna."

"Huh? What do you mean daddy?"

"Well first baby girl – uhhhhhhh – Lydia committed suicide. She overdosed on sleeping pills. They found her this afternoon."

"No daddy! That doesn't make any sense. Where's T?"

Daddy starts babbling ... why Lydia killed herself ... her adopted daughter showing up ... who she is and her relationship to Randall ... to Don Juan ... and then ... TiAnna... Dammit! I knew it was coming. OMG here we go again! Couldn't give me a break just for one moment! I break into tears when he tells me what happened. I'm relieved when Daddy says TiAnna's at a rehab facility north of Atlanta.

"Someone murdered Don Juan earlier tonight," says daddy. "I can imagine it's payback for what he did to your friend. The undercover at the scene says Don Juan snuck up behind him and knocked him out cold. Someone shot Don Juan while he was out. I'm guessing the unsub is close to home. No need to repeat what I said. I'm sure I can trust you to be discreet."

"My BFF is okay?"

"Yes. She's being treated as we speak."

"I'd like to go see her please."

"You can't. Not for a while. They'll let us know when she's able."

"Can I call her?"

"No baby girl. They'll let us know when. You gotta remember she's been through some deep shit. It's gonna take a while for her to get healthy."

"I need to be there then."

"Be there in spirit. Meanwhile write her a letter and I'll have it delivered along with some flowers."

"Really daddy? Thank you."

I pause then say, "Someone killing Don Juan makes me happier than shit! Good riddens!"

"Yeah. Ain't no love loss here. But he was Luanne's daddy."

I laugh and say "Really? Does she really give a shit after what he did to her and her mama?"

"A parent is a parent," he says. "She's a little shaken but she spoke with her mother who's handling it okay. Her mother wants her to go to Atlanta for the funeral. Luanne's taking care of the arrangements."

"Huh. Who's going to the funeral daddy? Paleeze! Wife or not I hope you don't plan on going?"

"Hell no! As for anyone else, I don't know and don't care baby girl. But we just won't have anything to say about the situation. Understand?"

"You know daddy, Luanne wouldn't show me the same respect. But okay. As long as she doesn't bring his name up around me. If she does it's over! This is my BFF we're talking about."

"No need to get upset. Luanne knows pimp daddy and her mama are off limits in our conversations," says daddy. "By the way Chelsea's disappeared. Police are looking for her. So she's a hot target."

Daddy assures me TiAnna is safe from here on out – from Chelsea and any of Don Juan's people.

"Mr. Donald Sutherland ain't no mob gangster with his backwards ass. I got more game than him," says daddy.

"Huh. Your uncle whooped his ass in high school. He and Donald about the same age. Donald got to talkin' crazy back then about being an OG, talkin' pimp shit to some girl your uncle was sweet on. Ray walked up to him in gym class, hauled off and clobbered his ass; knocked his ass down, daring him to get up. Other boys in the class said it was a damn shame. Donald looked like he wanted to cry. From then on Mr. Donald Sutherland was known as a sissy. His getting his ass whooped is probably why he went into pimpin' to control women since he can't defend himself against a man. Sheeeit! Anytime a man gotta make a woman do his bidding, he's nothing but a damn punk!"

Boy am I surprised at how daddy's talkin', but I'm glad he feels the way he does about pimp-daddy and his profession. I'm like daddy,

Donald Sutherland ain't nothing but a punk and I'm glad Unc Rae-Rae whooped his ass! What I can't believe is Luanne and her mama, giving his black ass a decent burial. Goes to show you how heartless the bitch is. Like her mama no doubt. My BFF may never be the same and they're celebrating the life of a man who may have ruined her life.

2:30 a.m.

When I finally get to sleep, I have another nightmare. But it's much clearer than before. When she comes at me with a knife, I hold out my hand and yell "stop!" She stops and drops the knife. I demand she tell me her name but she won't. It's 'cause she has no mouth; she's patting the place where it should be with her left forefinger trying to say "shush." Her eyes are brown and her face is – fading again.

I awaken the next morning feeling in control. The woman in my dream is someone I know. I can't wait to tell Dr. Ryan this next time I see her. Wow, for the first time, I'm can't wait to go to sleep.

I slept in

But once I'm up, I get dressed and head downstairs, taking in the wonderful smells of breakfast. Daddy's in the kitchen eating. He cooked this morning.

"Good morning daddy."

I kiss him on the cheek. Something I haven't done in a long time. He knows it, so he's grinning.

"Good morning, Tip. Want some breakfast? You know you should eat. You won't have no ass pretty soon."

"Ooo daddy! I ain't skinny and you know it."

"Ha ha ha! Keep it up and you'll be looking like Luanne."

"Not funny daddy."

Because of what he said I grab 2 big scoops of hashbrowns, 5 strips of bacon, half a hot link, 2 scoops of cheesy scrambled eggs – the way I like 'em – and make myself 3 pieces of toast. I know I can't eat all this, but I'm gonna try. Then I go to the fridge and pour myself a big glass of chocolate milk.

"Okay Miss Ella," he says teasingly. "Now we're talkin'."

"You ain't funny daddy. Anyway, I need to start working out again. Doing some weights or something."

"Yeah, Tip. Don't want no flub you'll end up with a scrub."

"Ha! Daddy that's corny. Give it up please."

I take a bite of my food, chew it up, swallowing it down with chocolate milk.

Then I say, "Speaking of rapping daddy, I've been asked to go to an industry party next Saturday night."

"Oh r-e-e-e-a-a-a-ly now. Who's asking?"

"Uhhhh. This white boy I met."

"A white who? Who are you and what have you done with LaTonya Ellis?"

"It ain't like that daddy. He's a rapper named DaMenace. He's gonna open for one of your favorite artists, Boss Amanishakhete."

"Say what? Is she coming here?"

"No daddy. Los Angeles next month."

"I may have to fly down. I hear she gives good concerts."

"Maybe we can go together daddy?"

"You don't saaaay. Uhhh, tell you what. I'd like to meet this white boy. Look him in his eyes and let him know I will kill his white ass if he does something outta line. You make sure he comes early enough so I can meet him."

"Gee daddy."

"That's the deal if you wanna go for real."

"Okay. Okay. No more rapping please."

"Maybe I should send the driver down for you just in case."

"You know if I had my own…"

"We have cars you can drive," daddy says, knowing what I'm getting ready to ask.

"But they ain't cute like me."

"Okay cute like me. How are you feeling this morning anyway?"

"Um ok." I'm tempted to tell him about my nightmare but don't.

"Well if you wanna talk about it. I'm all ears. I want you to check in with Dr. Ryan today. I made you an appointment."

"Yeah. I'd plan to call her."

"Oh? Any special reason?"

"No daddy."

"Okay then Tip. I won't pressure you. But I'm here for you."

Daddy mentions the brats Brittany and Jayden are upstairs with Luanne, who's packing and flying out this afternoon. The twins will stay behind for school. Daddy says Luanne asked him to go with her.

"I told her she must be high! How the hell could she even open her mouth to ask such a stupid ass question?"

I'm glad daddy told the bitch! And he stuck up for my BFF in his own way.

I grab a section of daddy's Portland newspaper. No news is good news. Thank the Big G there's nothing about the date rape. There's so much crap about the presidential election there's no room for other news. I'm glad daddy doesn't go off on a tangent about Romney but he does mumble saying, "Damn fool! 47 percent my ass."

The comment Romney made about the "47 percent of Americans think they should be entitled to healthcare, food and housing... think they are victims... mm, mm, mm. I don't know what it feels like to be poor, but I know mama would've turned over in her grave if she heard it. As for me, I'm looking forward to voting in 2016 when Hillary Clinton runs for president. Or maybe it'll be the Biden/Clinton ticket?

"Look here," daddy says grinning, handing me the news section.

There's a picture of daddy, icky Luanne and the Portland mayor at last night's event. Daddy says the mayor is quite the character. He's openly gay and made headline news after kissing a 17-year-old boy in the City Hall bathroom.

Daddy blushes when I tell him how good he looks in his brownish gold suit from his Steve Harvey collection.

Luanne has on a light golden dress, trying to match daddy. But I don't care how you slice it, she just ain't cute. The makeup she's wearing is too dark for her light skin tone and she needs to see a stylist about her hair.

Speaking of hair, I gotta call Shonny. We haven't spoken since she left Lincoln. But if I'm gonna be AJ's arm-candy, I gotta look extra good. I remember Shonny mentioning a stylist by the name of Miss T. Shonny says she's the best here in Portland.

Before I head upstairs, I think I'll try the "buy me a car" plea one more time in case daddy changed his mind in the last 5 minutes.

"Uh daddy. You know why you should buy me my own car?"

"Huh. I guess you're gonna tell me."

"Uhhh, well. You never did buy me a birthday present because you stopped speaking to me. A-n-n-n-d, you didn't like me for a long time. Do you like me now daddy? I mean do you really love me like you say you do. I am your first born you know. Annnd, I've been nice to you daddy, for a whole month now. Annnd, I've stayed out of Luanne's way. "

Daddy's just staring at me. Wonder what he's thinkin'?

"I guess it won't hurt to look. Hopefully it'll keep your mouth closed on the subject for a while."

Ooowee. I'm flabbergasted and afraid to say anything, in case it's the wrong thing. Don't want him to change his mind but gotta ask a follow up question. I'll take my chances.

"Uh when? Today? Tomorrow after church?"

He leans towards me with a smile and whispers, "I gotta work today and take Luanne to the airport later. How about we go early on Sunday? No need to waste time going to church. Luanne will be gone so we won't have to pretend," He winks. "Meanwhile, you've got an appointment with Dr. Ryan this afternoon you need to keep."

Ooh snap. I give my daddy a big hug and run upstairs. What's up with daddy playing nice all of a sudden? Maybe he has multiple personalities – the mean devil and the nice devil.

Whatever the case may be, I like not having to say – kiss my ass!

34

Give Me Strength

Before meeting with Dr. Ryan

AJ and I play phone tag, so we don't have a chance to talk. I also had to leave Shonny a voicemail.

Dr. Ryan's office is a lot different from Dr. Anderson's. The sandstone colored walls, light brown carpet, tall corner plants and table top ones, give off an outdoor oasis type affect.

Like Dr. Anderson though she also has a brown leather couch and recliner, which makes me think it must be the in-furniture for psychiatrists' offices. But I've only been in 2. Dr. Ryan likes Native American art and spends time in places like Sedona. She has 2 large purple crystals – one on the coffee table and the other on her desk.

Today I notice she has a new painting on the wall behind the couch. It's quite odd because it's more abstract than the others. The background color is plain white with several multicolored circles, crossing from the bottom left corner all the way up until it reaches the top right corner. The circles start large and get smaller. A dark-red swoosh stays the same size, seeming to squeeze through the middle of the circles. The swoosh looks stranded at the tip of the last small circle. Attempting to push its way through although it seems impossible.

Dr. Ryan is sitting in the chair next to me with her legs crossed. I see she's been tanning and her brunette hair is freshly colored. One thing about this 45-year-old white woman, she keeps herself in shape and spruced up.

She's quietly watching my expression as I study the painting. Huh. I'm guessing the painting was put there to get inside our heads. Rather than waste my time on a playing a mind-game, I start off by telling Dr. Ryan how I've been feeling since yesterday morning.

It had to do with my brief encounter with Luanne upstairs after breakfast. Right after my BFF was found, who was kidnapped, raped, drugged and god knows what else by Luanne's pimp-daddy, she made plans to go to Atlanta to help her mother with Don Juan's funeral arrangements.

I explain to Dr. Ryan, "I walk down to daddy's room on purpose to see what the wench and her brats were up to. Deep down I am hoping she starts somethin' so I have an excuse to whoop her ass! The door is open. She has a bunch of clothes on top of her bed and the 2 brats are on the bed too – Jayden is lying across the top of the big pillows with his back against the head board. In the middle, Brittany, hugging her legs against her chest."

Every now and then, Brittany picks up clothes and says, "Take this mommy. How about this purple blouse and these black pants? They'd be pretty on you."

And Luanne says, "Okay baby. Mommy will think 'bout it."

"I've been standing outside the doorway for about 10 minutes watching, when they finally notice me. I look right at 'em Dr. Ryan, with my eyes daring any of 'em to speak. But Luanne said nothin' and neither did her brats. Luanne also looks nervous; she should be. I am ready to pounce on her like a black panther, shred her to bits and her kids!"

Then she did the next best thing. She says, "Yaw mine yaw bizness. Stop staring. The 3 of them quickly looked away, hoping I'd disappear."

"I see how a warm interaction between mother and child would upset you," says Dr. Ryan.

A knot is forming in my stomach.

"LaTonya, I'd like you to lean back in your chair, close your eyes and focus your attention on your contempt for Luanne."

Dr. Ryan's helping me reflect on each of my encounters with Luanne dating back to before and after mama died. I notice I'm getting angrier and angrier as I relive each 1 and cry at times but not because I'm sad. But because I'm frustrated and feel powerless! Enough! I open my eyes, refusing to allow anymore old memories to come through about Luanne.

"What are you feeling LaTonya?"

"I don't want to feel powerless anymore. I felt powerless when Unc Rae-Rae got arrested on my birthday and when he later went to prison; when Jeremy moves to Florida and doesn't call me or tell me why he doesn't want anything to do with me; when Jerome gets gunned down in front of me; when TiAnna gets kidnapped and abused."

I take in a deep breath.

"Here's some tissue. Keep breathing."

"I especially feel powerless when mama gets killed because I should've tried harder to scream and fight back. I should've stood up for Unc Rae-Rae despite what he says. I should've followed my gut and told Jerome how I was feeling, maybe he'd still be alive today. Maybe if I would've been a better girlfriend to Jeremy we'd still be together."

"Breathe LaTonya."

"No! I don't need to! My BFF always talked about her mama and how she made her feel. Like how she felt suffocated and mistrusted. She didn't know why her mama acted like that but she wanted to know. All I could think too say was she's an ass like daddy. I should have listened to her and tried to help her. None of this would have happened if I would've had more courage to stand up and fight back."

Now I need to breathe and do so without Dr. Ryan coaching me.

"But lately, I've been standing up to Luanne more, challenging her, daring her."

"LaTonya, how does this make you feel?"

"I feel empowered and I'm not afraid of her anymore. Daddy can't take my power anymore either."

"Your father. This is the first you've mentioned him in a while. Why do you suppose that is?"

"Hm? I dunno. I guess I'm tired of being mad at him all the time. It makes me sick to my stomach actually. I like it when we get along, even though deep down I think he's up to somethin'."

"Why LaTonya?"

"Cuuuuzz, I know he's hiding somethin'. He looks guilty, like he wants to apologize and not about the normal stuff we've been going through. It's somethin' else and it's not good."

"Does this possibility about your father upset you?"

"Um. It makes me nervous. We already have a rocky relationship. But for some reason I think it's gonna make our relationship much, much worse."

"Do you care if things get worse between you and your father? More than it is?"

"Yes. I do actually. I want me and daddy to be close like we were when I was a child and when mama was alive. This is really important to me because I love my daddy no matter what he's done in the past."

"LaTonya listen, I want you to keep this in mind as we get closer to solving the puzzle. About what you just said about your father."

"Okay."

Dr. Ryan writes notes on her pad.

"Tell me about your last nightmare."

Boy. She sure changes subjects quickly. We go from Luanne to daddy without me sharing more about how I really feel about snow-bunny. I want to talk about her damn daddy who took my friend and did god awful things to her!

"Uh well it was different. I finally faced the killer and demanded her to tell me her name."

"Do you think the figure in your dream is female?"

"I dunno. She turned and ran before I could make out her face."

"LaTonya. You keep referring to the killer as she. Is the killer female?"

Uh, whoa! What did Dr. Ryan just say? What did I say? Ooo. I can't speak. I'm feeling sick! I think I'm gonna throw up.

"LaTonya. Are you all right?"

I'm down for the count
Until Dr. Ryan wakes me

"LaTonya can you hear me?"

I'm lying down on the couch with a cold cloth across my forehead.

"Nod LaTonya if you are okay."

I nod.

"Okay good. We're done for today. But I want you to lay here for a while until you feel better."

I hang for a while and dose off. When I wake up my head feels much better; the dizziness is gone.

"LaTonya do you feel okay? Do we need to call someone?"

"No. I have a ride waiting outside."

"Okay then. Before you leave, I want to remind you to pay extra attention to your feelings while you're awake."

Dr. Ryan breathes deeply through her nose then lets it out. Maybe she's showing me how to breathe again. I get it! I get it!

"LaTonya, you've identified the gender of the killer as female. You will soon know who it is even though you already know. When it's clear who it is please call me right away. Do nothing else but call me right away. Do you understand?"

I nod.

"I'm sensing danger and you know why. Do not share what happened today with anyone, not even your father, for now. We will handle what to do next together."

35

Ain't Over Until?

Quiet on the home front

Daddy and the twins take Luanne to a private airport in Hillsboro. They won't be back until around 6:00. Daddy says he plans to take Brittany and Jayden to the fun center – play some games, have burgers and ice cream to cheer 'em up. They've been pouting about their mama leaving without them.

Instead of going upstairs I go out to the back patio and stretch out on the hammock. We're lucky this part of our patio is enclosed in glass and is geothermal heated. The view is quite spectacular. Looking out into the backyard, which is also exquisite, we can see over the tops of the trees, giving us a panoramic view of Mt. Hood on one side and Mt. Rainier on the other. There's snow on both mountains. Hm. I wonder what skiing would be like.

Because it's late fall, the trees, Lady Ferns and Vine Maples are already turning colors. When we first got here, I smelled the air filled with wonderful perfumed smells. The backyard is fully bloomed with multicolored roses, a forest of daffodils, perennials, pansies, fuchsias, daisies, lilacs and beautiful white ocean sprays.

Daddy says Lionel Grayson, the landscape architect who designed and maintains the yard, won an award for this design. Daddy is so impressed he plans to use him on future commercial projects.

My mind is buzzing from meeting with Dr. Ryan. I blacked out, which I do sometimes when I get stressed and overwhelmed with thoughts about mama. Sometimes I blank out after a real intense argument with daddy.

When it first happened, I met with a neurologist, who sent me for an MRI. There's nothing wrong with my brain. It has more to do with my physical reaction to stress and mental anguish. It's my way of coping when things get too tough. But it can be dangerous, so I have to be extra careful.

Dr. Ryan reminded me again today. I have to work on my deep breathing techniques and meditation.

Hmm. My phone is ringing. I hope it's AJ.

"Hey baby girl," I hear a familiar voice say.

"Unc Rae-Rae!" Ooo now I'm sniveling like a fool. I haven't talked to my uncle in a grip.

"TiAnna's managing," he says. "I'm taking care of things. Mona's been a lot of help."

In Atlanta

Lang's partner, the undercover cop at the scene when Don Juan got shot, has the next few days off. He's healing from a slight concussion. Laying on his couch with a pillow propping up his head, he looks around at the small cramped space he's called home for several years.

"This place could use a once over. Those stacks of papers against the wall have been there going on 2 years. Shit! A fire hazard!" he says out loud.

The dishes have stacked up in the sink and the counters haven't been cleaned in a while. The bathroom is another story. The undercover's job continues to take a toll on his personal life, physical and emotional health. When he thinks he's had enough, he gets sucked back in by the adrenalin rush and what he perceives as a job perk, fraternizing with the "ladies of the night."

Like last night's assignment. He's wanted asshole Don Juan for the longest and was glad to oblige his demise. Being a part of the effort connected him to fond memories from the past he'd had with a young dark-skinned black woman named Mona. She gave the best lap dances while stripping over at the Serengeti.

The undercover is Mona's best customer. He tips her well. At one point, Mona figures out his MO but told know one. Instead she helped him bust some of the crazy pimps who took advantage of the girls. They were unable to get one pimp – Don Juan – who had Mona's best friend killed for refusing his offer. He got her drunk one night, led her outside, shoved her into the street in front of an oncoming car. Although they knew Don Juan ordered the hit, no one could prove it.

The undercover is surprised to hear from Mona, who left the life over a year ago. Mona needs a favor, so he agreed to meet her in a private location. The undercover said he had been contacted and he's in but would change the script for her.

6:45p.m. on the phone with Unc Rae-Rae

Who says, "I got some more good news. I'm getting sprung tomorrow. The DA overturned my conviction; don't know why – ain't asking."

"For real! Damn good news!" I say.

"Glad you're happy but watch your mouth," says Unc Rae-Rae.

There he goes acting like a daddy again.

"When can I see you? I wanna see TiAnna too."

"We'll see each other soon Tip. I promise. As for TiAnna, the rehab isn't allowing her visitors right now."

"I know, I know, daddy told me already."

"Yeah? Well not to worry. I'm in close contact and they give me regular updates."

Hm. I wonder how he's getting information. He's not her family. But my uncle has found a way so I don't ask.

"TiAnna knows you love her and you're with her in spirit, so no more worrying. You got to take care of yourself or you won't be able to support her when the time comes. Un-da-stand?"

"Yeah. I understand."

"Okay den. And say, don't feel you have to share my news with your daddy. I'm sure he'll find out soon enough. I'll get a chance to thank him in person for helping me locate TiAnna."

"Oh really? Daddy helped?"

"Yeah. He had his police contacts find her. If he hadn't, baby girl would've been gone."

"Oh. He didn't tell me. I'll give him a hug but won't tell him why."

"Okay den. Don't forget your daddy loves you."

She's leaving on a jet plane
From a private airport in Atlanta

Don Juan is dead and Chelsea doesn't know how she feels relieved or sad. Regardless, she can't go back to their place. Judge Simms told her the police want to question her.

"They'll take you down on this one Chili. So it's time."

Chili says farewell

To the man whose been there for her all these years. Thanks to him her dream is finally coming true. He's arranged for her new life as Stephanie Matthews: A $100,000 in cash, a private trust with another $300,000 and paid her tuition to attend one of the top fashion schools in the world, the Marcia Bodega Fashion Institute in Miami Beach.

He kisses the Chili good-bye he's known for years. She's his heart but nothing can become of it. She's dead to him now as he is to her.

Stephanie boards the plane content on leaving the memories of her life as Chili and Chelsea behind, which includes her sissy.

"If you survive you won't be the same sissy. You're weak like mummy! So all dat's left is one last score to settle in Donny's memory. But all in due time."

36

Woohoo!

October 20, 2012
In Portland

A couple of times I have to remind daddy this is about me and these BMWs and Mercedes ain't me. He thinks he's slick trying to shop for himself. At least the brats are behaving like they do normally when they're alone with daddy.

"Look daddy, I prefer something cute."

"Okay cute, whatever that means."

We drive out Highway 26 towards Beaverton and Hillsboro, take the Canyon Road exit and drive down car lot row, stopping in at several car lots. At one Chevy dealer, the salesman tries to push us to buy an electric car. Damn! Daddy just had to take one out for a test drive. Ooo. If I don't get me my own wheels, it's gonna be on again.

"You know Oregon is known for electric cars," says the salesman.

So what! I wanna scream.

"President Obama chose Oregon as one of 7 pilot states to put these cars on a fast track. The federal government gave the state over $150 mil in grants to build supporting infrastructure," he says.

"Yeah," says Daddy. "That's a great man. Oregonians should love him then and stop all this succession shit!"

Aw here we go! See what you did Mr. Salesman!

"Yeah a bunch of bull," says the salesman.

Yeah right. He probably started the petition. He just wants to sell daddy this electric crap!

"Oregon is a blue state anyway. The First Lady's brother is the head basketball coach at Corvallis University," the salesman says.

We know. We know. Not new news dude. Every time Michelle comes to Portland, we have to hear about it 'because the white folks complain about all the secret service. Like she can't have fun. Laura Bush, Clinton and all the other white first ladies had more fun time then she does. But she's black you know. Some white folks think she should be at the white house cooking.

"I do like this car. Tell you what. I'll come back in a couple of weeks and talk about getting one. I believe in being environmentally conscious."

Yeah right daddy. You smoke cigars.

Good we're finally leaving. I bet when we're gone, the salesman will have a lot to say about us black folks for not buying a car. I can imagine him saying, yeah. They couldn't afford it anyway. Probably on welfare, right Joe? You know they're those takers.

Not! We're rich you assholes!

We stop in at a Mazda dealer about a mile down the road, with signs promoting incentives for 2013 cars. We drive a couple of the ones I think are cute before I settle on a Convertible MX-5 Miata automatic.

My Convertible Miata is Dolphin Gray with rust colored, heated leather seats. It's the keyless kind with a push button start and you carry the key around in your purse or wallet. It's really cute and loaded down with all the extras like an alarm, satellite radio, blue tooth phone system and GPS. The total came to around $38,000 and daddy pays the whole thing with a credit card.

Daddy's card has no limit but mine does. Otherwise I could've bought my own car, which is why he probably caps mine at $5,000 a month and that's with an increase, which hasn't changed since I was 16. Before then he had me on only $3,000 a month. I didn't get my own credit card until I turned 13. Huh. As if we can't afford it.

It's easy for me to max out my VISA. I like to shop for clothes, do my hair and nails and go to the spa. And I can be generous when it comes to my closest friends like my BFF and Tommy Crumbs. I use to spend money on Jeremy too – clothes, tennis shoes and stuff.

When I first got here, I ordered some furniture from New York. Daddy wouldn't buy it. Says if I wanted crazy looking furniture, I'd have to buy it myself. He thinks anything fuchsia-colored is crazy. I opted to do a 90-day same as cash since the 5 pieces I bought – bedroom set and 2 comfy chairs – cost me $12,000. Shoot! Tearing into my spending money big time. Thank goodness I only have one more payment.

I also get a small check from working at RJ Designs. But it's laughable. Daddy has the nerve to pay me $10 an hour. Saying I should be grateful I get above minimum wage. He says he won't show favoritism and I have to earn my way like everybody else. If I wasn't interested in the business, I would've told him to take the job and shove it long ago!

I'm in my car gearing up to take a spin around P Town. The salesman shows daddy and me more about how the GPS works and gives daddy a code which he can input into his GPS. This way he can track my vehicle at all times. I don't complain. But then I also have to hear the 4-1-1.

"Yeah daddy. I'm going over to the Lloyd Center but not too worry. I promise to be safe."

"Don't forget you got school tomorrow, Tip."

"Yeah. I won't be out late. This ain't Atlanta you know."

I feel a sprinkle so I'm gonna keep my convertible top up. I hope at some point I can drop the top in this rainy city. I wave to daddy and Luanne's 2 brats from my rearview mirror.

My GPS takes me back down Canyon to get back to Highway 26. Boy this is a mistake! The traffic is hell! I swear it took me about an hour to get near downtown!

When get near the Market street sign, the GPS has me exit right, heading down I-5 south over the Marcum Bridge. This is one of my least favorite bridges. It has a weird angle, which makes me a little nervous. In some spots the railings are low and I feel like I could easily go over the side. I'd hate to be up here when it snows or gets icy. I hear it gets pretty bad.

Once over the bridge I take the Lloyd Center exit, drive up Weidler but when I get to MLK, I make a left. The GPS is trying to redirect me but I keep going. By memory I'm finding my way through northeast Portland up to Alberta Street, and then I think I go right on 15th. Yeah this is it. This should be Prescott coming up.

I stop at the red light but when the light changes to green, I can't move – my foot is frozen to the brake. I sit there until the light turns red, then green, then red again. The next time the light turns green, the driver in the car, which just came up behind me honks. I ease off the brake ready to turn left but hesitate. Phew! I'm glad I did. A car coming from my right runs the red light. Damn!

Okay. Here I go left and coast down Prescott on autopilot. If anybody comes up behind me this time, screw 'em. Ooo. My nerves are making me perspire. I haven't been here since it happened.

Look at all these flowers and balloons in front of Jerome's house. Déjà vu like I'm outside mama's gravesite. I'm stopped in the middle of the street with my foot on the break. Maybe this is a good time for some quick deep breathing. I close my eyes and…

Tap! Tap!

Who's knocking on my…

"Hey shawty. Whassup?"

37

Becoming Shawty Yo

It's good seeing

A familiar face – I roll down my window.

"Hey Darius."

"This is a nice surprise Miss LaTonya. You just passin' through?"

Ooo no he didn't just sound like Jerome.

"Sorta. I wasn't planning to come by."

"Sporting yo new drop. All sporty and shit."

Darius steps back to look at her from front to the back.

"Sweet. It fits you yo. Hopefully you can drop the top soon. Show yo pretty self. Love to take a ride wit'cha."

I think he's flirting, but I ignore his lines and say, "Yeah I like it. Thanks."

"You in a hurry shawty?"

Now I'm shawty again. But he sounds cool saying that too.

"Why?" I say.

"I'd like to invite you in. I could use the company. I get it if you don't want to."

"Uh-hum? Okay. For a minute."

Darius jogs over to the sidewalk and points to the curb for me to park. He helps me out of the car and my eyes go immediately to the spot where Jerome was...

"You okay shawty?" says Darius, holding me around the waist. "You don't have to do this ya know."

"Naw. I'm okay."

Darius keeps his arm around me leading me past "the spot" – filled over with flowers – and up the front steps.

We make it into the family room. I'm glad to be sitting down. The TV channel is on BET airing one of those stage plays they usually show on Sundays.

"You don't strike me as a theatre buff Darius."

"Oh really? What do I strike you as den Miss LaTonya?"

"Oh? I dunno. Some of those plays are corny though."

"You right about dat yo. Especially when they get ta sangin' dat gospel. I turn it off den."

"And here I thought Mr. Darius may have joined the church an all."

"Ha! Now I know you bullshitin' LaTonya."

I laugh too. I'm thinking about how he looked at Jerome's funeral.

"Yeah Darius I'm playin' wit' you."

"You go to church yo?"

"Yeah. Only 'cause I have too. I'm not saved an all. Me and the Big G don't get along these days."

"Yeah? Me and him got problems too yo. I just don't get why black folks go to church anyway. Christianity is a white man's religion forced on us during slavery."

"I don't know. I can't speak on it. But I can say the Big G doesn't answer me. And I can't stand pretentious ass black people who claim they're Christians. They smile in your face, say praise the lord, then talk about you."

"True dat. At Jerome's funeral I felt no love from those so-called God-fearing folks. Jerome's family is full of 'em yo. Pastor Jackson's is cool doe. But I ain't joinin' his church."

He sure likes the word yo.

"Did he ask you to join Darius?"

"Yeah he did. Ha. I tol'em not gone happen yo."

"He's your uncle, right?"

"He admits to it. He's the only one and Aunt Carole. She's nice to me and seems genuine. But I hear she's into somethin' else, so she don't go to church no mo."

Darius doesn't mention Shonny and I don't ask.

"This is nice yo. All I have is my mama and a couple of homeys. No friends really to speak of. No other family, so I appreciate you sitting wit' me."

"Well Darius, I don't know you well enough to judge you. And I don't judge a person because of what someone else says."

"They got Darius on blast. I know you've been hearing things shawty. They really hate Jerome left me this house and his trust fund. He had a living will so they couldn't contest it. If they knew how, they'd try."

"If you don't mind me asking, what is the truth about Mr. Darius?"

"Ha! How much time you got yo?"

Darius starts off talking about what happened when he got out of juvie for assaulting his father. His mother sent him to California to live with her brother and his wife. Darius was 15. He says his uncle was really cool and wanted him to succeed, follow his passion in music.

"But I got sidetracked. I was mad as hell because of what happened and I wanted to take it out on everybody. I showed my uncle and his wife no respect. Finally, they told me I had to straighten up or leave. I left in the middle of the night one night. I called mama so they wouldn't call the cops. I stayed on the streets for about 6 months. I could've been dead yo. If it hadn't been for this girl I met, no tellin' where I'd be."

"Oh? She must've been pretty special."

"Uh, I guess you could say dat. There were barriers to our relationship doe. Dats why we ain't together. But she got me to go home. Saved my ass yo. I was lucky my uncle let me come home. But he did give me an ultimatum."

"I end up enrolling in a music arts charter high school near Hollywood and graduated. I learned about producing, directing and song writing. Yep your boy is good at writing songs and creating beats."

"For real?"

"Yep. I sold one of my songs to Fella Jiles."

"Ooo snap! The dude who sounds like Luther Vandross?"

"What you know about Luther? You still a youngin'."

"Paleeze Darius like you old. Besides Fella Jiles is only about 28."

"True dat. Miss LaTonya how old are you if you don't mind me askin'?"

"I turned 17 in June."

"Cancer or Gemini?"

"Gemini and I don't have a split personality. So don't go there."

"Ha. I don't believe in dat. Just curious conversation mostly."

"How about you?"

"I'm coming up on 20. Dec. 10. Sagittarius."

Shit! So is Jeremy. His birthday is also Dec. 10 and he'll be 19! Damn! I hope this ain't a sign. Where the hell is he? What happened to him?

"Is dat a bad thing?"

"Uh no."

"Okay den. You turned yo lip up."

"Oh. I didn't mean anything by it. I just knew a Sagittarius once. Don't worry I won't hold it against you, ha!"

"Okay den. But I'm unique yo. There's no one like Darius."

Boy and he's modest. At least being full of himself is kinda attractive on him.

"Which one of Fella Jiles' songs did you write?"

"Mindless Intensity. It stayed on the charts for 8 weeks."

"Ooo I love that song." So, I start singing *you're on my mind all the time, so intense is your caress like angel silk, you're my Mindless Intensity.*

"Ha! Okay den. I like dat. You can carry a tune. At least you sound good crooning my words. You know we went platinum. I'm helping Jiles on his next album in the next year."

"Wow. Sweet."

"You know shawty there's an industry party being held here next Saturday. I'm playin' host for some friends I met in the industry. Wanna go?"

"Uh I'm already going."

"Oh r-e-a-l-l-y? Okay den. I'll leave you alone 'bout dat."

"Ha. Okay yeah."

Chatting with Darius I get to see a side of him his critics haven't seen. Then he brings up Shonny. He doesn't understand why she hates him so much.

"I don't even know the girl yo."

"Hmm. I don't know her well either. But I've seen her good and bad sides."

"Well Jerome introduced us once long time ago. She'd already been turned against me."

"Too bad. How's your mama Darius."

"She's cool. She's staying with me. Always talkin' 'bout leaving Portland yo. But I doubt she will. Mama helps me keep my head on straight. She knows I'm hell bent on finding my brother's killer. True dat!"

I'm tempted to tell Darius about AJ's suspicions about the Messiah. But I'll keep it to myself yo.

"Darius, what are you gonna do when you find 'em?"

"You ask a lot of questions shawty."

Darius is grinning, stretching his legs on the table in front of us.

"Oh sorry. Don't want you to get into any trouble. You did say you changed. You know because of a special lady an all."

"I just said I want to find out who did it is all. The cops ain't workin' fast enough. Don't want the trail to get cold yo."

"Oh. Okay. Any special lady keepin' you company these days. Yeah, I'm being nosey. Ha."

"Well yo, since you gotta pretty little nose you can be nosey. I'll let you know if it ain't cool."

There he goes flirting again.

"Haven't had anyone serious since almost 3 years ago when I met ol' girl."

"Ol' girl?"

"Yeah she was way older than me. She caught my attention one night outside a club on Hollywood and Vine."

"What were you doing there? Weren't you underage?"

"I told you beautiful I was in dem streets. I had fake ID too. Since you asked, you must be a good girl."

Wow. I'm Miss LaTonya, shawty, yo and beautiful. At least he knows how to transition Mr. Smooth Operator. Yeah daddy still listens to Sade.

"I'm not naïve."

"But you still a good girl doe. Ain't nothin' wrong with dat. I like good girls."

There he goes again.

"Ol' girl is married. Okay. Now what else?"

"Married?"

"Yeah couldn't help myself. Neither could she. I think it must've been her red dress and high, high heels. Mm, mm, mm."

Darius closes his eyes for a moment, shakes his head, savoring the memory.

"But like I say, she's married to some rich old guy back in Atlanta; they have twins. He also has an older daughter from his previous marriage. He was a widower so I get the picture he's much older."

"Ooo snap. Burrrr."

"You cold?" says Darius.

"Uhhhh, I'm okay. I felt this chill. It's gone now."

When Darius talks about ol' girl, it makes me think back a few years. Luanne went to Los Angeles on a weeklong spiritual retreat with the All Saints Church. Is the world really that small? What are the chances?

"Soooo, what's her name?"

Darius arches his eyebrows, looking at me curiously.

"Uhhhh, Anne."

Interesting. He sure did hesitate. Maybe it's too personal.

"Got any more questions Miss LaTonya?"

"Naw Mr. Darius."

"Well den it's my turn. Tell me about you den."

"What do you wanna know nosey Darius."

Now it's my turn to tease.

"Anything and everything yo. You intrigue me LaTonya Ellis."

Huh. Let me give him another name to add to his repertoire. "My nickname is Tippy. Maybe I'll bore you with why another day."

"Ha. I bet you use to sneak up on folks. Be all in the bitness yo."

"Ooo snap! How did you guess?"

"I'm psychic Tippy."

"Monsieur Darius eh?"

"Um. French. True dat. Like right now. I see great things coming your way."

He's closing his eyes like a fortune teller. "A new man is coming into your life. A great, fine looking talented brother."

"You're corny. How do you know I don't already have a man?"

"Don't matter. He ain't here."

Now I'm feeling sad. Maybe even turning up my lip.

"Yow. I hit a sore spot again I see," says Darius. "I'mo leave it alone yo. Tell me something good instead. I've already met your daddy. How's your mama doing?"

"Whoa. You sure no how to ask all the right questions. My mama was murdered when I was 7. I found her body."

I look right at Darius, blinking my eyes really fast so I won't cry.

"Aw wow. Damn."

Darius grabs and hugs me without warning. I don't get upset. I just go with it. He sits sideways facing me, stretching his arm across the top of the couch.

"Did they catch him?"

"Naw. I don't remember anything."

"What the hell. You was a little girl."

"I know but I still feel helpless. Then this happens too... You know."

"Say look yo I'm really sorry 'bout what happened to yo mama. If I can help somehow let me know. I can at least listen."

"Yeah. Thanks."

"As for my brother yo, you don't have to worry 'bout none of that ever comin' back on you."

Hm. I never thought about anyone coming after me. All I remember is the gunman had a mask on and the car was an old beat up rusty green Chevy. I told the police this. The police say if it was intentional the car couldn't be found anyway.

I then tell Darius about TiAnna and what happened. I also mention Luanne.

"I was hoping your Anne was Luanne. That would've made my day."

Darius arches his eyebrows. "You know shawty all dat what's been botherin' you, don't worry no mo. I gotchu." He winks.

I don't know what he means but it makes me a little less anxious.

"Now ain't I a rude host. I didn't offer you anything. Want somethin' to eat or drink? You should try my famous Jambalaya I made fresh today."

"So you're a chef like your brother?"

"He learned from me yo. Telepathically." Darius hands me the TV remote. "Make yourself comfortable. I'll be right back."

The play ended so I flip the channel until it lands on Bravo. They're running repeats of Atlanta Housewives. They can be corny too but I watch to see what NeNe and Phaedra are up too. Looks like I've seen this, so I turn the volume way down, kick off my shoes, throw my feet up on the table where Darius had his and lay back against the couch. I'm exhausted so I close my eyes. Got my nerve, but Darius did say get comfortable. Usually I wouldn't be so relaxed especially since I barely know him. But I know I'm safe here.

Jambalaya on warm

In the kitchen where Darius decides to make a quick phone call.

"Hey guess who yo?" says Darius.

She's surprised to hear his voice. But stays silent.

"Me and you have a mutual acquaintance."

She still doesn't respond.

"How 'bout dis yo. I'll come see you on Thursday."

Darius hangs up the phone. He then prepares 2 plates of Jambalaya, grabs a couple of strawberry sodas and heads back to the family room.

When he reaches the doorway, he sees Tippy laying back against the couch, which makes him smile.

Mm, mm, mm. Such beauty. Like one of those orange trees in Southern Cally beginning to bloom. Looking all ripe, ready to eat and shit. You've already gotten a taste Darius. No turning back yo.

38

Ready for Change

It's late afternoon at Darius's

Who's thinking about his past relationships with women. They were short and sweet with no commitment and he preferred it that way. At 19, he feels he's just begun to taste the lilies of the field. A field which seems to be getting wider with more variety, making him hungry for good, clean sex. But he can change.

"She ain't no ho and probably still a virgin," Darius thinks as he admires Tippy from where he's standing. "If my brother were here, Tippy would be his. Jerome always talked about marrying a girl like her – beautiful, sexy and smart with a whole lot of class."

Darius walks over and sets the tray on the table. He then steps behind it and reclaims his place next to Tippy. She doesn't move so he know she's sleeping. Darius closes his eyes, leans over and with his nose barely touching her cheek and moves it up and down.

Mmmm. You smell good like jasmine. Wherever you at girl, I'd like to be dare wit' you.

Oct. 25, 2012
At Atlanta-Hartford

On Thursday morning where Darius takes the airport shuttle over to one of the car rental ports and claims a pre-paid 4-wheeler in his name. He plans to return to Portland later tonight so he's arranged to meet her at a nearby hotel. As instructed, he would pick up a keycard to take him to the penthouse.

Luanne arrives to the hotel

A few minutes before Darius, checks-in and heads up to the penthouse.

Once inside she tosses her purse on the chair and stands near the window, watching the planes land in the distance.

"Why you cowling me Darius? Is you fo reals? You bet not ask for mo' money."

Stepping back a minute

Luanne hasn't seen Darius since their rendezvous in Los Angeles. But she remembers him fine and buffed, along with the good times they had during those couple of weeks. They played dangerously, had lots of sex and even made plans about having a life together. But reality set in for Luanne. She was married to Robert Ellis, a goal she'd set in motion. She also had his children.

Darius was also underage – only 16 – jail bait! Luanne had no idea – he didn't look or act it – and Darius certainly didn't volunteer the truth. Although Darius at first said he was 18, he later broke the news to her when she refused to give up her life to be with him.

Instead, Luanne sent money to Darius in L.A, feeling she was being blackmailed but Darius referred to it as, "helping a brother out." He would be forever grateful and their secret would be safe.

Darius finds the hotel

10 minutes from the airport. He chooses self-park rather than valet, so he can make a quick exit when the time comes.

Darius takes the elevator to the 21st floor; the penthouse covers the entire floor. The elevator stops, he gets off, walks up to the door and knocks – tap, tap, tap pause tap.

"I hope she remembers our signal."

Darius turns the door knob. If the door is unlocked it's safe to go in. If not he'd have to hightail it out of there just in case she had an unexpected visitor.

Like the time Luanne was in L.A. for a retreat. Darius was coming by 1 evening, so Luanne told the group she was staying in. Later, a church member decided to stop by unannounced.

Darius arrived at Luanne's room and before he could knock, the door opened. Standing there was an older, gray-haired black woman. She was the church member who had stopped by to visit and was on her way out. Darius was glad he had changed into more appropriate attire – brown cargos and a yellow polo shirt. He made up a quick cover story about his grandmother wanting him to thank Luanne for the flowers.

Luanne, who was standing behind the lady said Lonnie – a name she had quickly come up with – and his grandmother was staying in the hotel; she was confined to a wheelchair. Luanne told the church lady that she had met the woman downstairs in the women's restroom and helped her with washing her hands.

Luanne had easily come up with this story after recalling helping an older woman in a wheelchair at the Atlanta mall restroom once. The woman was having difficulty getting up to the sink. No one else would help her, not even her daughter, who was apparently waiting outside the restroom area. When she was done, Luanne wheeled the woman out of the restroom to her daughter, who didn't speak nor say thank you. Luanne was tempted to cuss her out but decided against it.

The penthouse is unlocked

And Darius opens the door and leans in. He grins when he sees tall, lanky Luanne. He slowly steps inside and out of habit, scans the room from side to side.

"I'm not tryin' da go da jail," says Luanne.

"Okay den," says Darius.

Clasping his hands behind his back, he strides toward her like he's Mr. Cool – stepping with the left foot, quick sliding with the right, stepping with the left foot, quick sliding with the right – trying to mimic the shy innocent boy look he pulled on her in L.A.

"Look at you girl, looking fine as ever, yo. Can I get a hug?"

Luanne keeps her arms folded, leaning on her right hip. Her mouth is pulled sideways into a half smile.

"Sweet," he says as he looks up at the glass chandeliers above the king bed topped with a black fur comforter. Darius gets excited wondering what Luanne may have in store for him later. After they talk bitness.

"Let's cut da shit. Who are we towkin bout?" says Luanne.

"Oh you wanna be like dat? Okay den," says Darius.

He stands up straight and folds his arms like Luanne. He then drops the smile.

"I'm here to talk about my soon to be wife. Your step-daughter, LaTonya Ellis. Miss Tippy."

Luanne stares at Darius, crinkling her eyebrows.

"Say what?" she says.

"Let me repeat den," says Darius, sarcastically.

"Oh paleeze," says Luanne. "Dat ain't necessary. How you know Miss Crazy?"

"Whoa now hollup," says Darius, dropping his left arm to his side while holding up his right hand signaling stop. "Can't talk like dat about the future Mrs. Broussard."

"So why you here. What she gotta do wit me? She's Robbie's daughter. I don't give a rip!"

"Ooowee girl. Damn! Trust me I get there's no love lost between y'all. Tippy already told me yo."

"What den Darius?"

"The what is, Luanne darlin', is dat my girl is struggling with her mama getting murdered sit-chee-a-tion. So being her man all, I can't have my girl being sad. I've been thinkin' about lending my help, like help her remember who killed her mama."

Luanne squints her eyes, lips tighten bulging out her cheeks.

"What dat gotta do wit' me."

"Dis is what Luanne darlin'. I recall somethin' you said to me in L.A. You say killin' dat bitch was the right move. What did you mean?"

Luanne tightens her arms, hutching her shoulders, she shifts from her right hip to her left. Her face hasn't changed.

"Did you kill her darlin'?"

"What!" Luanne says. Her eyes get big, dropping her bottom chin with her mouth wide open.

"I don't kill no damn body! I don't know what you tryin' da do, but you ain't gettin' no mo money from me. Robby didn't believe the last story I tol 'im."

"Ha! You say it don't matter," says Darius. "You get anythang you wont anytime. Or is Mr. Robby through playin your games?"

"Look. I help ya yella-ass outta a bine. I'm beggin ya leave me be. You say you would. Thought we had an un-da-standin'."

Darius leans back, half extending his arms out to the side with his palms up. He says, "Hollup. No need to make this personal. Besides you know you like my yella-ass."

"Come on. We have an un-da-standin'. Ain't here to hurt you yo."

Luanne relaxes, dropping her arms. "Whatcha up to?" Luanne says. "How you wont me to trust you?"

"Ya know with me in Tippy's life she don't have to remember," says Darius. "Girl, you may not've done it but I think you know more than you let on. Who did it?"

Luanne takes in a deep breath and says, "I'll tell you what I know."

39

Not My Stepmama

She's a rich skank

Whose grown accustomed to her lifestyle and has no plans to give it up – not without a fight. Luanne feels she deserves it, especially, after the hell she's endured most of her life. Luanne had to grow up quickly.

Sept. 1, 2001
Atlanta

Luanne had no childhood all because of the street life her parents chose to live. Their life landed her in foster care at 15.

Luanne's father Don Juan abandoned her and her mother the previous year, leaving them to fend for themselves. This happened shortly after her mother Cherry (street name) refused to let Don Juan turn Luanne out – his own daughter.

"Sheeeit," said Don Juan. "Ain't like she really mine. She'd bring in some good moola."

Cherry continued turning tricks even after Don Juan left to keep the bills paid. Within a couple of months, she started using crack. She did it to ease her depression and escape several years of memories with a man she thought loved her. She'd been with him since she was 17.

Now in her late 30s, he had no further use for her – threw her away like trash, never looking back. Don Juan was on the prowl, rebuilding his stable with some young fresh flesh.

The money Cherry made went to drugs. And when she had none, she'd turn tricks for a fix. She'd stay gone for days, turning into weeks, then months until she walked out 1 day and never returned. Luanne soon found her mother living at a crack house in 1 of Atlanta's most crime ridden areas.

For weeks Luanne lived without electricity, food and water. She shoplifted food at the grocery stores, hustled money by panhandling or running cons on older men – pedophiles – she managed to con her way out of sleeping with. But, despite her antics, Luanne had to escape with her life on several occasions.

The day she came home to an eviction notice was the day she decided to ask the school counselor for help.

The counselor arranged for her to stay with a wealthy Druid Hills couple, the Bradley's, the area's most trusted and respected foster parents. Living with the Bradley's turned out to be Luanne's worst nightmare.

Pastor Bradley ministered at the popular Methodist "Church on the Way." Church members thought the pastor and his wife, Sharlana Bradley, were a godsend for at-risk children.

Pastor Bradley took the foster kids to church on Sundays and paraded them in front of the congregation, "praising the lord for sending these kids to him and his wife so they could save their souls." He never missed an opportunity to talk bad about these kid's parents, saying they were lost souls damned to hell!

The church's predominately white congregation also hosted a small black membership. It included the Oliver family: Franklin, Jocelyn and their only child, Loretta Oliver.

Loretta Oliver discovered the Bradley's secret they'd managed to hide for years. Pastor Bradley was a pedophile. Although rumored, church members ignored it, convinced the devil was out to destroy their pastor's good name and good works.

When Loretta Oliver was 12, Pastor Bradley started acting inappropriately toward her. Like he'd comment on her beautiful eyes and fine lips and ask personal questions like, "Did she have a boyfriend; has she ever kissed a boy; or would she like to have a boyfriend." The pastor also invited Loretta to have 1-on-1 bible study with him. He said he could help her truly understand the Lord.

She refused him and told her mother.

Jocelyn Oliver refused to believe and said, "You're imagining things. Stop listening to the rumors!"

The next time it happened, Loretta told her father, who put an end to Pastor Bradley.

Luanne met Loretta Oliver-Ellis

At the Church on the Way youth center in Decatur, Georgia. She was the center's most dedicated volunteer who worked in the homework club. This gave staff and youth there a chance to know the loving, warm-hearted Loretta Ellis – easily approachable and easy to talk too.

Luanne enlisted Loretta Ellis as her confidant, someone she could talk to about her deep-seated resentment for her mom, dad and the Bradley's. Luanne told Loretta she wanted to leave the Bradley's home but wouldn't say why – which was the reverend took her virginity within the first month of living there. Mrs. Bradley knew about it and condoned it. That's how Luanne first learned about the love of God.

Finally, because she had no choice – Luanne is pregnant – she told Loretta everything. She even brought video-taped proof of her sexual liaisons with the reverend including those he had had with the other foster kids over the years.

Loretta Ellis wis shocked and outraged the pastor is molesting the kids entrusted to him. But she's not surprised. It almost happened to her. Loretta tells her mother she plans to turn the pastor in. Jocelyn begs Loretta not to tell.

"Just think of the scandal," says Jocelyn Oliver. "Your father and the other innocent church members would be tainted. We cannot afford this type of publicity!"

"You're joking right mama? How could you ask me to keep such a horrible secret?"

"We'll handle this in a different way. I'll have your daddy speak with him. Give me the videotape," Jocelyn demands.

Reluctantly Loretta Ellis gave her mother the videotape but told of her plans to bring Luanne home with her. She could mentor her, help her heal and turn her life around. And, she could use her help with Tippy since the current nanny was retiring.

"Now you're being absolutely foolish. You know the kids they take in have severe problems. You know what kind of home life she comes from? For all you know she seduced him. She's been taught you know," says Jocelyn.

"Mama!" says Loretta. "I don't care. She's only 16. No child deserves to be raped. And he's supposed to be a man of God! I'm taking my family out of his church. And if I ever hear he touched mine, I will kill the white bastard!"

"Enough Loretta!"

"No mama! What you are saying is enough! You'd better have daddy take care of it or I swear to God if I hear anything else, I will turn the son-of-bitch in. You and daddy will have to deal. No doubt you'll make out just fine. I'm sure of it."

Loretta Ellis made good on her promise – to take Luanne home with her and remove her family from the church. She told Robert Ellis her reasoning who said she did the right thing.

"I'm sure your dad will take care of things," said Robert Ellis.

Loretta arranged for Luanne to have a private abortion because of having to bear a child by a 50-year-old pedophile minister.

Meanwhile, Franklin Oliver confronts Pastor Bradley, who denies everything. He says Luanne is lying; she's evil and full of sin. Franklin Oliver shows him the video tape; the pastor breaks down.

"I know I've sinned," says the Pastor, picking up the bible. "I am weak but she came on to me. I swear to God. She came on to me!"

Now Franklin Oliver is no fool, but he promises his wife he'd handle things without a public spectacle. He knows Jocelyn Oliver was a proud woman and her public persona meant everything.

"What would people think of me Franklin? The women over at the foundation board I serve on? The Links? The mayor's wife?" his wife said to him. "Frank, you have to keep this under wraps. I need to convince our daughter you've handled things," Jocelyn said.

Franklin Oliver told the pastor he would keep what he knew to himself under 1 condition: He and his wife would give up their foster parenting rights and send the remaining children in their care to go back to social services – immediately by the end of day. The pastor agreed to the conditions.

Back at the penthouse

Darius lays it on the line.

"Look. I want Tippy. She'd be good for me," says Darius. "I know she's got the means to take me to the top in the music industry. The $200,000 my brother left me only gonna go so far. How much is she worth anyway? 10 mil? 20 mil?"

Luanne turns around and faces the window. Darius walks over and stands next to her.

"Why you so quiet yo? So what's the deal? I know she's got a trust. Her mama comes from old-money and her daddy's rich. Sheeeit she's probably worth more. So, give me the skinny?"

Without looking at Darius, Luanne says, "Yo future wife broke."

40

On My Mind

October 24, 2012
Phone tag ends

"Um, it's about time. Where you been hiding?"

"Trying to clean up my brother's mess. We had to get him an attorney."

I hadn't heard from AJ DaMenace since the night at his house – his brother's party. I've been missing this white boy. No joke.

"So what's going down?" I ask.

AJ explains, "The girl is accusing my brother and 3 of his cronies with gang raping her. Little bro says dat ain't true. He knows dis girl from school – Kim is her name. She shows up to the party wit' her girl Tanya. This Kim's been wantin' ta get wit' my little bro for a while. When she came at him, he brushed her off and starts talkin' to Tanya. I remember my little bro mentioning Tanya. He's been wantin' to peep dat since the beginning of school."

"My white friend Julie knows Kim. When she heard about the date rape situation, she says Kim probably consented to having sex. I guess she's had multiple sex partners at one time before. Julie says Kim has orgies with girls in the mix too. Me, I can't speak on it. You can be a ho but still get raped. We can't jump to conclusions."

AJ says, "I wasn't dair, but I know my little bro."

Of course, AJ's gonna defend his brother. Don't mean he didn't do it. But I'll be cool even though this is a sore subject for me. I hate it! Rape among women is on the rise, especially because of date rape an all. Now with my BFF being raped, this kinda thing really grabs me by the gut, making me want to hurt those damn rapists really bad!

"Innocent until proven guilty is all I can say on the subject AJ."

"Yeah right. Bro say he was wit' Tanya the whole time. The only problem I see is a possible civil lawsuit. The attorney says she could sue me for damages. The broad says it happened in my house. No one saw her do it. Someone would've seen a naked chick run out da house."

"How do your parents feel about all this? I can only imagine."

"Sheeish! They like ta take my head off. They like accuse me of corrupting' little bro. Ha! He don't need my help. My little bro is a smart dude when it comes to academics an all, but he does stupid things from time-to-time. Especially when he hang wit' doze little rich friends of his. Bobby and Lance. Then he got dis Arab friend. Now dem Arabs? I wouldn't put it past 'em. It's legal to rape women in Saudi Arabia, so the punk could'a had a flashback. Thought he was at home."

"My BFF got raped so if you don't mind can we stop talkin' about that part of it at least?"

"Oh I'm sorry baby. Here I am ranting' like a maniac and didn't even ask how you feelin'. How you been anyway? Have you heard from your friend yet?"

"She's not ready to see anyone."

"I'm here for ya. Let me know on dat. Hey, we still on for Saturday night?"

"Yeah. I finally got hold of Shonny, so I got a hair date on Saturday morning."

"Ol' Shonny wanna be Dale, hailing the dike life she's gonna see Gail," raps DaMenace throwing in some bee-boxing.

"Ha! AJ leave Miss Shonny alone. If that's what she wanna do, I ain't mad at her."

"She's glad, you ain't mad," AJ continues until I say "Okay boohoo." But why did I say that. Here he goes again, "You say boohoo, I say do you, ooo-we girl, make me wanna swirl."

"Ha! You corny." I don't know whose free-style rapping is worse, him or daddy's. If free-styling is his thing, he'd lose for real.

I tell AJ about my new car and meeting up with Darius. He wants to know if Darius said anything about Buster. I tell him no but he's keeping his ear to the ground too.

"Like you say, people are talkin'."

"When Darius comes up wit' it, Buster better channel the real Messiah for real yo. Ha!" says AJ, trying to mock Darius.

But there was seriousness to what he was saying.

"You don't think…"

AJ interrupts me before I can finish.

"Baby girl, don't forget ain't nothin' private. Feel me."

"Yeah I know."

I am glad for the reminder. With things like the Patriot Act, we've allowed the government to take our freedom.

Daddy says the "powers that be" will soon have a spy cam everywhere; they'll watch everything we do, to keep us in line. Daddy always talks about stuff like the New World Order and secret societies totally taking over and controlling us.

TiAnna says my daddy is just one of those conspiracy theorists. I don't know but when daddy talks like that it scares me. And the thought of it makes me wanna go get high. I don't even smoke dope – and never wanted to. But if somethin' crazy jumps off, I'm getting' with the dopers.

Daddy did say we stand a better chance than most because we have money. But he says they're trying to take our money, which is why the Bush administration crashed the stock market. Daddy says 50 percent of the millionaires and billionaires disappeared by 2008. The powerful elite want a smaller pool of folks with money. Easier to control the wealth.

"Stay sweet for me 'til Saturday girl."

I'm blushing for real. My face is really warm, but I manage to say in a shy voice, "Okay. I'll be thinking about you."

"Me too. I mean 'bout chu, ha!" says AJ.

Then we hang up.

Private rehab outside Atlanta

I'm nauseous, dizzy and sickened by you who has no name. I can feel you devouring my insides. Please hurry and leave my womb. Go back to hell from where you came.

41

You Know Me

At the penthouse

Darius grapples with the truth. This is not what he was expecting.

"Explain yourself yo! What da hell you mean my future wife is broke?!"

"I dint stutta Darius. Cows a da ecownyme Robby loss groun' in Atlanta and dat solar stuff. Robby wanna venture out, so he used her $100 million trust. He expand in Portland and plan L.A. fo' next year. He e'en inves' in new stuff. Say he wont to wean off the cu'ent business moldo."

Darius shakes his head like he's trying to snap out of a bad dream.

"$100 million! And what do you mean usin' my wife's money to invest!"

"She don't know. He make her sign it to him. She thowt it somethin' to keep her out of juvi. Her daddy cowzes a rif on her birthday. Set her, her uncle and friends up so he can steal it. Yeah he did. See ev'body think I'm the bad guy. Yeah. I'm gettin' mine but Robert Ellis a dawg. Ask 'im if he kill her mama. He had a reason."

Luanne pauses and takes in a deep breath, thinking she may have divulged too much.

"Keep it comin' girl!"

Luanne adjusts her stance and crosses her left arm underneath her chest with her right elbow resting on top of it.

"Robby not Tippy daddy. Her Uncle Ray is. Had an affair with her mama. Dats why Robby act crazy like he do."

Darius is shaking his head in disbelief.

"This is some bullshit! Sound like my daddy's motherfuckin ass! I ain't had no money to steal but he stole my childhood. Dat dawg motherfucka!"

Darius paces around the room, rubbing his chin. He walks back over to Luanne. Right up on her he points his finger in her face.

"I'mo get dat money back and you gonna help, un-da-stand!"

Luanne doesn't answer but Darius knows he can count on her help. He and Luanne are like each other in many ways. They both had it rough so life owed them – big time.

Darius picks Luanne up in his arms, carries her over to the king bed and throws her down on top of the comforter. He starts pulling off her clothes while she pulls off his.

Butt-naked their bodies collide like dancing wolves, howling and squealing in pleasurable pain. For Darius and Luanne, the world disappears, waiting for a new chapter to begin. Their stage awaits.

Oct. 12, 2012
In Portland

I'm at my new hairstylist's salon.

"My BFF's name is TiAnna."

"For real. She's tight den," says Miss T.

Miss T is Portland's top hair stylist known for hair weaves but does a variety of hair designs. Owner of Miss T Hair Design, she's also the lead stylist for the local film video industry.

"So why y'all come to Portland of all places?"

"My daddy expanded his business here." I tell her a little about the business and how long we've been here. "I really miss my friends and ATL."

"I like Atlanta. We're moving next year. Can't wait to get out of this broke down city. It's sooo boring here. And there ain't no men. Glad I got 1."

"Yeah. I've been talkin' to this white boy rapper since I broke up with my boo Jeremy. Jeremy's in Miami probably with some white girl. He's gonna play for the NFL."

"Why they do that shit. I hope your white boy got some money. Can't have no broke white boy."

"He's getting ready to go on tour with Boss Amanishakhete."

"Well hey den, I know that's right. Uh, umm, Boss is my mom."

"Whaaat? For real she's your mama?"

"Yeah she is. And her producer Anuff is my cousin."

"Wow. That's tight."

I've met some tight folks in Portland. But Miss T is right. This place is borrrring. There's no place for black kids my age to hang, like StoneRec back home. In ATL we have lots of teen dances, after game bowls, skating, something. The only time I saw a few black kids together was at Jerome's.

"I know this white girl at my school who thinks Portland's all that and a bag of chips."

"For them, yeah," says Miss T. "Most of them like the cold and rain and outdoor stuff like skiing, hiking and camping. My oldest son is 13. He goes to school around nothing but white folks. All his friends are white but he keeps busy doing things like camping."

"Do you hike or snow Miss T?"

"Girl paleeze. I can go camping in my own backyard. I did when I was a kid – had to go to outdoor school. H-a-a-a-ted it," she says, sing-song like. "I even went hiking one time with my uncle and cousins; it wasn't the truth. I don't like the rain, cold and snow, so sure ain't getting on no skis either. You?"

"Naw. You been living here all your life?"

"Born and raised." Miss T pauses but gets right back to talking.

She sure talks fast like my BFF does when she gets really excited about somethin'. Ooo I'm missing her.

"I did live in Seattle for a minute and I'm international. I travelled Britain and Europe because my mom lived in London at the time."

"Well it ain't like you've never been outside of Portland Miss T. I've been to Europe. We went last summer Italy, Spain and Austria."

"I was in Italy. Venice and Verona. All I wanted to do was shop. Forget about sightseeing stuff like my mom wanted to do. Ha!"

I had to laugh too.

"I was like that. Had to have somethin' no one else had in ATL. I've thought about learning how to ski though. I heard Timberline Lodge up at Mt. Hood is beautiful, especially in the winter."

Miss T turns up her side lip.

"Hm. I rode on this jet ski up in Seattle once with this crazy fool I use to hang wit'. I almost drowned because he was playin'. Folks play too much. My uncle's like that when he gets on his boat – all drunk. I meeean. I don't swim so playin' around water ain't cool."

I agree with her. I would be mad too, but I know how to swim. Unlike some of y'all black folks, ha! I'm open to trying new things, especially here since I have to make the best of it. It's beautiful, but I'm homesick.

Back home if I wanted to do some real outdoor stuff, we'd visit Savannah for something else besides pavement, red dirt roads, traffic and Waffle House.

"You should get your white boy to take you around then. He may like that kinda stuff. At least get him to take you to the beach. Seaside is the most fun and Lincoln City has a casino but not like Vegas. If you don't have kids it's okay. They have good entertainment from time to time. Oh snap! Chile, you ain't but 17. Shame. Trying to give you some pointers and you still in high school."

"Uh-huh. This is my last year."

But I ponder the possibilities. AJ DaMenace will be on the road soon. Do I really wanna be with a white boy for the long haul? Whoa. I'm getting way ahead of myself. Technically, we're not even an item.

"Your hair is so pretty and healthy. Dang it's long."

"Yeah. I thought about cutting it. I see all these cute short hair styles. Wonder how I'd look with short hair Miss T?"

"Uh, uh. Don't cut your hair. If you want short hair, I'll do you a short weave. Then you can wear your hair again when you get tired of it. I cut my hair once. Now it's grown back and I ain't doing it again. Takes too long to grow."

"Hm. That's a thought. Ooo I like this brownish, red color better than that burgundy I had in my hair."

"This color looks better on you. Everybody can't wear burgundy. There. You're all set."

"Thank you." I pay her and tip her $50 – 'cause I can afford it – and give her a hug. I tell her I'll see her in a couple of weeks.

I got some time left so I'll run over to Shonny's since she did ask me to come by after I got my hair done; she wants see it. I owe her a thanks anyway. I was starting to really miss my stylist back in ATL.

But heyyyyy. I found me a new hairstylist and not just any hairstylist. Miss T is Boss Amanishakhete's daughter, living in Portland, Oregon of all places.

42

Big B Ain't No Joke

On to Shonny's apartment complex near the Lloyd Center. These neighborhoods have no parking and from what I hear, landlords charge a whole bunch of money because of the location. Her complex has some parking but none for visitors. Maybe they don't get many.

Like my Auntie Maebelle in Savannah, GA. She rarely gets any because she's a recluse and a hoarder. When me, daddy and his family go to Savannah, we stay in a hotel. We're there mostly to enjoy the Savannah beaches, not to visit her. We went quite a few times without stopping by.

I meeean

When we do go to her house, it takes a while for her to answer the door. She's 70 years old with a hunch back and leans over frontwards when she walks. She wears a wig like gramma Ellis use to – she's gramma's oldest sister – and this bright pink lipstick she wears above her top lip. She pencils in eyebrows she doesn't have. And OMG she uses red lipstick for blush – I meeean – she actually circles it on and thick. Frightening. Oh boy, can't forget the sky-blue eye shadow I think she's had since they first came out with it. It's hit and miss on her eyelids.

It almost makes you wanna feel sorry for Aunt Maebelle until you walk inside – to a house buried in junk! She collects old black dolls. Many of 'em are broken, chewed up and missing clothes and she doesn't keep 'em dusted and cleaned up like most collectors would.

She's pitiful and ought to be ashamed. When you visit, she has to move stuff around so you can sit down. I think there may be some rodents nesting around there. I could've sworn something was gnawing at the back of my ankle while sitting on her couch. That was the last time I wore sandals and even pants. I would've died if something crawled up inside my pant leg.

Pays to be ready when you visit Aunt Maebelle. Daddy said one time he saw droppings in the bathroom. Ooo nasty! So, we go to the bathroom before we'd get there and then don't drink anything – not even if she offers – so we won't have to pee. And pray we don't take home bed bugs.

Parking finally

Geeish. I'm 3 blocks down and around the corner. I better remember this street named "Hancock." Okay Mr. Will take care of my transport. She's new you know.

I walk by several apartment buildings before I reach the front of Shonny's building. When I get there, I see a familiar face. It's the Latino girl I met at Jerome's, whose name I believe is Lucinda. Lucinda is also heading into see Shonny. I didn't know they were friends. They didn't act like it at Jerome's. But she was at the funeral and I think Shonny waved to her on the way out of the church.

"¡Hola! Lucinda?"

"!Si. Hola! Tippy. ¡Còmo estas?" Lucinda says. I didn't notice before but she has a warm smile.

Latinos love it when you make it easy for them. Speak their language. But one thing my grandparents, daddy and me agree on is everybody should speak English when in the U.S.A. No one should get special privileges. To cater to one non-English speaking race over others – many of whom have been here much longer like the Vietnamese, Koreans, Africans and Russians – really isn't fair. My daddy says when in Rome you do as the Romans do.

Daddy says Latinos expect you to speak Spanish in Mexico. I know when we traveled through Europe last year, we had to know at least language conversation. So I know conversational Spanish, Italian and German and even a little Japanese. My goal is to pick up on some Swahili and Chinese. I wanna be an international black woman. When I visit other countries I do as they do and don't expect them to give me any extra consideration just 'cause I'm American. But they can if they want. I'm girlishcious.

I don't mind showing out sometime. So I play along for a minute. So I say, "Estoy bien?"

"Ah… ¿hablas español?" Lucinda asks me do I speak Spanish.

I say just a little, "Hablo un poco español."

When we get to Shonny's door I hear strange voices.

"What are they doing, singing?" I say softly.

Lucinda says, "Shonny's mama is Buddhist. They're chanting."

"Buddhist? Isn't her mama black?" I say out loud, but thinking to myself, this is so weird.

Lucinda has her hand on the door knob. Right before she opens the door she lowers her voice and says, "Yeah she's still black."

The door opens right into the living room – like AJ's house – where about 10 people are sitting in a circle; most in chairs and a couple sitting cross legged on the floor. At quick glance I see the crowd is diverse with black and white folks and a couple of Japanese. Or are they Chinese? No maybe Korean? Anyhoo some Asians.

This lady says welcome. It's Shonny's mama Carole. She's sitting to the right of us near some tall brown cabinet looking thing. It's open with some funny looking cloth with Asian characters written on it. There's candles and incense burning and at the bottom next to the cabinet is this huge bell on top of a fancy looking pillow. Hm. Now this shit is really weird. Don't tell me I just walked into some occult crap, witches or those voodoo hoodoos.

I'm reminded about the time

I knew this girl at school who got mixed up into voodoo. She once was a member of our church. I ran into her one day at the grocery store. She had on this long white garb with a white head wrap. So I figured she joined the Muslims. I don't get why American women choose to wear archaic, oppressive head dress. Let Muslim men treat them like 2nd class citizens like in those Muslim countries. Paleeze. This is America – home of the brave, land of the free ladies!

When I ask her what's up, she started talkin' in some strange language, which didn't sound like any foreign language I'm familiar with. So, it struck me kinda funny. I don't know what made me say it, but I said, "Girl are you mixed up in voodoo?" She says yes and she's getting ready to marry some high priest named Usari. Now I didn't say nothing. I couldn't. I thought I'd better be careful so she wouldn't hex me or somethin'. She was looking kinda strange about the eyes, like she was lost.

I remember thinking, "Crazy ass fool. You need a man that bad?" She was 30, single and I think a virgin. She always said she was praying for God to send her the right man. If God sent her Usari, I think he must've been joking. Maybe testing her or something. Whatever the case, all I could think of is how do I get the hell away from her?

Before I could walk away, she invites me to her wedding. I didn't say yes or no. I just tell her, "Good luck" and turn to leave, but she tries to hug me. When she extended her arms, I say to myself, "Uh, uh" might be a trick. They touch you and you hooked like crack – the one hit wonder. So I wave and high tail it outta there.

I mentioned this to TiAnna and Tommy Crumbs.

TiAnna says "Ooo girl."

But Tommy, huh, he had a lot to say. He says at voodoo weddings they have snakes, rats, ferrets and other strange animals around on display. He says they drink blood and sacrifice one of the animals. Now I may not know a lot about voodoo hoodoos, but I think Tommy was referring to something he'd seen on television. I think I remember the movie he was describing.

At any rate, I did feel for the girl at first, then I thought, why should I? Her choice. No need of me feeling bad. Just wouldn't be my thing – to each his own.

Daddy would say, "Who are you to judge? Mind your business."

Shonny's waving too us

Wanting us to join her in the back of the room. To get to her, we have to step around folks sitting in chairs.

When we reach her, she motions for us to sit. I hesitate. I just came to show her my hair and have no interest in sitting with the Buddhist people. Now I may be mad at the Big G, but I ain't interested in following the Big B with the big belly.

Over the past several years Jesus has gone from looking like a long-haired white hippy to a curly haired black man with a beard. So, when I'm ready I may go back to following the black guy – gotta support the black man.

But to choose between I'm a Christian or I'm Buddhist would be tough. My black friends would think I'm wacked. Now Daddy would say, "Here she goes rebelling again." He'd definitely call Dr. Ryan and say, "Yeah Dr. Ryan, it's so bad she ran all the way to Buddha."

Lucinda sits in the empty chair next to Shonny who's pulling on my wrist to sit down. I give her one of my irritated, "What the hell looks." I hate it when people change the script and pull this kinda crap. We've gone from "Hey girl come show me your hair" to "Hey girl let's chant to Buddha."

So I sit on the floor but plan to leave real soon. I whisper in Shonny's ear on my way down to the floor, "I gotta get ready for my outing with my white boo." She smiles and nods.

Then I turn my attention to the group. This really dark, heavy set black guy is asking questions. His name is Paul and he looks to be around Unc Rae-Rae and daddy's age. He says he's not Buddhist and like me he's irritated. He says Rosie, who's Buddhist, begged him to come. She's been chanting for a year and has had good experiences.

Sitting next to him is this girl with black hair – wearing it long down to her chin on one side and shaved on the other side; her skin is white, white, white. That's probably Rosie. She put her hand on his knee when he spoke while looking at him sideways, as if she wants to say something like, "I understand, but please don't embarrass me."

Rosie's wearing a nose ring like a spike dike and a black tank top. It's almost November for goodness sake. And those tattoos up and down her arms. She could be twins with the girl who played in the movie The Girl with the Dragon Tattoo. I can tell she's younger than him and it kinda reminds me of daddy and Luanne. Like my daddy, he looks like an old fool, trying to be young. Look at 'im with those Derrick Rose sweats and Tennis shoes – same outfit Jayden has. I guess he'll be chanting soon so he can keep her.

He wants to know if they believe in God or Buddha. Good question I think and one I would've asked if I cared.

Carole answers Paul's question with a question, "What does God mean to you?"

Paul hunches his head back, surprised by her response. He shrugs. Carole doesn't say anything, giving him time to answer. No one else says anything either. It got real spooky quiet there for a moment, until a little girl about five years old, who had her head down on her mama's lap sleeping, woke up. Her head pops straight up.

Uh-oh. The sleeping giant awakes. I bet we'll get some action now. She's probably one of those bad kids like Jayden and Brittany, who whine and talk back to their mama. This little girl's mama is white too. White kids act up and talk back to their parents. All their parents say back is "Now little Johnny, now little Sarah I'm gonna give you a time out" instead of whooping that ass.

Ha! Who am I to talk? Mama never spanked me. But I was an angel. Daddy did slap me – once – not too long ago because I got at his wifey. The devil had got in him, so I told Unc Rae-Rae. Daddy never hit me again.

The little girl decides not to act up and lays her head back down. Dammit. I was hoping' for a show. Instead her mama begins to rub her hair and the side of her face. Mama use to rub my head and face to help me get to sleep at night. She'd sing me a song while she was doing it: Go to sleep, go to sleep, go to sleep my baby child. One little horsey, two little sheep, go to sleep my baby child.

Ugh! It's getting stuffy with those damn incense burning. Shonny must've read my mind; she gets up and switches on the fan. Shit! Just my luck! It's blowing from behind me, messing up my flat iron. I grab the back of my head shielding what I can of my hair from the monsoon. What is wrong with the girl? Just 'cause she decides to wear her hair in an old school afro, doesn't mean she should hate. I mean, didn't she just have braids?

I get up and move to the far side of the room furthest from the door. Better than having to kill somebody over my $150 do – without the tip.

Paul says something. Be a man. Aw paleeze. This is way too much.

I blurt out, "God is supposed be omnipotent be there when you need him, when you can't fight the battle yourself. Not abandon you in your time of need. Allow your mama to be murdered and the person who did it gets away. Let someone you just meet who has a heart of gold get gunned down in front of you and get away again. Your BFF gets kidnapped, raped, drugged and left for dead and God lets the person who started it, get away. When the man you love disappears and doesn't tell you why but God lets you suffer and wonder. When your daddy is supposed to comfort and protect you but he allows himself to be controlled by his devil wife. God lets it happen again and again."

I end my speech with, "So what does God mean to me? Nothing!"

43

Some Wacked Shit

October 27, 2012
Still at the penthouse

With Darius and Luanne.

"Phewwww. Cain't nobody suck my dick like you girl," says Darius who's lying next to Luanne. "I could go for round – shit. I done forgot how many times."

"Bet yo so-call futcha wife cain't do dat," says Luanne.

"Huh. Won't be nothin'. I'm a good teacher yo. You know I handles my business huh, girl?"

Between me and y'all yo

When I met Luanne, I was a virgin. Long time ago. She taught me a lot and because of her I'm a sex G. That part of my life the homeys knew nothing about. Yo, they would've called me a sissy; a punk.

The homeys lived dangerously and having sex was no different. I wanted no part. They didn't use condoms and believed, "Only sissy's catch shit. If you strong you won't catch nothing."

One of the homey's did catch an STD and passed it around to all the other girls he slept with. Didn't matter really 'cause those girls slept with anybody and everybody – crack hos needing a fix; gang hos who passed themselves around. Then there were the unfortunate ones. Girls who lost their innocence – gang raped.

Luanne rescued me from those dark days. Being a virgin was minor compared to some of the shit I'd seen. Like when I witnessed the homey's gang-rape a 12-year-old girl. I still get angry when I think about it. The one we called Dude, the leader of the crew, instigated the whole thing. Yo the little girl was his sister.

Dude brought her to one of our hangouts – a vacant dive on 31st street – and let his boys have his way wit' her. Claimed he was tryin' to toughen her up to survive the streets. She'd eventually have to give it up anyway. This way he could control how she did.

Five big niggas did her. Me, I refused to participate in the madness. Dude was mad as hell. Yo I couldn't stand to hear her crying, screaming in pain. They banged the shit out of the little virgin; back-door and everything. The shit made me mad as hell. Usually the bangers protect their own; don't allow anyone near 'em. Otherwise it's your life. Instead, Dude did nothing. I'm surprised he didn't jump in and get some.

After they finished, Dude had the nerve to threaten her not to tell nobody not her mama, which is his mama, who he had no respect for. His mama was one of those God-fearing religious fanatics – least she wasn't a crack ho. So many kids lose their childhoods because one or both parents is on crack.

Dude's mama acted like she didn't know what was going on right under her own nose. Dude was slinging drugs right in her face. When I'd see her she'd just say, "I'm praying for God to touch your hearts one day." Ain't happening for me yo. Not in my lifetime.

She should've worked on Dude. He'd rob his mama's friends while they were at church. Now I helped, but nobody got hurt. One time we entered a house and an old man in a robe – I swear he was about 90 – was sitting in a wheelchair in the back room. He was watching TV, so I thought, and didn't hear us come in. Dude wanted to handle it – take him out – no witnesses. I stepped in front of him and the old man.

Strike 2 for me yo

I knew my days were numbered, which is why I'm so grateful to Luanne. I ran into her that night and she pulled me. She schooled me on how to talk my way back into my uncle's house. He let me back in, but I had to toe the line. Good thing my uncle lived in Oxnard, far from the Dude and the boys.

Come to find out later the old man was dead. He died while his daughter was away at church – of old age; he was 92. When I saw him in the chair, his eyes were open but I figured he wasn't movin because he was too old. I've been around death but it struck me really hard when I heard. We were desecrating the dead by stealing his shit.

A few weeks later Dude got killed. He came home and ran straight into the barrel of a 9 mil, courtesy of his sister. Got it from under her mama's mattress. Surprise! This Christian God-fearing woman still believed in protecting herself. But she sho didn't realize it be used against Dude. He deserved it though. His sister was never the same after what they did. After she shot him, she called the police on herself.

The girl wanted to get away from her Christian mama, bad. Come to find out, she did tell on Dude but her mama did nothing. Instead she invited church members over to pray. Then she played doctor; called herself nursing her daughter back to health even though they messed her up bad!

She'll be in juvie until she's 21. No one cared Dude was dead, especially the cops. They wanted his ass dead. Check this out. The church had a memorial service for him, saying they wanted to put him to rest in God's hands. That's why I say, "Fuck them damn bible thumpers!" What he done was unforgiveable. He did it to family. Dude and my dead daddy would've got along great.

Luanne's lying next to me

Reminding me past is past. Gotta keep my mind on today, tomorrow and the future.

My first plan is to work on getting Tippy's $100 mil back from her daddy. Then gotta remove barriers to our happiness starting with DaMenace. I don't like the fact he's taking my shawty to the gig. I'mo have to let this slide for now.

"Tonight's the night, evrathang's gonna be alright," I'm Darius Winston Broussard and I approve this message.

44

I'm Awake

At Big B's house

I'm relieved. Like I can actually breathe. Now look at these folks y'all. They staring at me, but I could care less about what they think. Ha! If I could see myself, I'd be looking at me too. Hm. I'm wondering what came over me? I heard myself speak but felt no emotion, like I was floating above it all and looking down at the pitiful earth beings that once held me captive. But not no more.

Carole speaks. You'd think she'd say something profound but do you know what this older looking Shonny says? "Congratulations."

What the hell? We sat here all this time like quiet obedient little kids. Is this Buddha's wisdom? If so, ain't no worse than God's wisdom – you're on your own, LaTonya!

Carole says in Nichiren Daishonin's Buddhism experiences can be obstacles, but they help a person grow; they call this Human Revolution.

Sounds like some hippy shit to me. The guy she's talkin about turns out to be some Japanese fisherman who discovered the true essence of life: Nam Myho Renge Kyo, devotion to the law of cause and effect through sound.

Carole talks about the scroll – called Gohonzon – on the inside of the big wooden house sitting in the middle of the room. She calls it a Butsadan. The scroll represents the highest life condition any human-being can attain; it's within one's life, rather than outside like above in heaven somewhere.

Carole says, "The Gohonzon is not an idol, nor is to replace God. It's simply a focal point for one to commit to changing their lives for the better, affecting the world making it a better place. We work from the inside out," says Carole. "Rather than the outside in. We take responsibility for our own lives. I guess you could say we have a partnership with the universal law. The law is prevalent in all living things."

Carole pauses and then says, "The universal law is referred to by many names depending on the religious belief. Christians, Catholics, Krishna's for example call it God; Muslims call it Allah; Hindus call it Shakti or God; Eckist call it Sugmad; Jehovah's Witnesses call it Jehovah; Buddhist say Universal Law or universe mostly and so on."

"The Buddhist believers who practice this particular sect of Buddhism belong to SGI or Soka Gakkai International, a worldwide lay organization. Its roots are in Japan. There are about three hundred sects of Buddhism; SGI is one of many and part of Mahayana Buddhism – the new path."

"The meeting today is a district meeting, one of many held in many homes around the world in seventy different countries. Everyone who belongs to SGI chants Nam-Myho-Renge-Kyo and recites a daily prayer, morning and evening, from the same Lotus Sutra and in the same way. "

Carole wants us to also know there are other groups, chanting Nam-Myho-Renge-Kyo, but they not like the SGI.

Now I remember hearing those words in Tina Turner's movie "What's Love Got to Do With It," the one where Ike whooped Tina's ass over and over. Tina started chanting and fought back.

Carole then explains, "SGI is unique and different and focuses on individual humanity and world peace for the entire planet." Carole says, "We are connected to our environment and each other. This is why it is imperative to understand what affect our causes have on ourselves and others. Karma can be good or bad."

I know everyone sees me turning up the side of my lip. What she's saying sounds like an advertisement for Buddha and I'm not really interested. It doesn't explain why Buddha, God whomever have chosen me for the beatdown.

I put it like this, "What does this have to do with my issues? I've been living in hell and no will let me up for air."

"You're having obstacles." says Carole.

Gee no shit Sherlock! I hope she can read my mind.

"Everyone experiences suffering differently, depending on who they are and their karma," she says. "We do not have to suffer as victims; we can be victorious over every obstacle, every devastating experience no matter what. You Tippy can be the victor in your circumstances – over your mother's death, over my nephew Jerome's death and what's happening with others around you. Being the victor empowers you to win – solve your problems, helps you advance your mission, find answers to those pressing questions."

What she says fuels the flames, feeling like my head is on fire.

"I wanna know who murdered my mama and why. I wanna know why my daddy hate's me most of the time," I say sounding frustrated.

"Tippy, those answers are deep within your life. You need to open your life so you can see clearly what it is. You don't want to be disillusioned or defeated by it. You want to be victorious. When you are, your life will change for the better. You will no longer be angry or whatever you're feeling. But you have to be clear; otherwise when you find the answer you will still suffer."

"Be clear? I'm confused."

"Tippy you have potential to be a Buddha. A Buddha is a person. A person who understands the realities of life and their own life, so much in fact, nothing can destroy their happiness or spirit. Right now, you are on a journey, a very powerful one. You have experienced death up front and personal; there is a reason for it. Nothing is by chance. The reason has nothing to do with God or anyone else. It has to do with your life. You are to learn something from this. What you learn will be extremely powerful. But you have to open your life. Forget about your mind – it gets in the way. Listening to your heart will bring you truth."

I don't know how to respond; it seems like my anger has been zapped out of me. I don't feel hopeless right now. I get like this, then something horrible happens. But I'll work on keeping my heart open. Shut my mind off more.

Carole invites us all to chant Nam-Myho-Renge-Kyo three times to end the meeting. I decide to go along with it and chant with everyone else. In this moment, I am Buddha.

The meeting is over and I have to skedaddle so I don't have time to talk to Shonny. I see she's holding hands with Lucinda. I know she's Lesbo but I won't jump to conclusions. Besides, Lucinda doesn't look like a dyke. She's really cute actually – a tall, slender Latino with a booty like J Lo.

AJ did say Shonny gets the fine ones. Lucinda's got a Halle Barry haircut and her hair color is real, real black, making me wanna cut my hair again. I may be calling Miss T about it sooner than later.

I give Shonny, Lucinda and Carole each a hug and wave to everyone else while rushing out the door. It's getting late, it's 2:00 and I'd plan to be home much earlier.

As I'm driving home, I'm thinking about what I heard. I hear the chanting in my head. It's something to keep in the back of mind, but I don't think I'll be joining the group – getting a scroll. I'll just chill on the religious stuff for now.

At home Daddy's in the family room with Brittany and Jayden watching BET. What's on is the documentary Second Coming, about President Obama and whether blacks will vote for him this year. Daddy made me watch it already. It made me really sad listening to how nasty the black Republicans talk about our 1st black President. I should be used to it because of my grandparents.

Even more depressing is how the GOP is suppressing the vote. One in four blacks are affected like with the polls set to close on days blacks vote. Voter ID is required and they make it hard to get. Like this 90-year-old black woman, whose voted since blacks were given the right, was told she can no longer vote. They say her birth certificate and social security card aren't enough. She needs to find the marriage certificate and show proof of her married name. The woman has been widowed for 40 years. She says she has no idea where the certificate is and trying to get a copy is impossible. She can't vote and the black Republicans are okay with it.

I learn these things 'cause I watch what daddy watches like MSNBC – Rachel Maddow, Al Sharpton, Greg Schultz, and Lawrence O'Donnell mostly. It was on the Lawrence O'Donnell's show we heard about another stand-your-ground case in Florida. Another unarmed black boy was shot to death by a white man. Several witnesses say the white man shot the black boy for refusing to turn down his car stereo. The boy was a high school senior who was getting ready to start a new job. They caught the asshole with no help from the other white media which ain't talkin about it all.

Daddy also likes Bill Maher the comedian and talk show host on HBO. He's pretty good. He gave President Obama a million dollars to start his super-pact and I hear he's dating a black woman – heyyyy! And of course, there's Oprah. Daddy says she's not campaigning this year because her white folks got mad at her. Trying to destroy her reputation and her new OWN cable channel. She's back to giving away cars, trying to win 'em back.

"If more black folks would watch my girl's channel, she wouldn't have to worry about those damn Sarah Palin rednecks!" says daddy.

Daddy says it's a damn shame GOP can't win on their own merits. Instead they bank on stealing our democracy by stealing the vote.

"If those damn Republicans go in, we may as well pack our bags and head for the pearly gates of hell," says daddy. "Where they plan to send the bulk of us black folks and it won't matter how much money we have. If we don't fall in line, it's over."

Daddy told me the other day the Republicans have created a redlining-redistricting strategy to steal the presidential election in 2016. They've already started the process state-by-state which is why they control congress. Again, somethin' else the white media – except for MSNBC is refusing to talk about. We just may be in deep doo-doo if folks don't wake up.

I go into the family room, walk over to daddy and kiss him on the forehead. He smiles then says, "Larry Hughes invited us to attend a dance performance at Jefferson High School and have dinner with his family next Wednesday, the day after the election. Put it in your calendar."

Daddy's been talkin' about introducing me to Mr. Hughes' daughter Debra who's a senior at Jefferson. She's one of the world-renowned Jefferson Dancers.

"Look don't forget to bring your date in here to me," says Daddy.

"Yeah, yeah," I say.

"And you still got a 12:00 curfew or else I'll send out the posse."

"Yeah daddy."

Right when I get ready to walk away daddy says, "Have you heard from your Uncle Ray?"

My back is to him so he can't see I'm lying.

"No, why?"

I crunch my forehead, attempting to look serious then turnaround and face him. Daddy stares back at me like he's trying to read my expression. Hm. I ain't giving the devil any excuse to start acting. I'm getting close to being sprung – my night with AJ.

I know he don't believe me. But I'm ready for the interrogation.

"Well okay. I'll see you in a bit, LaTonya."

I ignore the devilish smirk on daddy's face and hurry outta there before he asks me anymore trick questions. When I get to the foot of the stairs, I here President Obama's voice coming from the television.

"We've got to move forward not backwards."

Yes Mr. President. Onward we must go.

When I get upstairs, my cell phone is ringing, displaying a private number. I debate whether to answer it.

"Hello." No one speaks but I hear breathing. "Hello," I say again. Still nothing and I'm getting really annoyed. "Who the hell…"

"Tip uh, it's me."

45

Is This for Real?

At a rehab outside Atlanta

My BFF found a way to call me.

"Um Tip. I... uh...can... huh...can I..."

I'm so shocked to hear her voice, I can't speak either. Finally, I say, "I've been hella worried. Been feeling bad 'cause of what hap..."

"Tip... um... phew... uh it's hard to say words."

"T. Where are you? Are you okay?"

"They gave me... those uh, for pain and calm."

"You're still at the hospital?"

"I'm... uh... being released, Tip."

"When T? I'll come th..."

"Um. Soon. I'll come... there... Portland."

"Are you able T?"

"It don't, don't matter, Tip. I ain't, I can't go home. No more."

I know TiAnna is still hurting and not only from what Don Juan did. But her mama's suicide and her daddy's involvement with Don Juan's girl, Lydia's supposed daughter she put up for adoption. A daughter she conceived out of being raped at 14. Another crime committed against a black woman where the ass got away.

"I'll help you get here T. Can I send some money or charge whatever you need to my card?"

"I uh… it's arranged, Tip. Call you soon… K?"

TiAnna hangs up before I can say good-bye. I don't know how she is really and how she plans to get here. Who's helping her? I wanna mention it to daddy, but I'll wait to hear from T, make sure this is for real. It could've been the drugs talking.

It's show time

And Aj's here.

"Hey daddy this is AJ."

Daddy stands up. AJ extends his hand; they shake. Then daddy looks AJ up and down.

"Yeah. He's white all right."

"Ooo daddy."

"Ha! So, I've been told sir. I promise you Mr. Ellis, the serial killer gene passed me up."

I smile. AJ's funning', alluding to the fact most serial killers are white. But daddy isn't laughing.

"Well you better not be young fella. This OG will find your ass."

Oh, know my daddy didn't just claim he's a gangsta. I knew he had some thug in 'im.

"Oh, I understand sir. I also suspect your daughter has learned a few tips from you."

Daddy glances at me from the corner of his eye.

"Yep she is like her daddy. Don't let her sweet innocent look fool you."

"But I am sweet and innocent daddy."

AJ looks at me grinning. Then back at daddy.

"What time shall I bring LaTonya home sir?"

Um. Trying to sound all proper. Daddy would knock you out if he knew you was kissing on me last week.

"She has a 12:00 curfew," he says.

"OMG daddy!" Shit. Now I look like a little kid.

"Okay sir. I'll make sure she's home on time," says AJ.

He then leans around daddy to acknowledge Brittany and Jayden who are laying on their stomachs with their arms and hands propping up their chins. They're watching one of those Harry Potter movies.

"Hello there. You must be Brittany and Jayden."

They roll over finally and acknowledge our presence. They're smiling because they're getting attention. I rarely introduce my friends to 'em.

"Hi," they both say.

Okay enough of this meeting the family stuff. I give daddy a kiss on the cheek.

"See you daddy."

"Remember, I know how to find you."

"Nice meeting you sir. Bye Brittany and Jayden."

"Alright then. Take care of my daughter."

"Bye," say the twin brats in unison.

I broke free LOL

And ooo the white boy is trying to show me some class. Get this. We're riding in a stretch limo and the driver is waiting outside the door.

I also have a chance to really peep what AJ has on. He's g'd up with dark green jacket, black shirt and slacks. The top two buttons of his shirt are unbuttoned, teasing me with a little of his chest hairs.

Jeremy has little curly hairs on his chest I'd run my fingers through while going down on 'em. But boo on Jeremy. It's AJ time. On to "I may give this white boy some, song."

AJ gives me a hug while the driver opens the door. "Ooowee girl you look real sweet. And smell good too."

Yep. I'm wearing Jasmine, my favorite scent and this satin, fuchsia A-line girlishcious dress. It was made by a designer I saw on Project Runway, who lives in Atlanta. The dress hangs three inches above my knees with a black lace lining, hanging an inch below the hemline. The modestly low-cut front has a 2-inch opening down the middle, exposing the black lace in between, starting from the top, down to my waist. The back has crisscrossed diagonal straps down to my mid-back and is sleeveless with 1-inch straps crossing the shoulders, connecting the back and front. The dress comes with a long sleeve short bodice length jacket.

The designer, who made my dress, asked me and TiAnna too model one of his dresses at the designer showcase last year in ATL, spotlighting new designers.

I ended up not going 'cause I had really bad cramps, which use to happen at the wrong time. I'd bleed really bad to where I'd be afraid to go out of the house. When I did, I wore a super pad along with a tampon so I wouldn't leek. My doctor put me on birth control to regulate and control the bleeding. But those damn pills make me gain weight. LaTonya doesn't do fat so no more birth control.

The doctor also wanted to give me some prescription pain meds. Daddy wouldn't let them. He didn't want me strung out on opiates. I take 800 milligram tabs of Ibuprofen instead. But within the past 6 months – knock on wood – it's slowed up a lot.

It all makes sense

Why daddy is really leery about opiates. Gramma Ellis overdosed on pain meds when I was 13 around the time, I started my period. Daddy doesn't like to talk about it, but I heard him and Unc Rae-Rae talking after it happened.

The autopsy showed high levels of Oxycontin in her system. A few months earlier she'd been hit by a car while crossing at a cross walk. The guy who hit her was drunk. He got arrested and come to find out, his license was suspended for having several DUIs. Gramma Ellis was lucky. She says the lord was with her.

My gramma Ellis was overly religious too. One thing about black folks they love the Big G more than anybody –'so Unc Rae-Rae says. He says he don't know why since black folks still suffer the bulk of the problems. He thinks it's also because when you go into black communities there's a liquor store and church on every corner. More than any white community.

Unc Rae-Rae says he can't see himself praying to a God who enslaved black people. A religion taught to us during slavery. He and Darius think a lot alike on this. Unc Rae-Rae says in Africa black folks lived from the earth, honored and prayed embracing the natural laws and environment. He figures if black folks get back to their old spiritual ways, things will change for the better.

"Can't wait for the white man and you sho can't wait for his God," says Unc Rae-Rae.

My uncle feels black folks won't change their beliefs, 'cause black preachers make way too much money. They'd rather keep enslaving their own kind for the almighty dollar.

Because of his views, Luanne of all people calls him a heathen but not to his face. The nerve, if she really did sleep with daddy while he was married to mama, she's an adulterer, which makes daddy a... don't wanna go there.

46

Girlishcious
in the house

Downtown Portland

Is where the event is being held at Diamond Ballroom.

On the way, I ask about the situation with his brother. AJ says it looks like they're gonna get off. Tanya gave his brother an alibi. She also told the DA she heard Kim talkin' to one of the guys near the bathroom. Said she'd meet them someplace and give 'em all a duck sick. Sounded like she was planning on having consensual sex.

It turns out Kim did have the date rape drug in her system. The DA can't prove who or if anybody gave it to her. This makes me cringe. Kim may have put herself out there, but to have to run down the street naked, I know somethin' else funky went down. But AJ's brother's friends are sticking to their story.

AJ says he's relieved there's no chance she'll file a civil suit against him. Can't prove it happened at his house.

The driver pulls up in front and comes around to open the door for us. I feel like a celebrity.

We step in line behind this black guy in a black suit who's with this black woman who's wearing a long burgundy sequined gown and black fur wrap. You know they old folks dressing like that. This is about hip hop y'all I wanna scream.

Inside the 2-story ballroom of about 1000 people, large screens hang from each corner, playing music videos of the latest rappers. But the music is low enough for folks to converse. On the first floor, tables with white tablecloths displaying 3-candled centerpieces, Victorian loveseats and chairs filled with people, surround the edges. Up top is the same set up with some people standing looking over the banister while others are sitting at tables talking and drinking. The green and gold low-lit back light soothes rather than blinds the eyes.

I notice many more suits and ties, figuring they must be the music execs. Then there are quite a few hoochies. Mm, mm, mm. Look at hoochie over there. She should know she's too damn big to be wearing a tight-fitting strapless dress. There goes another and another. This is why I don't like the hip hop scene. These hoochies are embarrassing. Make rappers think we're all like that. I bet they all begging to be video vixens and will do anything. I'm the classiest looking girl here. Even the older women look better than they do.

Me and AJ DaMenace make our way through the crowd to see who's who. Aj's "whaddupin" and introducing me to fellow rappers. We run into Tao Phat, who's popular in Japan, looking to break in over here AJ says. Phat may be able to build a big fan base among white folks. The South Korean one-hit wonder rapper, Gang Nam, got popular quick with his silly dance. And can't forget William Hung – don't hate.

The hip hop game is still run by black rappers but AJ DaMenace is fairing pretty well for a white boy. I'm glad he doesn't do just hip hop. He sings pop and soul too like Robin Thicke, but I think AJ can give Robin a run for his money.

"Ok, hollup." It's Darius. "Whatcha' doing wit' my girl DaMenace. I don't remember you asking my permission."

Oh no he ain't looking sideways at AJ while staring me up and down. Sheeish. You eat a man's Jambalaya and all of sudden you belong to 'im.

AJ with his big ass boyish grin is looking at Darius like, on the real? Who the hell are you?

I like this AJ look. It saves me from having to read Darius like, "Excuse you."

Besides, y'all know I can't ruin my celebrity hello smile. The 1 where I slowly lower my head, turn it to the left; then look up with my eyes and stare; then slowly bat my eyes once; nod – down, up and pause and do the same looking to the right. Got to be selective when you do it. Like if I see a dude standing alone eyeing me. Or there's a bunch of 'em standing together checking' me out, knowing they can't help but notice my fineness. If I feel like being bold I do it when the hoochies are standing around trying to get noticed by some dude standing near 'em. I grab his attention and watch the hoochies sneer.

Darius is waving to someone, who's pushing his way through the crowd, coming this way. It's this light-skinned dude like Darius and who's medium built, wearing jeans and an Atlanta Falcon jacket. Ooo making me miss home. It's football season and we'd be at a game right now me an... dismiss the thought Tippy. This guy has these Asian-looking eyes. He looks familiar.

"Whassup D," he says, grabbing his hand, giving him the black bro hand shake – they pull each other forward quickly for one of those half manly hugs, slap each other once on the back and step back.

"What up Anuff," says Darius.

Anuff says the same to AJ and AJ says "What up."

They introduce him to me saying he's a former Portland hip hop producer who lives in Atlanta now.

"Okay," I say to him. "I know who you are. You were at the Falcons end of the season bash last year. Yeah?"

Anuff leans back and squints his eyes as if he's trying to remember me. I don't expect him to. I was amongst a crowd of folks, like he was, and I was with Jeremy.

"You fine. How'd I miss you," Anuff says, ignoring I'm holding onto AJ's arm.

"Probably 'cause you were with your lady," I say, my way of getting back at him for dissing AJ. I did want to laugh when he said that though. Negroes and their lines. They can't help it. I'm fine.

"Ha. Yeah okay. But I see you noticed. Ladies can't help it," he says, rubbing his chin.

OMG he's one of those who think they're the shit. He is fine though but damn. Don't be frontin'.

Darius is shaking his head at him like, "niggaaaa..." And AJ, well, he's still grinning. Must be his celebrity smile because it hasn't changed since we've been here.

"Say DaMenace, me and Boss lookin' forward to you opening wit' her. This tour is gonna be the truth. Full of surprises."

I read in the Atlanta Constitution recently an article about Boss Amanishakhete. She finished writing her first novel, geared toward a young adult audience. It's about a 17-year-old black girl, who comes from a wealthy background but has a pretty tough time of it because her mama was murdered. After reading the critique, it sounded a lot like my story so I plan on reading it when it comes out. The critics are saying it's gonna be a hit. Shoot! When they do a movie maybe I can play the lead.

"Yeah me too," says AJ. "I got some new stuff."

"Ha! Okay, slick. Don't forget it's the Amanishakhete show. She'll remind you."

"Got it. I ain't interested in upstaging the Boss."

"Okay cool. In a minute man."

Anuff then heads off to mingle with some of the other rappers. Our cue to keep walkin' and whaddupin' some more folks. Darius walks off in the other direction.

We've been walking, standing and talkin' for about an hour. We finally go for a couple of Pepsi's since we can't drink alcohol. Gotta have ID and AJ won't be 21 until January. Every now and then I grab an hors d'oeuvres from the passing trays. Mm. These crab puffs and salmon ones too, are gooood. I could nibble on these all night but gotta watch my figure. It's hard maintaining a girlishcious figure.

It's time to do a make-up check and while I'm at it, wipe my peepee with my feminine wipes to make sure I still smell sweet. Can't smell fishy like some girls. Soap can't get rid of the smell.

A note to my girls

I know men can stink too, but as for women, I asked my doctor about the fishy smell we have sometimes. She said it's a vaginal odor which happens when a woman is stressed. It can also be from eating certain foods and having sex. She said washing with a feminine gel and using a spray from time to time will kill the odor. But be careful with douching. It can reduce vaginal liquids which are important to keep the twot-twot from drying out.

I wish doctors would discuss hygiene with their female patients more often. I had to tell TiAnna about it. She was smelling it up one day, to the point she even had to say somethin', "Girl you'd think I'd been doing-the-do."

Gotta pee bad

I tell AJ. I'm going to find the girl's room.

"Want me to go wit' ya."

"Naw. I'm a big girl."

I make my way towards the neon restroom sign up ahead. On the way, dudes are grabbing my arm saying "hey" and nodding. Shame. They don't care if you're with someone. Girls are the same way so I'd better hurry back before one of these hoochies kidnaps my white boy. A whole lot of stray hoochies have come in over the past few minutes.

Speaking of which, I pass this Gypsy looking hoochie with long brunette hair parted to one side and wearing this red lace mini dress.

It's so short if she bends over I bet you'll see her ass. Probably what she wants. At least it'll distract the dudes from noticing the thick foundation and blush on her face. I meeean. What's she trying to hide?

Dang all she had to do was go to Nordstrom and have 'em show her how it's done. They do it for free hoping you'll buy their products. Like the blue eye shadow across her eyelid and lavender shadow underneath her thick brows gotta go. Then she has the nerve to put eyebrow liner on those thick things. While she's staring at me, she should be taking' a few pointers – I keep mine waxed.

To top it off she has on this bright red lipstick, pulling my eyes right into the mole above her lip. I can't help but to look right at it when I pass her. It doesn't look natural. It's slightly smaller than Chrissie's mole on Love and Hip. Look at her with her arms crossed, scrunching her lips and nose like she's saying "ooo you stink!" Huh. She must be smelling her bottom lip 'cause I take showers using expensive body and bath shit.

Next to her is this other girl – she's staring too. Paleeze. This short plump winch looks really trampy. Her make-up's on thick, an awful almost black looking lipstick. Her hair is long, black, stringy and oily-looking. Ewe, ick! And her disgusting too-tight dress – shame – is faded black and strapless. She must be about 48F. I don't know how she's holding that dress up. Wow no class. She could've at least changed those nylons. The whole on the left ankle screams hello.

She and the other hoochie look kinda alike; must be from the same clan. Now there they go whispering, making me feel paranoid. I'd better be on guard.

Aw. Here's the bathroom finally, way on the other side of the ballroom. I'm 'bout to pee my pants. The women's bathroom is a few feet from the men's, down this long hallway. Why make women's bathrooms harder to get to and the furthest away?

There's more than 1 stall open. I run in, barely get my panties down, squat and phew! Didn't even have time to grab a seat cover. Good thing I got strong legs so I can squat for a while if I need too.

Where's my wipes. Here we go. Wipe down with a couple of wipes – front to back. That ought to do it.

When I come out of the stall this Grecian looking woman, who looks about 40, is still sitting on a stool; she greeted me when I first came in. After I wash my hands, she hands me a paper towel, which I wish she hadn't done. No tellin' where her hands have been. I'll have to use the hand sanitizer I have in my purse once I'm outta here. Don't wanna hurt her feelings, but she should know better.

In the left corner of the counter, there's gum, hand lotion, tissue and an empty tip jar. She's expecting a tip, so I reach into my clutch and hand her a 5-dollar bill. She's grateful but paleeze. This ain't the Ritz Carlton.

Glad I came when I did. There's a line outside the door. I make my way out past the line, heading down the hall then…

It's time for the hoochie twins. They're walking towards me. You can hear mole hoochie's heels clicking against the hardwood floor. Probably because she wore the rubber off the heel and too cheap to replace 'em or buy another pair. She's carrying a half glass of wine. I bet she ain't 21 but promised the bartender she'll duck sick 'im later.

Those 2 are up to somethin; I hope they don't think I'm scared. I keep my head up and stare back at 'em. I stop when I'm up on 'em. They're blocking me. I step to the left so I can step around 'em, but the plump one takes a step to her right, blocking me again.

"Excuse me," I say. I don't have time for this shit I'm thinking.

"Excuse me," says the one with the mole, mockingly.

I step right. Then mole hoochie steps to her left.

"Don't know who you think you is," says mole hoochie. "Dissing me."

"What the hell…" I start to say. Then I shake my head. I got too much class for this and can't be messing up my designer dress. They can afford to ruin their flea market shit they're wearing.

"You think you all dat, one of those high society bitches," says the plump one.

I know they're trying to start some shit. Just any shit. Let 'em keep it up. I have somethin' for their asses. I look good and they hatin; I got a man they don't; they hoochie, I'm not; they hos, I'm girlishcious. Need I say more? Shit these bitches probably got a gun or somethin'. They look like gypsy trash I've seen on those trailer park slasher movies.

Let me try this again. When I try to move further to the right of mole hoochie, she throws her red wine on me! Oh no she didn't! I look down at my designer original with my mouth wide open, then back at her. That does it! With my clutch in my left hand, I ball up my right fist and sock her dead in her face! Mole hoochie drops the glass – crash – and falls backwards, holding her face.

The plump one starts swinging but I kick her dead in the crotch, Taebo action. She falls on her back, spread eagle. Mole hoochie regains her balance and comes at me with a knife in her left hand. Memories of my mama the night she was murdered flashes before my eyes. I see the murderer stabbing her – over and over again.

"Not this time you asshole!" I say. "Bitch you're going down!"

47

Hoochies Down

Back from the zone

Darius says, "Hey shawty you cool?"

This ain't daddy's voice. Who is it? I look over my left shoulder to see who. Is Darius holding me? His face is really close to mine looking at me.

"You cool LaTonya?"

Ooo, those hazel eyes of his. What's he yammering about anyway? And why is he holding me like this? Could've sworn I came with AJ. I turn around, facing him. His left arm is still around my waist.

"Let me holla at you," he says.

"Wait, Virgil? Ain't you supposed to be in jail? Why do you wanna holla at me? I ain't TiAnna. Oh. TiAnna's on her way I think."

"You alright. Okay," he says.

It's Darius again. What happened to Virgil? Darius is leading me down the hall; then up the stairs, into a room like office. It has a desk on the left but in back against the wall is a green velvet couch, coffee table and end table with a brass lamp. He leads me over to the couch, where we sit next to each other. I lay my clutch on my lap and start massaging my forehead.

"Ooo my head's foggy and I don't feel right."

I need to close my eyes. I wish the room would stop spinning. Like I'm drunk. I know the bartender didn't put something in my Pepsi.

"Is TiAnna here now? She told me she's comin."

He puts his hand under my chin and turns my face towards his.

"Hey beautiful. You alright now. I gotcha."

"Darius?"

"Yo."

"Okay Darius it's you. Shit. What are we doing?"

"Chilin'."

"Why? Where's AJ?"

"Don't know yo. You need to chill."

"Why? What do you want?"

"For you to be calm. You need to chill."

During the fight

Darius says he arrived at the men's bathroom in time to see me taking off 1 of my heels and wailing it upside the head of 1 hoochie's head! She fell down and I stomped her with my bare foot. She rolled over on her stomach, shielding her head while I kept stomping her.

Darius says someone in the crowd should've stopped it or called security. I saw a crowd of people but I thought they vanished after I hit the 1st hoochie.

"Fake ass niggas," says Darius. "But you was handlin your bizness. But..."

"But what Darius?"

"Well shawty you kept screamin' you killer bitch! Stay away from my mama! You looked lost when I grabbed you."

"Hm," I say. "I don't remember."

Darius is quiet. I bet he thinks I'm wacked y'all.

"You was spankin 'em. Where'd you learn them moves yo."

"My daddy has a black belt. He showed me some self-defense moves a few years ago so I can defend myself. I still practice with him."

"Well he's a damn good teacher. What the fuck happened anyway?"

"They started the shit Darius. I passed 'em on the way to the bathroom. They were gawking at me and stuff. Then when I came out the bathroom them two hoochies walked right up to me! One had a knife!"

"The shit is wacked yo! Don't worry I'll handle them hos."

Hm. I'm smelling alcohol. Where is th...

"Will you look at this shit! All on my designer dress!"

Now I remember the mole hoochie, throwing the glass of red wine at me!

"Ooo! This is why I don't like being around the hip hop scene. There's always problems with these trifling bitches."

"Can't blame the game beautiful. Blame DaMenace for not handling his bitness."

What does Darius mean? And where is AJ anyway?

"The girl in the purple is Uriella, DaMenace's wife."

I know Darius is bull-shittin'. "What do you mean wife?"

"I didn't stutta shawty."

"You know what Darius. Where the hell is AJ? I'm ready to go." I get up but Darius grabs my hand.

"Hold up shawty. We need to talk."

"I'm ready to go Darius."

"Tippy look. Somethin' happened to you for a minute. You was gone yo."

Shit. Darius did notice.

"I don't know what you're talkin' about. I was just mad," I say.

"Girl, you called me Virgil," says Darius.

I never mentioned him to Darius. Repeating what I said about mama, what the hell. I don't remember much from the time I ran into those 2 hos until a few minutes ago when we came in here. I need to straighten this shit up.

"Uh, what's the big deal. I got jumped by 2 bitches."

"Yeah. I know. But you had me worried beautiful."

"So what? You think I'm wacked?"

"Naw. The shit wit' your mama is making you crazy. Shit I remember being really mad when my mama got sick and almost died. The pain was killing me. Girl you are still in pain, but you can't let it break you. You gotta take control yo."

"Yeah I know. Damn Luanne's always insinuating to daddy he needs to commit me. I'm always afraid daddy's gonna send me away."

"That ain't gonna happening, yo."

"What Darius. You gotta a magic wand? What can you do? Shit I feel like I'm by myself in this mess."

"Look shawty, you got me in your corner."

"Reeeeally," I say, looking at him.

"Look here yo. Remember the time we was talkin' about ol' girl I was wit' in LA?"

"Yeeeah." I'm getting really anxious about what Darius is getting ready to say.

"Between me and you shawty, that girl was Luanne. Your step-mama."

48

That's Gangsta

Darius comes clean

"Ha! I knew you knew her, Darius. That's scandalous. Why you trying to hide?"

"I ain't hiding nothin' yo! I had to make sure. So now you know."

"Ooo, I can't wait to tell my daddy."

"Now hollup yo. This gotta be between me and you for now. Otherwise I can't help you."

"My daddy needs to know about his triflin' ass wifey."

"Look shawty. This is serious bitness and could be dangerous. There's more to this than you know."

"What then? Tell me and stop playin'."

"Tippy look. This involves your daddy. Trust me he won't care nothin' 'bout Luanne and her indiscreets. She's got him in checkmate."

"I know all about that Darius. So what."

"Oh do you really?" Darius is looking at me like I really don't know nothing. "You may think you know but don't know the 4-1-1."

"Yes I do," I say. "Luanne was my babysitter and she had an affair with daddy when she was underage. I figured that out long ago."

"Huh. Like I thought. You're not even close. Your daddy's pulling shit right under your nose and I don't like what he's doing. Remind me of my old man."

"So what don't I know?"

"Look beautiful, this ain't the time or place to go into dat. As long as we keep this on the DL, we can smoke out your mama's killer. Isn't that what you really want?"

I'm nodding my head even though my heart is saying something else. I wanna get Luanne really bad. Daddy's been much nicer since she's been gone. It feels like we've been rebuilding our relationship but now Darius is trying to tell me daddy's been up to no good. I knew it. I told Dr. Ryan I suspected somethin'. I wonder if what he knows has to do with what I've been feeling.

"Tippy, you gotta trust me on dis. I gotchu. I gotchu."

"Hey, Tippy are you in there?" AJ's hollering and banging on the door.

Darius looks over at the door briefly then back at me. "Shawty between me and you un-da-stand? We gonna handle this together."

"Alright, alright. I'll trust you for now. But I'm not holding' my mouth forever."

"You won't have to yo. I gotta plan."

AJ storms into the room all wide-eyed, looking all concerned.

"What up girl. I've been worried like hell!" He comes over to me and kneels in front of me. He glances at Darius out of the corner of his eye then says, "Girl you had me worried."

"Nothin' to worry 'bout. She's in good hands," says Darius.

AJ DaMenace wants to say something. He's not pleased that I'm in here with Darius but I can care less. I know he knows damn well what happened. How can he miss this huge red stain on my designer dress? I know it ain't upped and disappeared. I can see it without looking at it and smells stinky – damn alcohol strikes again.

"Worried about me? Paleeze! Should've asked your wifey what happened? Oh yeah, maybe she can't talk. I hear I whooped her ass pretty good."

AJ DaMenace snarls at Darius. "Should've known you was in here putting me on blast. To your advantage no doubt."

"Look man, I ain't the one wit' a wife I can't keep in check. I'm just trying to watch out for my girl yo."

"Yeah I bet. I know what's up D."

"Forget this back and forth shit!" I say.

"It's not like that," AJ says.

I'm not even looking at Darius right now but I bet he's thinking "white boy please."

"So what's it like then?" I say.

"I'd prefer we don't talk in front of company," he says, nodding at Darius.

"Well Darius ain't company but that's not the issue. That skank and her skank friend jumped me and messed up my dress. Have me looking a hot mess. My image is screwed."

"I'll take care of the dress," says AJ DaMenace. "Let's get you out of here."

"That sounds like a plan, but I ain't going with you. Darius can you take me home?"

"Not a problem shawty. I gotchu."

I get up, grab Darius by the hand and stepped around AJ's kneeling ass! The nerve of that white boy. That's what I get for thinking I can crossover. Thank the Big G my twot-twot is still intact.

Looking like a fool

"I bet you set this fuckin' shit in motion didn't you Darius?" AJ's is thinking once they've gone. "You up to no good I know it. You ain't getting away wit' it."

49

Making Moves

November 4, 2012
Miami Beach

Jeremy's hooked already?

"Ooo yeah, that's how I like it. Keep going, yeah like that. Ooo yeah. Woo! Almost. Yeah baby, yeah. Ahhhh. Oh Oh Oh Oh Ohhhhhhh shit! Woo."

"Mmmmm. Been a while huh baby. You was full up."

"I guess you could say that. I ain't been down since me and my girl... never mind. Don't need to talk about dat."

"Good 'cause I'mo make your dick hard again. Make you forget. Now don't this feel good."

"What you tryin to do Stephanie, kill me? No more suckin', no more fuckin'. I gotta get some sleep. Tomorrow's a big day and I need more than an energy drink in the morning."

"Okay den. I'll just have to settle for you wrappin' yo big, strong black arms around me den."

"You sleep?" Stephanie asks Jeremy. He doesn't answer. Hmm got you snoring already, Stephanie's thinking. Dis just too easy. I got big boy as long as turkey baster does its job.

Nov. 5, 2012
A crazy morning in Miami

Jeremy's running late. It's almost Election Day and he knows traffic is worse than ever. And the world is watching. In the news, voters suspect Republicans plan to steal Florida – impede the President from winning the electoral votes. Lucky for him, he's eighteen and still considered an Atlanta resident. He voted for Barack Obama by absentee ballot.

The election though is not Jeremy's main concern. Tonight's game is crucial. As the team's starting quarterback, he's got to make this one count. NFL scouts will be there. The team's back up QB – Lawrence Munson – is pretty damn good and Jeremy plans to give him a run for his money.

Stephanie comes up and grabs him from behind after he pulls on his team jacket. She kisses him in the middle of his back and lays her head on him. She's dreaming of being Mrs. Simms and having a real family for the first time. She knows his love for Tippy is a challenge, but she's up for it.

"Gotta go," says Jeremy.

"I'll be rootin' babe," says Stephanie. She watches Jeremy until he jumps into his Range Rover and drives off.

On his way to practice, Jeremy glances at his cellphone. No more calls from Tippy. In her last message, she told him to go to hell! He wants to call her – tell her why he hasn't called – but he can't. He has to bide his time until Tippy turns 18 and graduates high school. Then she'll be out from under her father. Then I'll tell her everything. I know she'll understand. Then she'll fall into my arms, say how much she loves me and forgives me. She'll move to Miami and be my wife. You better hope that happens, Robert Ellis. If I lose Tippy, you'll pay.

Portland calling

"Who dis?"

"You don't know me, but I know your niece LaTonya. I'm a friend. She needs are help."

"What do you mean our help. Who the fuck is dis and how'd you get this number?"

"My name is Darius. Darius Winston Broussard and I'm real close to her. I thought I'd call you 'cause you her real daddy, right?" The other end is silent.

"Look I don't know what kinda game dis is Darius, if that's your name, but I don't find this amusing."

"Uh look sir. Or can I call you Unc Rae-Rae? Or would you prefer Raymond or Mr. Ellis. I don't want to show any disrespect. Like I say, Tippy and I are close."

"You not answering my question!" Ray yells.

"I know Tippy is your pride and joy and we both want what's best." Darius knows he's playing a dangerous game. But he's done his homework and knows Raymond Ellis is streetwise and would do anything to protect Tippy, which is why he's gotta keep him close. He may come in handy one day.

The word on the streets is Ray Ellis may have ordered the hit on Don Juan. If true, Darius hasn't figured out the connection. He also knows he's walking a fine line and has to be careful not to throw Luanne under the bus.

"I'm listening. So get ta talkin' young fella," says Ray, getting annoyed, knowing if Darius were in his presence he'd jack him up.

"I don't think we should have this discussion on the phone. Can we meet sir? I'm happy to come to where you are?"

"Naw. I'll come to you aw'ight?"

"Okay cool sir," says Darius continuing the cordial act with Ray after calling him out as Tippy's father.

"I plan to be in those parts in the next couple of weeks. No need to tell Tippy. I'll tell her. I hope we have an un-da-standin'."

"Yes sir."

"And look Darius. Tippy's got a lotta friends 24/7. On my end and my brother's. I hope we're clear."

"Enough said sir. I'll wait to hear from you."

"Right." Ray hangs up.

As Darius contemplates on his next move, Raymond Ellis is busy calling around about Darius. In the streets no one knows his real name. Nor all the shit he pulled while gang-bangin', can be traced back to him. He never got busted and has no case.

The leader of his old crew is dead. His other homeys all got killed a few months later. Although Dude's sister didn't finger the rest of her attackers out of fear, she told somebody. The somebody knocked his homeboys off one by one execution style, leaving a body to be found each day and strung up in the neighborhood park. They were hung by the neck, butt-naked, with their hands and feet bound.

Police found a note nailed to their chests, which said, "I'm a rapist atoning for my sins. Next stop hell!"

None of this has come back to haunt Darius. He's glad he had nothin' to do with raping the girl. He couldn't have helped her anyway. Her brother stood right next to him with a gun to his head, threatening to kill him if he didn't take a turn. Darius told Dude, he'd rather die. He wasn't no rapist nor pedophile.

Unc Rae-Rae on snoop

"So nothin'? Airbody got somethin' to hide."

"No Ray. He's legit. Into the music biz. His brother was the one got gunned down in a drive by. The one your niece was involved in."

Ray closes his eyes as a sense of sadness comes over him. He remembers how helpless he felt. He couldn't even be with his daughter to help her through it. Then the thought of TiAnna crosses his mind.

"Okay man," says Ray and hangs up.

He can't shake off feeling uneasy about TiAnna. The last he checked she was struggling with treatment. Then she had a meltdown after the abortion. And now this Darius is calling. His gut tells him to keep a close watch on him.

"It's the right time to take a trip" Ray says talking to himself. "Gotta make my presence known."

Ray's cell phone rings from a familiar number. "How's she doing?"

"It's a really good day Mr. Ellis. She opened her eyes," says the voice on the other end.

Ray closes his eyes tight, letting the tears fall fast and furious. He's waited a long time for this day – 9 years. He can breathe again, live again and love again.

50

Almost Home

Nov. 6, 2012
Rehab outside Atlanta
"Bebe`caliente. ¡Cómo te sientes?"
"Ready now."
"Okay bebè. Midnight express."
"¡Gracias! Te amo."
"Te amo. Espero estes bien. I'll be in touch."

Nov. 7, 2012
Early evening in Council Crest
I'm certainly glad the election is over. We got President Obama for another 4 years thank the Big G. Glad he's doing something right for a change. Daddy is happy too. I thought last night he was gonna bust waiting for the results. When it was over, he tears-up but mans-up quick.

"Now you see, that's what them damn Republicans get," daddy says. "They played dirty; tried to keep black folks from voting; talked about women like a dog; told the Latinos to self-deport; the Muslims to kill themselves; gays to go to hell and now they're blaming their boy Romney. Huh, they threw away $400 million to buy people's votes and got nothing. Could have put the money to good use but noooo, greed took over! But we the people told 'em to shove it up their asses! And go to hell Fox News! I'm surprised those billionaires didn't beat the shit out of Karl Rove for stealing their money."

Daddy can barely breathe, he's so excited. "We have to protect the president's legacy. These racists aren't gonna sleep until they succeed in destroying him and his family. Huh. Now some of them racist states, including this one wants to succeed from the union. What bullshit! We gotta be ready to fight back when the time comes."

Daddy also doesn't like black folks being ignored. Now the Republicans are harping about how to appeal to Latinos but say nothing about black people – they know we ain't stupid. We had a greater turn out than in 2008 despite trying to keep us down. Few news stations except for MSNBC are talking about it. Most everyone else is ignoring black people – again. As if we don't count.

Daddy says he hopes the Latinos don't get fooled by those damn Republicans. All they care about is building a power structure to turn us into slave labor. What daddy says reminds me of the movie the Hunger Games. I hope it never happens. If so, I'll be one of the ones, along with daddy, getting thrown into those concentrations camps they keep talking about on the internet. Like daddy I ain't bending.

I know my grandparents are pissed. I wonder what they're doing anyway. Since reconnecting, we've been communicating through email. We use a private account Unc Rae-Rae set up. You need a password to access it – in case daddy gets a hold of my phone – with "ATLgo.gp" for Atlanta grandparents Oliver God's people.

Unc Rae-Rae doesn't like to use email.

"I prefer to reach out and touch someone," he says.

My uncle doesn't trust putting private bizness on email regardless of how secure they say it is. He doesn't believe it. He's also leery about phones, so he tries not to handle important stuff that way either.

I've been waiting for Darius to finish what he started to tell me on Saturday. But he's in L.A. He left on Sunday and will be back late tonight. He's been meeting with record company executives. about working with some of their artists on beats and lyrics. Looks like things are moving along for Darius. I'm glad given what he's been through.

Meanwhile, I'd lost interest in attending the Jefferson Dancers' performance tonight with daddy 'cause of what Darius told me. But he says be cool. I will for now. Fortunately, daddy and me are still getting along thanks to Luanne being in Atlanta. Darius says I can count on her staying out of my way.

5:20 p.m.
Running on time
The Hughes' live off of 17th and Northeast Knott in the Irvington neighborhood where there's lots of older style Portland stucco and brick homes. A few blocks up there are a group of historical landmarked homes with owners who host an annual tour of their residences. Many of the larger homes, house some of Portland's affluent families. A prominent judge and city council member live in the area, including doctors and CEOs.

Daddy says some of the home prices go to upwards of a million plus. From what I've seen so far in Portland, you don't get much space for the prices their asking. Like in Atlanta where folks can buy an average 5,000 to 10,000 square-foot home for next to nothin'; some around $500,000, depending on the area.

Since leaving Druid Hills – mama and daddy's 100,000 square-foot house with three hundred acres – we've settled for smaller spaces. Like our Stone Hill house was only 10,000 square feet – 20 acres. And our house in Council Crest is the smallest with barely 10 acres.

In the Portland house, I feel cramped even though out of the 6 bedrooms we have, we only occupy 5. I talked daddy into letting me turn one of the vacant rooms into a TV room for me. Just in case I ever make enough friends to invite over. It does make the north side of the house seem more inhabitable. I'm the only one on my end. On the other side of the stairs – the south side – is Daddy and the 2 brats' bedrooms. It's nice I don't have to share space with them.

Such is life when your daddy marries poor trash, who thinks manufactured homes "are to die for." She toured a couple back home and wanted daddy to purchase this one out near Buford. Daddy told her she'd be living there by herself. Gotta give daddy credit for not allowing her to destroy this house with her design ideas.

We arrive at the Hughes' with 5 minutes to spare. Daddy believes in being punctual. "I don't go for the 5-minute leeway rule," says daddy. "As far as I'm concerned, you're still late!"

Daddy parks on the street directly in front of the Hughes updated home. The 2-story house with rustic siding, sits on top a small hill like many of the houses I've seen. You have a choice of walking up the driveway or the 10 cement steps connected to the pathway. Tall bushes cautiously cover the house on both sides.

On top of the roof is a chimney stack set behind a peek-a-boo window. The kinda window I always see on top of big houses in scary movies. The ghosts hide there, spying on unsuspecting tenants and guests. I'm glad in the real world I've never been privy to "haints" like daddy calls 'em. Not even mama's ghost. She did use to show up in my dreams after she died. Up to when I was around 12. Then she stopped. Probably 'cause I was dealing much better with her loss.

Inside it's warm and cozy. The small entry has a staircase off to the right. At the top the stairs connect to a 5-foot banister on the left.

The dark cherry wood floors match the staircase rail and six-inch siding, traveling around the bottom of the brilliantly, light rust colored walls. This same pattern is seen throughout the house. The Hughes decided to maintain the character of the old fashion interior from when the house was first built in 1906.

After initial introductions, we sit around the big wood fire place before Mrs. Hughes calls us in for dinner. Debra, the Hughes daughter, the 1 who's part of tonight's performance, is tall and skinny like a ballerina and keeps her hair in shoulder length Rasta braids. She has the face for it and she looks like her mama. Both mama and daughter have perfect oval shaped heads with high cheek bones, barely-there eyebrows and really dark healthy-looking skin – it ain't ashy – LOL. They have these noses like baby pig snouts, small brown eyes and round lips.

They're both beautiful women who have the greatest smiles. I can tell they're really close like me and mama were.

The Hughes oldest is in college. Terrance is a freshman at Howard University planning to study law. His goal is to be a defense attorney for the underdogs. Mrs. Hughes says she's proud of his decision. Mr. Hughes thinks he should think about making money first.

"Shoot where is he going to live when he practices law? With us?" says Larry Hughes. "He won't be able to live nowhere else – he'll be broke. We already have to pay his law school bills."

Time for a home cooked meal

But first, Mr. Hughes leads grace, which was short and sweet. At some black Christian dinner tables grace becomes a sermon. The food's cold by the time you eat.

We pass around platters of food, serving ourselves a choice of – roast beef, salmon, crab cakes, rice pilaf, garlic mashed potatoes, sweet potatoes, fresh mustard greens, string beans and rolls – phew! Mrs. Hughes already warned us to save room for the peach cobbler.

If I don't know you, I won't say a whole lot right at first. Debra and her mama do most of the talking among the 3 of us. I answer questions when they ask me.

Brittany and Jayden are behaving and haven't said much since their mama's been gone. At least they got table manners. Secretly, I'm always wishing daddy would just send 'em on to Atlanta with Luanne. Oh well. C'est la vie.

Daddy is in deep conversation with Mr. Hughes about some business interest. Mr. Hughes is able to multitask 'cause he weighs-in on our discussion, then turns his attention back dad without missing a beat. Like when Debra spoke about her dream to be a professional dancer. He jokingly says, "Maybe she'll make a couple dollars and can give one to her brother."

But then he says, "Dancers don't make much either. Dancing's not a career where there's a lot of opportunity. Good thing we bought a big house. I can forget about retiring."

Daddy chuckles but doesn't comment. He knows LaTonya Ellis won't be a burden. Mama left me a big trust fund.

Debra tells me Jefferson High School is predominately black. She says she's the only Jefferson Dancer to attend Jefferson. The mostly white kids attend other schools and its always been that way. Kids in the group have no desire to attend Jefferson but respect the dance team. It has a great reputation and a great start for kids interested in professional dancing as a career. Debra also says they're supposed to change this by 2015. Anyone interested in the dance team and dance program there, will have to enroll at Jefferson fulltime. Except they may "grandfather" those already in the program.

"Hmm. Sounds like to me like the white kids think they're too good to go to school with black folks," I say.

"I don't believe that's totally correct, even though there may be some truth in it," Larry Hughes says. "Having a history of being a black school means the school doesn't get the same attention and quality of teaching as with the other schools. This is generally the case in most inner cities. The current supporters are doing their best to change the perception. The community surrounding Jefferson is now largely white so it will change sooner than later."

Jefferson High is a college preparatory school for kids, who may have barriers to a college education. The school is across the street from Portland Community College on northeast Killingsworth, which is where many of the students may attend once they leave Jeff. But they have options to attend 4-year universities in Oregon; some plan to offer full paid tuition for eligible students.

Larry Hughes says the district should've considered turning Jefferson High into a healthcare prep school or at least made it a significant part of the curriculum. Healthcare is supposed to be a growing field and the industry is having a hard time filling certain types of jobs, like nurses and technicians. The healthcare industry also lacks people of color. He says Legacy Emanuel is in the Jefferson neighborhood.

"Legacy could've adopted or sponsored the school," says Larry Hughes. "But with these teachers' unions, they wouldn't have allowed it. They don't like business influence even though kids got to find jobs."

"You know having business involved in public schools makes too much sense," says daddy. "Teachers do a lot of political posturing too."

Daddy and Larry Hughes talk business through the rest of dinner. But me, Debra and her mama find other things to talk about like our feelings about Portland. Like me, they miss home and have found this black community – especially the ones born and raised or who've been living here for a long time – cliquish. Debra did say she's managed to make a few friends at Jeff. The kids have been pretty friendly.

At least I'm not alone in my thinking. Given how small the Portland black community is, you'd think they'd be more welcoming. Maybe I'd have a better experience at Jeff. But daddy wouldn't let me go there anyway 'cause of my GPA and career objective.

I thought it would never end

The performance is over – finally – and I'm glad as hell. To me, it was booorrring, but Debra was the star; she's a good dancer. As for the rest of the dancers, I wasn't feeling 'em. I am use to seeing more blacks on stage.

We stick around to congratulate her on a job well done. She's cheesing big time. The audience did give her a standing ovation.

Time to say our good-byes.

I say to Debra, "Looking forward to staying in touch."
She says, "Same here."

Can I get some peace?

"What AJ! What! I wish you'd stop blowing up my phone! Shit! I gotta go to school in the morning!"

"Well you won't talk to me Tippy. Let me explain."

"Are you married or not to hoochie bitch, AJ?"

"We're not together. It wasn't even a real marriage. I filed for divorce after 3 months because she lied about being pregnant."

"Ha! So, you gotta a wifey but you didn't think to tell me. So instead I have to find out from your bitch and her pawtner trying to jump me and trashing my one-of-a-kind designer dress."

"Wow girl. What's up with you and your designer dress shit? Yeah, I'm mad as hell she came at you. It shouldn't have happened. But you can bet it won't happen again."

"Look DaMenace I don't expect you to understand, given how trifling your wifey is. I see you ain't use to someone like me with class. If you were, you wouldn't be dissin' on my designer dress. Bottom line, you disrespected me by not saying anything."

"Girl you know what? You and my soon-to-be ex have more in common than you know. You both have big-ass mouths, flapping in the wind over bullshit!"

Oh know this white boy didn't just compare me to his skank ho. And he thinks what happened is just bullshit?

"Look white boy, I don't know who the hell you think you talkin' to, but you can kiss my ass!" I say. Then I hang up the phone.

The scene reminds me of my last words to Jeremy. Shit! This wanting to give up my twot-twot ain't working at all. Not at all.

After hanging up the phone with Tippy, AJ DaMenace turns on the stereo and pulls out his marijuana stash underneath the baseboard by the stereo. He lights an already rolled swisher, takes a huge hit and holds it in. He hits it a couple of times until he relaxes; then kicks his feet up and stretches out on the couch with his hands behind his head. He smiles when he thinks of Tippy's last words.

"I wouldn't mind kissin' your pretty ass LaTonya. I ain't through whichu yet."

Who the hell is calling now?

Better not be AJ DaMenace trying to call me from a private number! Trying to trick me into answering his call!

"Who is this?"

"Hey Tippy it's me."

"TiAnna? Where are you?"

"I'm outside your gate. Please don't tell your daddy I'm here."

51

Busta Ain't Rhyming

Nov. 7, 2012
Earlier in Conyers, GA

"Mama you gon' be fine. Me and Joshua's tess be back anytime. Ya know one a us will match."

Joshua nods his head. He knows his sister is scared but kidney transplants are common. If they are a match, Cheri won't have to go on a list. Her doctors say siblings and children are probable donors.

For years now, Cheri's gone back to using her real name rather than her street name Cherry.

Until Cheri receives a transplant, she has to succumb to kidney dialysis. Today turns out to be one of her toughest days because of having to also battle a viral infection. The doctors gave her antibiotics and said if she's not better in a couple of days, they'd admit her as an inpatient. Cheri wants no part of a hospital and isn't looking forward to the month-long stay she will have to endure after the transplant.

"I don't like hospitals," says Cheri.

"Don't worry mama. I'll be right here," says Luanne, holding her mother's hand.

She looks at her uncle Joshua whose been sitting quietly for the past few minutes. He's thinking about Luanne's request. He agrees to go to Portland and pick up some more of her things and check on the kids for her.

Joshua laughs to himself "I like kids."

11:30p.m.
Back in Portland

Darius returned about an hour ago. He's been thinking a lot about Tippy, who's anxious about what he has to say, but he wants to talk to her uncle first. Whatever he plans to say has to fit into his plan.

He thinks about calling her. He looks at his watch. It's late. "She's asleep. I keep forgetting she's still in high school."

For November the weather in Portland ain't bad and Darius thinks it's a great night to be out. He usually takes walks when he has a lot on his mind.

He turns the corner on 7th and Prescott and walks down to the corner store. In the distance, he sees a familiar face – Buster!

"I ain't seen the nigga since I've been lookin'."

Buster doesn't see Darius until he's right up on him.

"What up, Messiah? Thought you'd be at the hop on Saturday. All the big producers were there."

"Yeah I hear. I've been out of town."

"Hm. Outta town or hidin' man?"

"Whatchu mean hidin'. What I gotta hide for Darius?"

"I've been askin' around Messiah. We need to talk."

"Look maybe later man. I gotta run som'in to my girl. She's pissing a bitch for dis bud. "

"Sheee-it. Don't I know women. Say can you run me home? Then we can plan to hook up later this week," says Darius, using a fake smile.

Messiah hesitates. He knows it's a bad idea to run Darius anywhere. But he also doesn't want Darius to get the impression he's trying to avoid him – even though he is.

"A'ight den?"

Darius hops into the passenger seat of Buster the Messiah's old '82 350SL Mercedes. Buster drives up Alberta and makes a right on 15th. Darius is quiet until they reach his house. Buster pulls over to the left curb to let Darius out and glances at the driveway where Jerome was gunned down.

"Hard to believe bro is gon'," says Darius.

"Yeah," says Buster without looking at Darius. "Look man I got ta…"

"You had my brother killed," says Darius.

"Naw man. I know that's what you heard, but it wa'ent me."

"Who den Buster? And you better come clean. I got folks on standby. I hope your last words to your mama, sister and girl was nice."

"It's like dat huh. You just don't know."

"Well then tell me somethin' Messiah. And don't try no bullshit. I have guardian angels."

Right when he says that, 2 black dudes appear from outta nowhere and come up to Buster's car. 1 stands in front and the other on the driver's side. Both have their jackets open touting guns tucked on the side of their pant waist.

"Come on man, it wa'ent me."

"Get to talkin' den."

"Man, it wa'ent my doing. She said she wanted to talk to him. Just talk to 'im. Says the family wouldn't put her in touch. She asked me to bring him outside."

"What the fuck man, who she who."

"Aw Darius man. You ain't gon' believe me man."

"I'm 'bout done with this shit B…"

"Yo mama Darius! Yo mama had your brother killed!"

52

Hey la BFF's Back

The tears are rolling

"I can't believe you're here T!"

"Yeah, yeah stop with the boohooin'. Make me wanna cry but I can't. They took my soul Tippy."

TiAnna breaks free of Tippy's hug, takes her coat off and lays it across the empty chair opposite Tippy's bed.

"Girl you and these fuchsia colored walls. Even your bedroom furniture is fuchsia – nightstand, dresser, bed headboard and all – whew! How'd you manage?"

"I special ordered it from Jacob Maroni in New York. Me and Jeremy strolled through there when we visited Manhattan. They have modern, colorful and eclectic household furniture."

"You know Tip. I've always liked your table lamp and floor length one. It amazes we how they made the statues look like you, turn 'em into lamp posts, using the lamp shades as hats. At least the statue is wearing a fitted cream dress and hat. I'da been fuchsia dizzy."

"Ha! Yeah. I know. I tried to be careful on how much fuchsia to put in here. So, I opted to have the fireplace, bedspread, curtains and throw rugs match the color of the statue. The cream stucco ceilings and cream and black marble floors work too. You know I got to thinking, if I add any more colors it would look a hot mess like the Stone Mountain House."

"Ooo Tip, you ain't never lied. Shameful what yo step-mama did to the Stone Mountain house!"

"Alright T. Don't start."

"Okay, I'll let you alone. Girl, let me get out of these clothes. Put on somethin' comfy. Where's your dad? You didn't tell him, did you?"

"No. Of course not. He's out meeting a friend. Probably Larry Hughes. How'd you get here? When did they let you go?"

"Earlier today," says TiAnna.

"Virgil made arrangements for me to come."

"Virgil? He's out?"

"Naw. He's still awaiting trial. They want him to cop a plea but he's refusing. You know how stubborn he can be."

"So how did…"

"Virgil has hookups. He wants me to be okay."

"Alrighty then. I won't ask questions either. I'm just glad you're here so we can do this together."

"Come on Tippy enough with the tears okay. I can't take the feeling sorry for me shit."

"Sorry T that's not my intention. I'm just happy to see you. You know you're my girl."

"Yeah you my girl too, Tip. But you gotta know, I'm not the same person you once knew. What I went through changed me. No matter what you say or anyone else says, you can't change what happened to me."

"I know I can't change it T. But I do know what pain feels like. My pain may be for a different reason but it's pain nonetheless."

"I know, I know Tip. Remember my mama's gone now too. So I'm feeling the same pain of never being able to see her again. But Tip, this other pain is deep. The things they did to me. I was raped and raped. Tip I was still a virgin. They took my virginity and all I can remember is being in so much pain and shame. It wasn't supposed to be like this."

"Tip, you know how we use to romanticize about our first time? Well it won't be like that for me. I was nothing but a fucking bag for every filthy stinking man who wanted to fuck a young girl. It didn't matter what I said to him. Hmm. I even tried to appeal to their sense of dignity. You know maybe they had a daughter or something. You know Tip they didn't care. They wanted me even more. I kept thinking maybe I'm saving their daughters in case they daddy wanted to fuck 'em. I tried to make it all better but it was never better. The only good thing is the drugs they gave me. And you know Tip? While I was in rehab, all I could think of is how to get a fix."

"T you've always been there for me. It's my turn. We'll do what it takes to get you through this – together."

TiAnna sits quietly holding her head down.

Then she says, "I had to get an abortion Tip. I was 6 weeks pregnant. None of 'em would use condoms. I couldn't bring myself to having a baby fathered by one of several men who either raped me or paid Don Juan to sexually abuse me. Now I have to wait 6 months Tip to see if I have aids or somethin'. I already had an STD."

"Tip, tell me how we gonna do this? How am I going to ever be able to live my life without fear? How am I ever gonna to love again? Especially since I hate myself. I hate my daddy. And I still hate my mom even though she died because of all of this. She was raped too Tippy at 14 by the lawn maintenance guy who worked for her parents. You can't trust no damn body. Nobody can keep you safe. So you gotta do it yourself."

"Guess what T? I say, changing the subject. "I ended up going to this Buddhist meeting. Remember the chant Tina Turner was doing in the movie about her and Ike? You know, Nam-Myho-Renge-Kyo."

"Ha! My friend the architectural designer Buddha," says TiAnna, grinning and shaking her head.

"Notta T. I don't think I'd be a Buddha even though my friend Shonny's mama says we're all Bodhisattvas who can become Buddha. But every now and then I say those words and it makes me start laughing. Why don't you say it? Maybe it'll make you laugh."

"Girl, I don't think so. But thanks Tip and thanks for not rubbing God in my face. Daddy had the nerve to send Reverend Jacob to visit after I told daddy I never wanted to see him again. It was right after my abortion too Tip. I ended up cussing him out when he said all of what happened to me was God's plan. God had something special for me to do. All bullshit. Ooo it makes me mad every time I think of his ass and his God. I tol' 'im Tip I want no part of a God who let a bunch of nasty men fuck me, sodomize me and make me suck their nasty ass dicks. Are you fuckin' kidding me? I said to the sorry bastard!"

"I'm feelin' you girl. The Big G and me ain't on good terms lately. I've been questioning my relationship with him a lot. Carole, Shonny's mama did say I can't blame God. But it's easy for me to do right now."

"I thought she's Buddhist. Why she talkin about God?" says TiAnna.

"Carole says everyone has their own idea about what God is. And it's not necessarily the Christian point of view. She believes God or the universe is within everyone. Not up in the sky in some heaven far away," I say.

"Well he can stay up in the clouds," says TiAnna. "Just leave me the fuck alone. He's done enough for me thank you!"

"Why don't you get some sleep. I gotta go to school tomorrow but you can hang out up here until I get back. Daddy and the twins will be gone all day too. You'll have free reign of the house. We'll talk tomorrow about when to tell daddy. He's been pretty cool lately and really did his best to find you."

"I know I heard Tip. And your uncle helped. I'm grateful, but we'll see how I'm feelin' okay? I know I can't hide out up here forever."

"Meanwhile I got you covered. Do you need me to bring you anything T?"

"Um. How about a joint and a beer, ha!"

"For real T if you want a joint, I know I can find one tomorrow. Daddy only keeps the hard stuff like brandy, scotch..."

"Naw girl. I'm just foolin' witchu," says TiAnna.

I'm relieved. I'd do anything for my BFF, if it would make her feel better. But I know I gotta be careful. Don Juan hooked my girl on smack. She's always loved weed, which should be okay. Weed didn't make her crazy.

"Nam-Myho-Renge-Kyo. Goodnight Buddha. Ha!" says TiAnna.

"Back at you Buddha," I say.

I'm glad to see my friend smile even though I know that's gonna change. I just hope not for a while.

53

Say It Ain't So

In Conyers

Luanne is glad her uncle Joshua agreed to go to Portland for her. She'd go herself but Darius insisted she stay away from Portland for a while.

"My girl hates you fo reals yo. I don't want her to snap on your ass!"

Luanne feels the same way about Tippy. She's hated the spoiled brat since she first met her. And she's glad she's been able to manipulate Robby's feelings.

Luanne has also witnessed Tippy's rage and thinks perhaps it's getting worse. Darius got upset when she mentioned Robert Ellis was close to committing Tippy several times. Luanne wasn't responsible for his actions, but Darius threatened her anyway.

"If anything happens to my girl, I'll make both y'all lives a living hell yo!"

Luanne knows Darius intentions toward Tippy's is about money. But she also gets the impression he has feelings for her. And she'd be happy if Darius found someone he could really love and would love him back. But why did it have to be her spoiled crazy-ass stepdaughter?

Shoot you a whole new Darius. So I'mo have ta watchu.

Despite his threats, Luanne knows they have a bond. Her body tingles when she's close to him or thinks of him; the same feeling she felt when they were together before. Her Darius has swagger but she's drawn to his street smarts and his drive to go after what he wants like her. Luanne's also seen the loving side of Darius like when he speaks about his brother Jerome. She can see the hurt in his eyes.

Luanne's cellphone rings.

It's the hospital.

"Dis Luanne."

"Hello Luanne. This is Dr. Staplemeyer from Atlanta General. We have the results of your test."

Luanne holds her breath, hoping it's good news.

"Luanne I'm sorry to say but you are not a match."

Luanne crunches her forehead, dropping her mouth wide open.

"Wha ya mean? I'm her daughter, why not."

"Uh Luanne, I don't know how to say this but you have an entirely different blood type. Your blood type is AB negative. Because it's so rare your parents would have to be AB negative."

"What you tryin' da tell me docta," she says.

"Luanne, we ran your tests 3 times. Including re-ran your swab sample. I'm sorry Luanne but your DNA just doesn't match your mother's. You're not your mother's biological child."

Nov. 8, 2012

12:05 a.m. Portland

Darius let Buster go with a warning, "If I find out ya lyin' I'm comin' after you and yours yo!"

Darius plops down on the top porch step of his house; his eyes focused in front of him, arms dangling between his legs. He's smiling to himself – proud about being prepared like tonight. He has his boys

— he met when he first got back from L.A. – on speed dial. They live down the block, running a quiet drug operation, supplying street pushers.

Darius takes in a deep breath and goes inside.

"Is that you Dari?" a voice says once he's near the living room.

"Mama please don't call me dat yo! I ain't no baby; no punk neither!" Darius says, once he's in the back room standing in front of his mother.

Jill sits on the loveseat with her feet kicked up on the coffee table.

"Well you still my baby Dari."

"Why you sitting in the dark mama. What you been up to?"

He reaches over and turns on the lamp next to her. Jill blinks her eyes and holds her arm up over her face, shielding it from the light.

"Why it gotta be so damn bright Dari."

"Mama look at me!"

But Jill keeps her face covered. Darius grabs her arm, pushing it down away from her face.

"Look at me yo!"

Jill looks at Darius. He can tell by her sluggish red eyes she's high.

"Dammit mama, you just got out of rehab!"

Darius feels like pissing bullets. Since moving back from L.A., he's had to face a drug-addicted mother, who he found passed out on the bathroom floor with a crack pipe lying next to her. She was breathing, but he couldn't wake her so he called 9-1-1. Jill was taken by ambulance to the county hospital where she stayed in detox for a couple of days.

Darius looks down at his mother not knowing whether to be angry or sad. Jill's crack addiction has ruined her life. Her once beautiful looks are gone. No one would believe she was a woman who attracted lots of attention because of her once Miss America looks.

The Jill today is a hot mess! Her now drooping face has rapidly aged, sprouting deep wrinkles and puffy eyes, which make her look 60 rather than barely 40. Her weight loss is extreme, brought on by a poor diet and lots of coffee. Along with smoking crack, Jill chain smokes causing an irregular cough. Doctors say is a sign of early emphysema.

Darius moved his mother into the Prescott house with a condition she'd stay clean. In the past 2 months, Jill's been in rehab twice.

"Don't look at me like that Dari. I can't stand it."

"Mama you promised yo! I told you, I ain't having none of dat shit here! You gotta get straight! You my mama but you a grown ass woman!"

"You got your damn nerve Dari! All I've done for you! You even got money now!"

Darius is suddenly reminded about his conversation with Buster.

"What the fuck are you talkin about mama!"

"Aw stop it Dari. You know your uncle says you was outta there when you turn 18. What were you gonna do? Go back to the streets? Fuck around get yourself killed? Aw Dari. Your brother wants you to have the best of... aw Dari. You good boy." Jill starts crying.

"Damn mama. You can't be saying what I think yo. Not my brother."

"Wait Dari."

"I ain't yo motherfuckin' Dari, mama!"

Darius reaches into his pocket and pulls out a wad of cash.

"Here! Dis what you wont yo!"

Darius holds the money in front of his mother's face; then drops it on her lap.

"Stop pretending you give a damn about me. You ain't gave a damn since you been on that shit yo!"

Darius has his answer – his own mother killed his brother! His eyes moisten as he allows his anger to swell.

"I wont you da fuck out of my house by tomorrow mama! I'll move you anywhere, you want but not here! I'll even give yo ass some money! Den you on ya own, yo. Let me get outta here before I do somethin' I'll regret yo!"

Darius reaches down, picks up the coffee table, and throws it across the room hitting the wall right below the hanging big screen television. Then turns and walks out.

"Please don't go Dari. You all I got. I'm sorry Dari."

Darius heads directly to the front door. Once there he opens it. To his surprise Five-0 is standing there with Detective Brannigan, the lead detective investigating Jerome's murder.

"Hello there Darius," says Detective Brannigan. "We're here to see your mother."

9:30 a.m.

Ooo snap! Someone's here. Who is it? Tip said I'd have the house to myself. I guess I won't be going downstairs yet. Let me back away from these steps. Whoever it is knows the alarm code. Shit. I think he's coming this way? No. The footsteps are fading. Phew! Good thing Tip and them got hardwood floors so I can hear what's going on. Hm. It's quiet. Wha..

Uh-oh! Here he comes whistling that damn tune? I know… Dang! Let me get my ass back to Tippy's room. I hope whoever it is can't see me peeping through this cracked door. But I gotta see who it is.

OMG who is he? As long as I've known Mr. Ellis, he's never whistled. Ooo. He's almost to the top of the stairs I think… Ooo snap! It's a familiar white man? This ain't good. I back away from the door.

Dang whose cell phone? Oh. Michael Jackson's "Bad" ringtone. Not mines. Phew. Oh wait. Is my cellphone on? Okay he's answering.

"Yello. This is Joshua."

54

No Means No!

November 8, 2012
Miami surprise

When Jeremy says to Stephanie from the shower, "Say babe get the door for me will ya!"

She runs to the door knowing, Jeremy's expecting 1 of his home boys from Atlanta. When she opens the door, she's surprised to see a familiar face.

Stephanie has to play this off so she won't risk being exposed. Maybe he won't recognize her. After all, she changed her appearance – her hair color is different and really short. She's also wearing green contacts and she had her nose done. She always hated her wide nose so she had it thinned. And she no longer puts Botox in her lips, making them look thinner.

Finally, Damon speaks, "What up Chili."

Upstairs in Tippy's room

Breathe T. Gotta turn off my phone before it rings.

Okay which suitcase? This one. Good my satchel's still intact with all the right stuff. Ooo I'm tempted to shoot up right now. I brought some just in case I couldn't hang. This Joshua shit is making me wanna zone out. I'm scared shitless.

Girl stop! Stay focused! You know the damn john is wacked! Yeah. You're the one. I remember now. I thought I could appeal to your sense of decency. But instead you rambled on about "the blacker the berry the sweeter the juice. You sick bastard! You even told me you had, had your way with a 14-year-old black girl. When you were a landscaper for her family. You said she loved how you laid it on her. When you were done with me, I'd be hollering for more just like she did. Now I know she was my mother you son-of-a-bitch! Yeah. You were brutal. I ended up hollerin' all right. But because you started beating me with your belt. Calling me your little black slave. Don Juan had to throw you out – ah-ha! Here's my special present from Virgil. Suzy, you are so pretty but I know you'll do the trick.

Only minutes have passed

Why is it so quiet? Where's the bastard! Maybe I should go and find him. Make him pay for what he did to me and my mom. Do what the police should have.

"I thought I heard someone. Hey miss."

Okay girl. Breathe. He's behind you over by the door. Don't turn around. He'll recognize you. I'll just wait until…

"Hey don't you hear me talking to you? Are your deaf or what. Ha. All the better for me. You sure look good from behind. I can only imagine what you look like. A black beauty I'm guessing."

He's coming. Closer, closer…

"Hey you!"

I turn around quickly and…

"Bam motherfucka! How do you like my Suzy!"

"Awk!!! You black bit.."

"Get 'im Suzy. Go Suzy go!"

Huh! The bigger they are, the harder they fall. You old fat slimy motherfucka! Didn't know what hit you did you? Yeah. Ooo wait. Missed a spot. Bam! Yeah. Gotta remember to thank Virgil again for having his friend drive me out here. Otherwise I wouldn't have been able to bring all these goodies like Suzy.

10 minutes later

"I think I'll take Suzy back now," says TiAnna as she pulls the blade from Joshua's crotch. "Ooo. Lots a pretty red flowing everywhere! Say fella, don't move. I'll be right back. Oh ha! You can't. I'll deal with you later then. After I take my shower and clean up a few things. Thanks to you I don't think I'll be needing my goody stash. I feel vindicated. You can't hurt me or nobody else!"

Oops. Tippy's callin'.

"T where you been?"

"I was downstairs getting somethin' to eat Tip."

"Oh okay. I was getting ready to come home."

"Yeah I know. No need to worry Tip."

"I called to tell you my friend Darius will be by shortly. I told him to check on you. He has a swisher for you."

"Oh girl. Not necessary. I'm cool."

"I gave him the code to get through the gate."

"Gee Tip you trust him like dat?"

"Yeah. He's cool. And he's helping me out. You can trust him. I'll tell you about it later."

"Okay Tip, I better get dressed before he get here."

"Okay T, see you about 4ish."

TiAnna hurriedly takes off her bloody clothes, throws them on top of Joshua's body. Runs into the bathroom to take a quick shower.

She's dressed and ready when the doorbell rings. TiAnna quickly glances over at Joshua's bloody corpse on her way to answer it.

"What up TiAnna I'm Darius."

He extends his hand. TiAnna nods, shakes it and steps back to let him in.

"Say are you a'ight?" Darius says.

TiAnna's feeling of serenity turns to panic.

"Um, I... Tippy's gonna hate me. She can't hate me. I didn't mean..."

Darius grabs TiAnna as she falls into his arms. She's shaking and crying uncontrollably.

She says, "I didn't know what to do. I couldn't let him hurt me again. He hurt my mama. Ooo, I just.."

"Hey hol'up. Come on. You among friends girl. Tippy's my family, so you my family."

TiAnna looks into Darius eyes, pleading for his help without saying anything. Can she trust him? Or would he call the police. If he did, it be over for her. She'd lose her friend. But it was all worth it. Joshua's dead.

She then grabs Darius's hand, "Can I show you somethin'."

Darius nods. He sees how scared and confused TiAnna looks, hoping she doesn't go crazy like Tippy. Darius is also amazed at how similar the 2 of them look.

"Hm? She reminds me of Tippy. Her face is shaped like Tippy's; she's got the same eyes, nose and mouth. Damn they could be sisters."

Darius follows TiAnna upstairs. She pauses when she gets to the door of Tippy's room.

Before opening it she attempts to explain, "Ah Darius I, I... ha, had to." Rather than continue she opens the room door and walks in with Darius close behind her.

Inside he sees a bloody dead body in the middle of the floor.

"Aw man. Girl what did you do?" Darius rubs the back of his head. She's wacked too. Her and Tippy gotta be related.

TiAnna holds her head down trying to show remorse. But deep down she could give a damn. "I'll understand if you call the police."

Darius scratches the back of his head. "Naw. Tippy would never forgive me if I turn you in. The motherfucka wa'ent nothin' but a rapist anyway. I'da killed 'im too."

"Look I'll take care of dis. We ain't gotta tell nobody. Not even Tippy. This would freak her out and she'd feel bad she wa'ent here. Un-da-stand?"

TiAnna nods.

Darius pulls out his cellphone, hits send. The line on the other end picks up, Darius says, "Say, I need Spic and Span and Mr. Clean."

55

U Don't Know Me

Miami reveals

Stephanie's trying to play it cool but she's nervous as hell. She even tried to change up on her infamous British accent and went back to using more ghetto slang. But it's been hard to adjust. Jeremy prefers her British speak over her ghetto girl act.

"Naw baby, I'm afraid you got the wrong girl."

"Huh. I swear you look like this girl I knew back in ATL."

"She musta been some girl den."

"Ha! Yeah. She gave the best lap dances among other things."

Damon plays along, but he knows Stephanie is not who she says. She's Chili, the stripper, he met at a bachelor party a couple of years ago. Jeremy wasn't there, so he knows his buddy wouldn't be with somebody like her. Jeremy likes his women clean. Damon's thinkin' either he doesn't know or does and he's down about Tippy.

"Hey D," Jeremy says, walking in from the back with his robe on.

"Wassup my nigga," Damon says, giving Jeremy a high-5.

"You know I'm down here representin' D."

"True dat. True dat. I know they hatin'. Specially Mr. sideline number ten. He waitin' to get in but you killin 'em, J."

"Ha. True dat, D."

For the past few weeks Jeremy has stayed true to the game. He's made several touchdowns and has come on strong as the new quarterback this year. The industry is buzzing about Jeremy Simms.

Stephanie's happy too. Her plan has been working. Her and Jeremy are getting closer by the day. The more she fucks him, the more he stops missing Tippy. But now Damon's here. The Damon from her past. The Damon she gave "head" to and all of his friends the night of the party. Stephanie knows Damon didn't buy her story. This means she has to take care of the Damon problem before he leaves town.

A couple of hours after
kicking it with Jeremy
Damon makes it back to the hotel. He's in town for the next couple of days for his girl Delinda, whose brother had gotten into some trouble here. Delinda begged Damon to go find out what. She nor her mama can reach him. Damon didn't want to, but Delinda pleaded while laying a guilt trip on him, "He's my only brother baby. You know we didn't have it as good as you on your boo-zhee friends."

"Least you have a daddy who cares about you Damon," Delinda would say when she wanted him to feel sorry for her and her brother.

Damon cares for Delinda but doesn't give a damn about her brother. But he agreed to go to Miami for her and while there, he could stop in to see his boy; Damon's glad he did. He plans to tell Jeremy all about Chili when they meet up for a drink tomorrow night.

Damon phones Delinda to let her know he made it in and saw Jeremy. He plans to see her brother tomorrow, will call after he visits.

"Thank you boo," Delinda says attempting to be coy.

"Yeah. Yeah. You owe me."

Delinda laughs. "You know what you got waiting when you come home," she says. "How's Jeremy?"

"I don't know Delinda. He's with this chick. I know, I know 'er."

"What you mean you know her!"

"Nothin' like dat girl. This was before I knew you anyway."

"Well who is she den?"

"I know she's this girl Chili my cousin Tyrone hired for my cousin Leon's bachelor party. She's a ho."

"Whaaatt?" Delinda says. "Not Jeremy."

"Yeah I know. That ain't my boy. Somethin's up and her name ain't Stephanie."

"Well you let me know how it goes," Delinda says. "Mama's callin' me so I'll have to holla at you later."

"Later den girl."

There's a knock at the door. Damon wonders who it is. It can't be room service. He didn't order anything and he doesn't know anyone else in Miami.

He opens the door and it's Stephanie, the girl he knows as Chili.

"Somehow I thought you'd show Chili."

"Can I come in?"

"Yeah you better. We need to talk about your exit strategy. "

Conyers

Luanne wonders why Joshua hasn't called. Where the hell is he? Luanne's pacing anxiously. She hasn't heard from him since they spoke this morning. She hoped he didn't forget to shut off the security camera while he was in the house and set it back a few minutes before his arrival at the gate. Then set the timer for the time he planned to exit which would be around 2:30. He has a 4:30 train to catch.

Portland in Council Crest

Darius's people moved Joshua's body and finish cleaning up the murder scene. They have everything back in order a few minutes before 2:30 and quietly leave the scene. Darius will wrap things up with the later. For now, he'll keep TiAnna calm and in check before Tippy comes home.

"You wanna hit this," Darius says.

With his lips tightly around the tip of the swisher, he pulls in and holds.

"Naw Darius. But thanks. I think I'mo leave it alone. I need to get straight. I think I can now. Move on."

"I hope so yo. We don't need to be cleaning up any more dead bodies un-da-stand?"

"Yeah." TiAnna smiles. "Tip did say you was cool and I can trust you. Thank you."

"Like I say girl, you family."

Darius takes another hit. While holding in the smoke he says, "Maybe one day you can return the favor."

"You got it Darius."

Darius nods, lets loose of the smoke, thinking "Making Tippy mine is going down real smooth. Real smooth."

2:00p.m. over at Abraham Lincoln

I wonder what's up with the principal calling me down in the middle of the day. Shit. I hope nothing bad has happened. Naw. Can't be. Daddy would've called me on my cell phone.

**At the office I speak to
the snooty receptionist**

"Principal Davies asked me to come down," I say.

Without speaking, the old white hag points to Davies' office.

How rude. Daddy's right. He says expect more white folks to show their true racist selves since their boy Romney lost. I knock on Principal Davies' door.

"Come in," she says.

When I walk in, I'm surprised to see police officers – a tall stout white man and a butch looking white woman. By the look on Principal Davies' face, this isn't good news. I hope nothing's happened to daddy.

"LaTonya, I've called your father to inform him you're being arrested."

I raise my eyebrows, leaning my neck and head back.

"Excuse you," I say.

"LaTonya Ellis you have the right to remain silent. Anything you say can be held against you in a court of law. Do you understand these rights?" says the female officer.

Huh. The bastards could've at least said hello, I'm thinking.

"No. I don't, but does it matter? I know I'm black an all." I say playing the race card. I don't like cops.

Ignoring my comment, the female officer tells me to put my hands behind my back. I'm tempted to tell her to go to hell. But daddy says if I ever get in trouble, never resist arrest unless I plan to die. And I don't – not today – but I can't stop talking.

As I turn around for her to put the handcuffs on I say, "Are you gonna start arresting and killing black folks now because your damn Romney lost?"

I say it especially for Principal Davies's benefit. She's a staunch Republican. I overheard her say to one of the teachers she hopes the Muslim doesn't win again. Until then I use to wonder why she never had much to say to me.

The police don't say nothing as they lead me out of the office.

"If you hurt me you'll be in big trouble. My daddy's a rich man and he'll own this whole Portland by the time he's done."

The kids have just gotten out of last period. The officers parade me down the crowded hall for all the white students to stop and stare. Don't matter. I'm on a roll so I keep talkin to 'em and also yellin' at the students along the way.

"I bet you all think I stole somethin' huh! It don't matter what you think. The President is still black!"

On the way, I see Julie who turns beet red when she sees me. Figures. They act like they your friend until somethin' happens. Then they start acting like the rest of 'em. Julie rushes over and walks alongside me all the way out to the police car.

"Tip I don't know what's going on but let me know if I can help. You're my girl," she says. Then she looks at the cops and says, "Don't try anything stupid. I got your badge numbers. And my daddy knows your boss you jerks!"

Oh no she didn't! Check out the white girl. Teaching me all white folks aren't alike. Like daddy says, white folks helped get President Obama elected his first and 2nd term.

Moments later

They put me in the back of the police car. Once they slam the door, I look out the side window and smile at Julie, who's waving. Now she's one bold white girl, but I hope she didn't get me in more trouble.

Once we're on our way I say, "Officers I heard about the recent DOJ report scolding the Portland Police Bureau. Uh-huh. You're like the rest of the cops around the country if not worse. You racially profile blacks and the mentally ill at a higher rate than the 2 populations combined and then some."

I still don't get arouse outta 5-O. They probably get the picture this black girl ain't one to mess with.

Like my daddy ain't either. He got stopped once since he's been here. The traffic cop accused him of not turning on his blinker one hundred feet before making a left turn. Daddy swears he did and I believe him. Luanne was with him. Daddy figures the police stopped him for driving while black and with a white lookin' woman. The cop gave daddy a ticket but he swears he's gonna fight it.

The cops take me to a juvie holding place for girls. Inside they take me to a briefing room with a 2-way windows. I meeean. Like I don't watch TV. I'm going to laugh my ass off if they start the good cop bad cop shit.

The door opens and in walks daddy with a tall suited, ball headed white man. The white man is smiling; his face is smooth and shiny. I bet he gets face peels. His teeth are slightly bucked and he has these bushy but manicured eyebrows and deep blue eyes.

"You must be LaTonya," he reaches over to shake my hand but I show him I'm still in cuffs. He frowns. Now he looks like daddy, who's frowning and hasn't said a word. He opens the door and calls out to 1 of the officers.

"I'd appreciate it if you'd take the cuffs off my client," he says.

His name is Leonard Gross. He's articulate. I'm guessing he's straight since he doesn't have a gay lisp.

The police take off my handcuffs then leaves the room. Then he and daddy sit across from me.

Daddy's quiet; his arms are crossed and he's still frowning. What's pissing me off is daddy's looking at me like "What the hell did you do now Tippy?"

So much for me and daddy getting along. He never gives me the benefit of the doubt. He hasn't even heard my side. Hell, I don't have a side 'cause I don't even know what's going on.

"Do you know why you are here?" says Leonard Gross.

I shake my head no.

"LaTonya you've been charged for assault against a woman named Uriella Novelli. She's currently at Gates Memorial Hospital with broken ribs and bruises. Apparently, this happened last Saturday at some music event," he explains.

AJ's bitch I say to myself.

"Are you kiddin'," I say.

"No, I'm not," he says. "This is serious. Oregon has Measure 11. Assault carries a mandatory sentence of 5 years."

56

Yo Mama

At Jeremy's

Stephanie has returned from seeing Damon. They now have an un-da-standing, which means she won't have to worry about him exposing her to Jeremy. I knew those photos would come in handy one day," says Stephanie smiling to herself after meeting with Damon. Reminiscing about old times brought back colorful memories.

Back in the day

Chili loved to dance so being a stripper was a bonus. An associate of Don Juan's hired her on at an ATL adult club despite being underage. The club is where she met Damon's cousin Tyrone, who hired her and her Mexican girlfriend Patrice, known as "Sunday Surprise," for a bachelor party.

Party time

When Chili and Patrice arrived to the bachelor party, they walked right into a room full of drunken party hounds – loud talking and music blasting. Chili and Patrice went about doing their thing – Chili stripped all the way and Patrice down to her panties. The big tippers – those willing to pay $200 – received a private lap dance and a duck sick in front of everybody; the way the guys wanted it. Chili and Patrice also did 2 on 1 for a thousand dollars but never alone, for safety reasons. Some boys just didn't like surprises!

The guys threw in a $1,000 for the groom, who went with the girls for a private 1-on-1 for about an hour. He returned, grinning. Damon and the boys wanted details but all they got from the groom was, "What happens in Vegas stays in Vegas!" Moments later he stumbled to the bathroom and missing the toilet, threw up all over the floor.

"We ain't in Vegas!" Damon yelled at the groom. But he was curious. "Sheeeit! Is they that good?" he said to the fellas.

Damon had $2,000 on him, which he earned doing commercial work thanks to his talent agent. Damon is a football jock whose parents count on his work to pay for college. They also bank on him pulling a football scholarship as linebacker for a prominent college.

Because of his lucrative career, Damon loved to brag about being a fine buffed black brother all the ladies wanted.

"Every time my commercial runs, it's pay day," Damon said to 1 homey, who was wasted and could care less what Damon said.

Damon rubbed his chin, contemplating on taking the girls up on their offer.

"Say Chili, I'm in," said Damon. "And this better be good."

He stood up pushing out his chest. With his arms stretched out to each side, he bent his upper arms and pumped his muscles. The boys cheered when he walked away with Chili and Patrice. Damon glanced again at the groom, hoping to read a final expression. The groom had already passed out.

In the back room, Damon didn't notice Chili had pulled out her cell phone to capture the moment. Rather he went straight for Patrice who was teasing him over with her forefinger. She pushed Damon onto the bed and pulled his clothes off, leaving him positioned butt-naked on top of the blankets.

Patrice then straddles him, plopped 1 bare breast over his mouth. Damon attacked like a hungry lion. He then pulled her breast from his mouth, replacing it with her thick round lips, which he parted quickly, then stuck his tongue all the way into the back of Damon's throat.

Patrice then pulled off his red lace panties, then rubbed Damon's crotch. Boy's getting hard. Looks like he's ready for my surprise, Patrice is thinking while still tongue sucking Damon. Here goes my…

"What the fuck!" said the startled Damon, pushing Patrice away. Patrice rolled over on his back, laying spread eagle; his hands behind his head. Damon's eyes quickly travelled down Patrice's long lanky legs straight to his crotch – Patrice was a man!

Present day reality

Finds unsuspecting Damon ready to kick Chili to the curb. But Chili has the upper hand.

"Say boy? I forgot to give you deese," says Stephanie, handing Damon a set of photos.

Damon snatches them and quickly scans each 1. "You funky bitch! I shoulda known!"

There's Damon, laying naked with Patrice, a night he wanted to forget. Once he found out Patrice was a man, he wanted his money back. Chili said if he tried anything, she'd send Patrice out with no panties and let the other guys in on their secret.

Damon decided he wanted his monies worth. They could all have fun as long as Patrice didn't "stick her dick in his ass!" So, for the next hour it was on. Damon went so far as to have anal sex with Patrice with him as the aggressor.

Damon recalled the disgust he felt after it was over. No one could ever find out what happened. They'd think he was a fag or on the D.L.

"You was too drunk and eager to fuck anything," says Stephanie.

Stephanie doesn't have to say much more, knowing she has extra photos safely tucked away. Damon knows it too.

"I'll tell the whole world about your undercover gay ass Damon!"

Damon balls up the photos and tosses them at her. He wants to haul off and slap the grin off her face!

"I'm a man! I ain't no gay motherfucka!"

"Try tellin' Jeremy and your boys. Huh. The press would have a field day. You could kiss goodbye to your stellar career. I hope we un-da-stand each other."

Stephanie slowly backs away from Damon until she reaches the hotel room door. Before she exits, she smiles wickedly and waves to Damon, leaving him to wallow in self-pity. He feels like crying, but like he says, he's a man. A man who fucked up big time. Now he's in a situation where he has to choose between his career or saving the life of his best friend.

Back at Jeremy's

Stephanie says, "I wouldn't have to keep running back and forth if we are unda one roof Jeremy."

"Yeah but I ain't quite there yet Step. Thanks for bein' good to me. Not pressin' me and things girl."

"Uh-huh. Yeah, I'm cool. Hopefully we won't have to wait too much longer baby."

Stephanie's determined to be Jeremy's baby mama really soon.

57

No Place Like Home

November 12, 2012
At the Atlanta estate

Ray says to Dr. Stanwick, "How's she doing?"

"The same when her parents were in here earlier. She's awake; seems to be alert but she hasn't spoken. You know we can't hope for a whole lot. She's been in a coma for several years. There will be brain damage for sure."

Ray wonders if she'll recognize him despite her possible brain damage. He takes off his hat and coat, carrying them with him into the room. The patient in the bed looks over at him – his eyes moisten. He wipes them before he walks over to her bedside. Laying his things across the chair, he pulls the chair closer to her bed and sits down.

"It's good to see your eyes open, girl."

She stares back at him and blinks her eyes several times. Her mouth begins to move but no sound.

Ray leans over and grabs her right hand. "What you trying to say?"

She continues to move her mouth, "Laaa.."

"Take your time beautiful. I got all the time in the world."

She still tries to force herself to speak, "Laaa… Laaadiiiaa."

"Ladia?" Ray repeats.

She says, "Laidia."

Ray pauses momentarily then he says, "Lydia?"

Her eyes blink faster and faster. She knows Ray understands.

"Aw man," Ray says.

He falls forward, dropping his head to the edge of her bed. This time he lets the tears go without stopping. She lifts up her hand and slowly places it on top of his head.

"I sor Lydia."

Falling asleep

Ray sits with her until she closes her eyes and drifts off to sleep. This time things are different; she's no longer in a coma. He leans over, kisses her cheek softly and whispers, "I won't be gone long. You're safe my love at home where you belong."

Outside her room, her father is waiting. Ray says, "I'll be out of town for a couple days in Portland to check on Tippy."

"Be careful," says the father. "We'll care for things on this end."

On the way to Portland

Delta has reached flying altitude so Ray leans back in his first-class seat and closes his eyes.

Damn I'm exhausted but we're off to a great start. You remember me good. Real good. But I still gotta a lot to do and think about. What's my move when I meet with Mr. Darius? One thing I'mo do for sure is set his ass straight. Then there's Tippy. I made her a promise. Gotta get her away from my brotha without him starting shit. And now TiAnna's missing. Yeah. I'm sure her sister Tippy knows where she is.

Ray smiles, making this his last thought before dosing off.

Portland

Black artists are still chanting, "Obama's our black president, oh yeah, oh yeah. Obama's our Black President for another 4 more years!"

Even Portland's white rappers are high-fiving each other while waiting for their next gig. Unlike AJ, who's getting ready for his big opening with Boss Amanishakhete. He's packing the last of his things when he gets a call.

"This is your wife, Uriella. How come you haven't come see me?"

"Uri, stop callin' me. Sign the papers and stop bullshitting."

"Well I think you'll change your mind given what I have to say."

"What Uri?"

"I had your black boo arrested for assault. She's going down unless you and I come to an understandin'."

"What the fuck did you do! You know you deserved to get your ass whooped! You and Debbie jumped her!"

"I did it for us. I don't want a divorce and you don't either. Unless of course you want your princess to go to prison."

AJ cringes. Uriella is like a bad nightmare that won't go away. Now she's using what happened with Tippy to keep him locked into a marriage he never wanted. What's worse, she lied about being pregnant which is why he married her. He discovered Uri was in fact sterile. Years earlier she suffered from a bad case of endometriosis, leading to a hysterectomy.

Uriella's call is a bad omen for AJ, putting a damper in his plans. Last week, he sent Tippy a bouquet of fuchsias. He hoped she'd give him a 2nd chance. At least see him before he goes on tour.

"I'll be over shortly Uri. You'd better be straight with me about dropping the charges. The next time you lie to me…"

"Ok poppy come to mommy," Uriella says mimicking a Latina. "I'll be waiting."

COMING THIS WINTER: LaTonya 2: Fathers Maybe

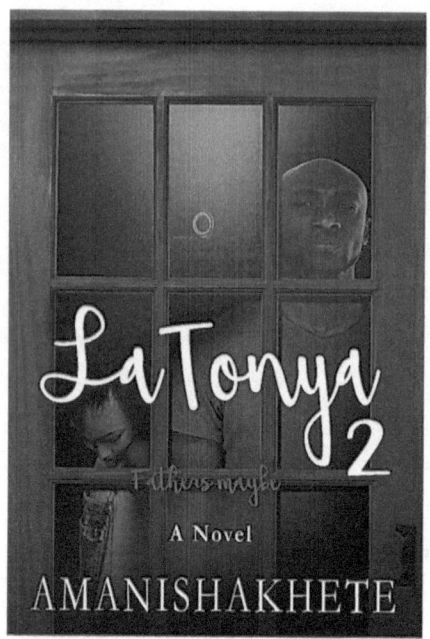

Loaded with more surprises leading LaTonya into dangerous territory filled with deception, hate and violence. She even experiences her first sexual encounter, as a resident of Portland, Oregon attending Abe Lincoln High School where she's arrested. A lot goes down in this small city town and she owes it all to her controlling father who has his own reasons for holding her close.

LaTonya discovers a whole new world unlike her own, but friendly thanks to new friendships. Like Darius who wants her badly knowing he has to cool his jets until he finds a way to gently capture her attention. After all, this young lady has class and money, money, money and Darius find's out just how much. Then there's Shonny, a known Lesbian who is engaged to a Latina, white boy DeMenace, a Portland hip hop artist who LaTonya has a brief encounter and, of course, TiAnna her friend from Atlanta who makes her way to Portland under awkward circumstance and after escaping her kidnappers.

Despite the love hate relationship with her father and wanting to murder his wifey Luanne, LaTonya has these friends—old and new—from all walks of life who remain by her side through the toughest parts of the hell she's reliving from the day her mama left.

LaTonya finds out that things are not always as they seem, or are they? Like the true identity of the killer. Is it Luanne? Robert Ellis? Or some other SOB? Find out in LaTonya 2.

About Amanishakhete

Inspired by her own life, Atlanta Author Amanishakhete (Uh-ma-nee-sha-keet), named after the ancient Nubian Queen Amanishakheto, conjures up an imagination full of colorful characters that make up the LaTonya trilogy. Readers never know what's coming next when they turn the pages of her amazing new series filled with characters from all walks of life – characters she feels she channels.

"They speak to me," says Amanishakhete. "I definitely hear their voices and let them say and do as they please."

No wonder this fresh new fiction writer captures the attention of readers from 16 to 60.

Along with fiction writing and authorship, Amanishakhete is a Word-Soul artist who writes and performs her own lyrics underscored by original music composed by Portland hip hop artist and producer Anuff. Amanishakhete plays herself in the series. Fans can purchase her music at CD Baby and iTunes.

Born in Osaka, Japan to an Air Force family, but raised in the states, Amanishakhete holds an Associate of Science and Bachelor of Science degrees in Business and Communications supported by Business and International Relations graduate studies in London, England and a Master of Fine Arts in creative writing.

Amanishakhete.com
Ashakhete@gmail.com

Amanishakhete